WHAT JANUARY REMEMBERS

THE JOLVIX EPISODES

FAITH GARDNER

MIRROR HOUSE
·PRESS·

For my family.

CHAPTER 1
UP ON THE HOUSETOP

JULIANNA

It's been two long years since I've been back to the Pink Castle and as soon as I pull up in front of the iron gate tangled with ivy, cursive *The Jaggers* adorning the top, my stomach twists like it's too soon. Because with my family, everything's always too soon.

I jump out of my car into the sunshine, leaving the engine running as I punch the code into the keypad out front and the gate pulls open, beckoning me and my old-ass Honda Civic inside. Breath held, I inch the car up the pebbled driveway, passing rows of palms on each side, strung with rainbow lights. The koi pond and fountain with the mermaid statue, wearing a Santa hat. I let out my breath. Okay, we're festive this year. Interesting. We haven't been this festive since my mom was alive—though the intensity of celebration depended on her mood. Some Christmases there was fake snow and inflatable snowmen on the lawn and family pictures with matching holiday sweaters. Others she never got out of bed.

Parking in front of the garage, my mouth drops as I notice two things. The first is, the Pink Castle is no longer pink. It's stark white, blank as a cloud. Dad should have prepared me for the shock of this, because since I was a little girl doing cartwheels on the lawn out here, this has always been the Pink Castle. The second thing I notice is January standing high up on the second-story roof. She's among those light-up reindeer that, in the light of day, look like white reindeer skeletons. I count nine of them. January waves and climbs to the edge of the roof closest to me, bare feet on the shingles, fearless. If she were human, I'd worry for her safety.

"Julianna, is that you?" she calls. "Welcome. How was your trip?"

"It was fine," I call back, shielding my eyes from the obnoxious sunlight.

"Traffic was all right?"

"Not too bad."

"I am just finishing up decorating."

"Looks like you went all out this year."

"Jeremy thought it would help send a visual message that he cares."

Showing us he cares. By making his bot put a bunch of reindeer skeletons on the roof.

"Great," I say.

"Yes," January answers, my sarcasm sailing far above her head.

And then she strolls straight off the roof. Walks off, like a person walking the plank. She lands on the lawn in front of me with a soft thud. And yes, I realize she doesn't have human bones. She can withstand falls from roofs and blows to the head. As we learned two years ago, she can be stabbed, kicked, punched in the face, and yet she remains. But watching someone walk off a roof and fall two stories still gets my heart thumping.

January stands up, dusts herself off, and walks up to me.

"Jesus," I say, hand to my chest.

"Did I upset you?" she asks.

"I'm all right. Are you?"

"I am always all right," she says with an impeccable smile.

January has a plain, heart-shaped face with no distinguishing marks—no freckles, no dimples. She's pale as porcelain with something edging on a hint of blue. Her color reminds me of a moon and her eyes are a deep blue, with the silver pupils characteristic of bots. She has shoulder-length hair that used to be blond but is now a chestnut brown. And she's wearing one of my mom's dresses, the denim one she used to paint in, but I try to not dwell on that.

"Looks like I'm the first one here," I say, trying to mask my disappointment as I gaze at the driveway with just my car in it.

"Indeed."

She keeps her eyes fixed on me, her smile unmoving, and I put my fingers in my pocket, feeling the folded-up note there. Wondering if she sent it. Debating if I should just ask her right now and get it over with.

"Shall I get your bags?" she asks.

"That's okay," I say. "I've got it."

I turn to the car, pop open the trunk, grab my backpack and my heavy Le Chaudron pot. I love to cook. I love my pot. I've been with my pot longer than I've ever been with any lover or job in my life. The whole time I gather my things, January just stands there, hands folded, her gaze relentless. I shut the trunk. Somewhere, I can hear my dad yell, "I can't find my other slipper!"

"Julianna is here," January shouts back.

"Kiddo," he says, strutting out on the upstairs balcony, pajama-clad, his robe open, one slipper on. "Didn't even hear you drive in. Figured I'd have heard you pull up since you're still driving that shitmobile." He squints at me over the top of his reading glasses. "What do you think about all the decorations?"

"It's great," I say, squinting up at him. "Really sends a visual message that you care."

"She say that? Jan takes everything I say so literally."

Jan. I get a cramp. January stands on the lawn, arms akimbo. She could be a mannequin there, wind rustling her hair.

"Want some nog?" Dad asks, raising his glass in the air. "Or you just going to stand out there all day like a weirdo?"

"Sure," I say. "To both."

"Meet you down there in a few," he says. "I'm trying to find this slipper. Jan, you want to help me find my motherfucking slipper?"

"But you told me my first priority over the next seventy-two hours was attending to your children," she says. "Would you like to reassign priorities?"

"Oh, never mind," he says, waving his hand in the air and disappearing into the room that leads to the balcony, Josiah's old bedroom.

"Shall we go inside the house now so I can continue attending to you?" January asks.

"Sure. Great."

Damn it, why'd I have to be the first one here? I have no siblings to pad the awkwardness. Well, Jada's somewhere, of course. I cast a look at the guest house we call the Little Pink House—still bright as a cotton candy, like the main house used to be. There's a bicycle parked out front, but no signs of life otherwise. If I had to guess, my little sister's probably sleeping the day away. I fight the urge to burst in there and jump on her bed to get her up. Another part of me is afraid of what I might discover in there.

I trek up the brick stairs to the front entrance, the familiar wooden door with its stained-glass hummingbird in a glass panel up top, the porch swing where my mom used to sit and watch the sunset. I hesitate before opening the front door—is this even my home anymore? But yes, even now, even after everything, even when it's white and not pink, it will always be home.

January follows me inside. Everything's the same as it ever was. I stand, sucking in a breath at my mom's portrait still lording over the foyer. Her wavy, chestnut-brown hair to her shoulders. Her peacock feather earrings and blue-green eyes to match. The slight smirk on her full, red lips. I exchange a glance with the painting, an ocean of feeling seeing her there.

"She was a very beautiful woman," January says as she stands next to me. "I love this painting."

January stares up at it with such reverence. I think about how, two years ago, my brother Jesse stabbed her with a knife and a hot poker and kicked her until we could see wires and now it looks like nothing ever happened. I shiver, wondering how the hell this is going to play out. Are we going to pretend it never happened? That was the last time we were all together. It seems bizarre to just move on breezily and celebrate Christmas without acknowledging the fact there was basically an attempted murder last time. Then again, everything about my family is bizarre.

January turns to me before I can say anything. "Would you like a beverage?"

"Sure," I say.

I follow her into the living room, where the Steinway gleams in the sunshine that streams through the picture windows. I can imagine the ghost of my mother pounding the keys and belting out lyrics in a throaty voice as I and my brothers and sister sat on the couch, her ever-captive audience. There's a blank space in the corner.

"No tree yet?" I ask, pointing to the blank space.

"Your father thought it would be a fun time to go get one together," she says.

A fun time. Sure, that must be it. My dad's richer than I'll ever be and yet so stingy about the little things that he gets his trees as late as possible for the discount. There's holly on the banister leading upstairs and stockings hung on the fireplace this year, but I guess some things never change. Dad's a haggler. Everything has to feel like he's getting a deal. After Mom died, that was the Christmas tradition—drive down to the tree farm on Christmas Eve when nothing but sad, browning trees were left, get one at a discount, and come home to brood and drink too much in the home theater as he watched *It's A Wonderful Life* on repeat. Me, Jesse, Josiah, and Jada received cash in envelopes on Christmas morning.

Everything's the same in this room. Same Persian rug, same twin potted palms, same painting of the Pink Castle above the sectional couch. I can see the beginning of the long line of family portraits up the staircase. Odd, really, that the art in the house is of the house itself and the people in it—as if insisting, "We are the Jaggers. This is the Pink Castle. We exist!"

The fire crackles in the fireplace even though we're in Southern California and it's sixty-eight degrees outside. I wince, my eye catching the sight of the pokers—but we continue on to the kitchen, black marble countertops and gleaming silver appliances. January goes to the refrigerator and asks it for a cup of ice with filtered water and when it delivers it with a *ding*, she thanks it.

Do robots consider appliances friends? I take the water and thank January and wonder if it's just as pointless to thank January as it is for January to thank the refrigerator.

"Would you like some eggnog, cider, beer, wine, bourbon, sparkling water, milk, tea, coffee—"

"Water's fine," I say, waving my hand in the air.

There's a long silence as she watches me drink. It's uncomfortable, being with January. I try to be nice about it because I know that having her around has brightened Dad up. But it's like you're in a room with someone and yet utterly alone at the same time. There's something so chilling about her relentless stare, her still expression.

"So, how've things been?" I try, sitting on a barstool,

wondering how long this is going to have to go on before either my dad or my siblings rescue me.

"Things have been good and we have been well," she says, folding her hands and sitting next to me on the barstool. "Your father's blood pressure has gone down. We got the deck repaired. Jada enrolled in cosmetology school."

"Again?" I ask, raising my eyebrows. "How is she?"

"She is well," January says.

I don't know why I would expect January to be able to answer that question. Even we humans, Jada's siblings who know her best, can never tell how she's really doing. My sister is a brilliant, gorgeous flower. She's also an addict who will lie until the end of time claiming she's not an addict. But the years in and out of rehab and the scars on her arms don't lie. She moved on to pharmaceuticals a couple years ago, following in Mom's footsteps, walking a line between treatment for her issues and a plain old addiction to pills in orange bottles. It takes a keen eye to know if she's high or not, to be able to scour her medicine cabinet to see if all the prescriptions are in her name. January is oblivious to our history. Lucky her.

"And you?" January asks. "Are you well?"

"I am well," I say, feeling like I'm practicing conversation with someone learning English for the first time.

"Still tutoring?" she asks.

"Yep, for now."

"Are you seeing anyone romantically?"

I almost spit the water I'm drinking, so surprised by the question.

"Your father was saying that you are twenty-seven years old and he expected you to be married by now," she says. "Your mother was a mother at twenty-five."

"Mmm. What else does Dad say about me?"

She smiles and says cheerfully, "He says that you are

throwing your life away at the tutoring center and that you should get a real job."

"Does he now."

It stings, but it's nothing I haven't heard before. Of course, when Dad dishes it, it comes as a half-joking jab. I guess that's a plus of having January around. She's a bot. Bots can't lie. They can only tell you the straight-up truth.

"Perhaps it is time for you all to grow up and be adults, like Josiah," January says, in a voice like she's trying to be helpful.

I kind of understand why Jesse chose violence with her.

"Josiah," I muse. "Ever think about how it rhymes with 'messiah?'"

"That is an interesting fact," January says.

She watches me gulp the rest of my water down with the blank fascination of a thirsty dog. I put the glass down and look over my shoulder, making sure my dad's not there. And I pull the note from my pocket, hand shaking just a little, and open it up. I put it on the counter between us.

It says, in typed all caps, YOUR MOTHER WAS MURDERED.

"January, did you send me this?" I ask. "It came in my mailbox yesterday."

"I did not," she says, peering down at it.

No reaction. No gasp, no nothing. Not a flicker of recognition in her face. I frown. "You sure? It's got a stamp that came from Santa Barbara."

She stares back at me unblinkingly. "Yes."

I let out a breath, folding the note up and putting it back in my pocket with disappointment. I was sure it had been January. It's just too strange, too out of nowhere for it to be anyone else. But she can't be lying. All bots are programmed not to lie.

"Maybe it's a joke," I say, thinking through the possibilities.

"That does not seem like a very funny joke," January says softly.

Even though her face doesn't change, there's a shadow of something resembling empathy there.

"Don't mention it to anyone, please," I say.

"I will not voluntarily mention it, but if I am asked directly, I will have to answer truthfully," January says.

"Fair enough," I say.

Robots gotta robot.

January gets up and refills my water glass at the refrigerator. "Do you think your mother was murdered?"

"No," I say, offended she would even ask.

My mother died by suicide twelve years ago this January, when I was fifteen. There was no mystery surrounding her death, no suspicious circumstances, no investigation. And though it was of course tragic and heartbreaking, it wasn't entirely unexpected. My mom was hospitalized so many times she referred to Lakewood Hills Mental Facility as her vacation home. She had tried to kill herself multiple times before she succeeded.

"Would you like some cheese and crackers?" January asks. "Popcorn?"

I look at the sunburst clock on the wall. Good Lord. Is it only noon? I don't know if I can take three days of this. "Hey, actually, is there bourbon down here?"

"In the wet bar," January says. "Cocktail? With eggnog? On the rocks?"

"Straight," I say.

She disappears around the corner. I'm relieved to be alone, away from her stare. I don't mean to be mean, discriminate against her, but ugh. I text Jesse, *SOS. You'd better be here soon.* Getting up, I peer out the window.

"Jada home?" I ask.

"You can try her," January says from the other room. "Her schedule is unpredictable."

Mmm-hmm, all that not working and not going to school really eats up the schedule.

"You know where it was, Jan?" my dad asks, walking down the stairs and holding his slipper. "It was at the bottom of my hamper. Was that you?"

"It was not, Jeremy," she answers, coming around the corner and handing me a highball glass with an amber inch of whiskey. "I know well that slippers belong in the closet and not in the hamper."

My dad is enormous, broad-shouldered, with salt-and-pepper hair that's cut flat on both sides and longer on top. He has a permanent smirk on his face and twinkling dark-brown eyes. Right now, he's in sweatpants and a Humane Interest T-shirt. Humane Interest is the app Josiah designed. You can rack up points for random acts of kindness, then redeem those points for coupons and discounts at various big-box stores. It's the reason my brother's a multimillionaire at the age of thirty.

"Drinking already?" Dad asks, impressed, clapping me on the back.

"I'm on vacation," I say.

"From that hard-knock job you have helping pipsqueaks with algebra."

"That's the one."

"Come here, my jellybean," he says, folding me into his arms and squeezing. My dad gives amazing hugs. And he doesn't give them out often, so I close my eyes and soak this one up, hugging him back hard. "I've missed you," he says quieter, into my hair. "Good to have you back."

When I open my eyes, January's standing there at the counter, staring at us blankly. I get a chill.

"Why the hell'd you do that to your hair?" Dad asks, pointing to my pixie cut.

"Because I wanted to."

"Looks nice," he says to me. He turns to January and points to my glass. "I'll have one of those, too. With ice."

"Where's Jada?" I ask.

"I don't know. You check the Little Pink House?"

"No."

"Probably better not to." He opens the fridge. "I went in there the other day to deliver her mail and there were four naked people sleeping on her floor."

"Ew," I say.

"None of them were her, thank God."

"Who were they?"

He takes out a bag of baby carrots. "Well, I didn't exactly stop to ask their names."

"But ..." I search for something, but all I can come up with is, "why were they there?"

Dad drops the baby carrots on the counter between us with a plop and rips them open. "I don't know why. I don't want to know why. Your sister's a grown girl. Her orgies are her business. Baby carrot?"

Still trying to wash the image out of my head, I reach out and grab a handful of carrots. January joins us, giving Dad the bourbon, then standing with her hands folded on the countertop.

"I am proud of you for eating your vegetables," January says to my dad.

They stand close. Very close. She talks to him in a tone that falls somewhere between mother and wife. I get a shiver up my spine.

"I'm trying," Dad tells her.

He pats her hand so tenderly. With my mom, it was loud smacking kisses on the cheek or goosing her from behind. Let's be real, it was a lot of screaming and yelling and sometimes it was my mom throwing things at his head. There used to be a china cabinet in the corner until one day there wasn't much china left. How sad, really, that I've never seen that tenderness in him until now. Was it my mom's fault, for being too much all the time, the black hole that sucked all our energy and joy?

"You're being soft," was one of her favorite insults.

YOUR MOTHER WAS MURDERED.

Who would have sent that to me? And why? Twelve years later? I look at my father, chomping a baby carrot. I consider showing him the note. There's no way it was him who sent it, but maybe he would have an idea of what it means or where it came from. Then again, it would upset him. He might get weird and call in a favor to his buddy Walt over at the police station to look into who sent it and make it a whole thing. And for once, it would be nice to have a visit home, a normal holiday, without family trauma bubbling up like a volcano under our feet.

"I hear an engine," January says, perking up.

"Supersonic hearing, this one," Dad says, pointing to January.

Oh thank God, an engine. I hurry to the front door with the speed and desperation of a puppy. Out the window, a midnight-blue Sunray, one of those new luxury solar-powered cars, pulls into the driveway; it's blasting with a meditative voice saying, "You are successful. Forget your competitors. Your uniqueness is your gift."

Damn, I was hoping it was Jesse.

Josiah pops open his falcon wing door. He's wearing some kind of kaftan and sandals and has shaved his head. He pulls out two enormous rollaway suitcases and beeps his car closed, coming up to greet us at the door.

"What the hell happened? You join a monastery?" Dad asks, giving him a hug.

"Did I join a what?" Josiah doesn't take off his mirrored aviators, giving me a one-armed hug. "What's he talking about?" he whispers.

"I guess he's wondering what you're wearing," I say.

"It's called a kaf-man." Josiah pulls away from me and shows off his outfit. "A kaftan for men."

"I think it's lovely," January says, watching us from inside the doorway.

"That you, Jan? Come here, you." Josiah abandons his suitcases and goes into the doorway to engulf January in a hug. A bigger hug than he gave me. I look at Dad, raise my eyebrows.

"They've gotten close," he says.

"Get my bags?" Josiah asks her, and heads inside.

We follow, all of us walking by the portrait again, no one making eye contact with it. We pass through the living room, which feels so much smaller with all of us in it, and go to the kitchen.

Though it's been remodeled beyond recognition—my mother's red walls painted over with a steel gray, the old-fashioned appliances replaced with stainless steel, the walnut dining room table with dainty legs replaced with something glass and more modern—the kitchen remains my favorite room in the house. It's the oasis, the watering hole, the place we casually gather, the place I can escape to and cook for everyone and find a sense of purpose. It's the place where I have the fondest memories of my mother, who went through occasional baking flurries. Elaborate three-tiered cakes. Latticed fruit pies. Braided chocolate bread. During these flurries, I was her assistant, she was directive and patient and kind. It was one of the rare places she gave me her undivided attention, invited me into her world.

Here, Josiah raids the fridge first thing, stopping a moment first to admire the many Christmas cards stuck to it with magnets.

"The Hansens look ancient," he says. "And what the hell are Bob and Abigail wearing in that picture?"

"Christmas sweaters," Dad answers. "I think that's supposed to be a reindeer."

"It looks like feces," Josiah says, slightly horrified.

I come and look over his shoulder. "It does."

Josiah points to one of our neighbors with his companion bot. "I got one of those."

"He sends them every year," I say. "I got one too."

"Did you get this one?" Josiah asks me, pointing to a card from Dad's former co-workers at the hospital. It has their mangy-looking cat with Christmas lights strung around it and just says *Meowy Cat-mas.*

"Sadly no," I say.

Josiah opens the fridge. I spend a moment behind him dreaming of something I can whip up for us all for dinner. Cream, Parmesan cheese, broccoli—alfredo, maybe. I take a seat on a stool at the counter again. January and my dad stand watching Josiah, a rapt audience of two.

"Nice shirt, Dad," Josiah says.

Dad pats his Humane Interest shirt proudly. "Thanks. You want bourbon? We're drinking bourbon."

"Not yet. Too early for me. You really went all out on the decorations this year."

"That's all Jan," Dad says.

"You asked me to," January reminds him.

"True," Dad agrees. "Team effort."

"Fridge, I'm looking for a protein-heavy snack," Josiah says to the refrigerator.

"Ours isn't one of those high-tech ones like yours," Dad says. "Just ask Jan to fix you something."

"Cheese and crackers?" January asks Josiah.

"Cheese and fruit?" Josiah counters.

"Grapes?" she asks.

He shuts the fridge door. "Spectac."

Ugh. My pet peeve with Josiah: the way he shortens words like he's creating some cool new slang. He's done it since he was twelve. He's thirty now. I would like to kick him. I wish Jesse were here to make fun of him for me, because I'm too nice to do it. I smile as he takes a seat next to me at the counter.

"Good to see you," I say.

"You too, sis. What's up with your *hair*?"

"What's up with your lack of hair?"

"There's this fashion movement in the Bay Area right now," he says, rubbing his head. "Buddha couture, they call it. I've gotten a bit swept up in it, as you can see."

"I live in the Bay Area and I've never heard of Buddha couture," I say.

He smooths my hair. "Mmm. Well, we swim in different ponds, love. Or maybe it's a South Bay thing." He smells his fingers. "Your pomade smells weird."

"I'm not wearing pomade."

"Ew, what is this, then?" He smells his fingers again. "Grease?"

I shrug. "Who knows."

He gives me a look and goes to wash his hands at the sink.

"I came up with this idea for an app," Dad says, sitting on the stool on the other side of me. "You ready, Josiah?"

"I don't know, Dad. Is this like your idea for a dating app for pets?"

"No, I was joking about that. This is real. I was thinking, what if there was an app that could tell you how much estimated lifetime you had left, based on your choices? Like I eat a baby carrot—my lifetime goes up. I eat a burger, it goes down?"

Josiah sits back down next to me. January lays out a plate with grapes and cheese cut into little cubes in front of him. "Thanks, Jan. Hmmm, Dad … people don't want to know that."

Josiah rattles on for a while about his interest in branching out into angel investing, my dad and January enthralled by his every boring word, which gives me some time to stare out the window at the bougainvillea twisting over the arbor and wonder how Adriana and my cat Jarvis are doing back home. I live in Oakland and have recently started dating my next-door neighbor in a rent-controlled apartment, which has been a great decision in the short-term but who knows how wise it is in the long-term. Can you imagine being heartbroken by someone and then having to keep hearing the timbre of their voice through the wall? She's hilarious, though. A bit of a space cadet, a lover of animals, a stoner with bad tattoos, a professional dog walker, and a free spirit who doesn't give me a hard time about not being motivated to do more with my life. Who thinks life's just for enjoying and living and not about pursuing anything higher than that. Who thinks tutoring is a noble and worthy career.

Who I like far too much for her to meet my family yet, so I didn't invite her here.

I look sadly at my empty bourbon glass and at my phone. Jesse hasn't responded. There's some knocking on the sliding back doors and it's Jada, looking forlorn and pale in a black dress that could be a nightgown, her hair dyed fire-engine red. January unlocks the door with a beep, letting her in.

"I have a migraine," Jada says. "Sorry. Hi everyone."

Josiah comes over and gives her a big hug, which Jada merely tolerates by not moving. When he's done, she tolerates a hug from me. I step back to give her the once-over, noting that she's thin, but not worrisome thin. That her eyes have circles under them, but small ones. That there's a pimple on one side of her face but otherwise her skin looks clear. I'm always on the lookout for signs that she's falling apart.

"Let me try to find your pressure points," Josiah tells her. "This woman I know does bodywork and it *cured* my migraines."

"Okay," Jada says, turning her back to him in offering. "How are you all?"

"Doing well," I say.

"Same," Josiah says.

"How was the drive?" Jada asks. "Did you come down together?"

We shake our heads. I can't even imagine five, six hours in Josiah's self-driving car, filled with mantras and too much air conditioning. I prefer my dirty little beater and singing loudly and off-key to the oldies station.

Josiah's squeezing the sides of Jada's neck between his hands as she scrunches her brow skeptically.

"Feel that?" he asks.

"Yeah. Ow. And where's Jesse?" she asks.

Swear to God, January flinches at the sound of his name.

"Good question," I say, keeping my eyes on January.

After The Incident two years ago, January had to go to a specialized robotocist to get repaired. Companion bots are becoming more common each year, but they're still relatively new and rare and only manufactured by Jolvix. January was one of the earlier designs. When they repaired her damaged head, they also wiped her memory so she wouldn't remember what Jesse had done to her. It was for her own benefit—companion bots are sharp learners and fierce defenders. They have been known to hold grudges. It's rare, but to be sure, they thought it best to wipe her memory of that Christmas.

But the way she looks now, there's a glimmer of fear shining in her silver pupils, and I wonder how much a robot really can forget. And what would happen if she did remember.

"Ow," Jada yells to Josiah.

"You have to remain *still*," he says.

"You're making it worse." Jada breaks away from him. "I'm going to get ibuprofen now."

She stomps up the stairs in her fuzzy slippers and I watch her, thinking, I can't believe they let her go through their medicine cabinet. I hope they hide the good stuff.

"More cheese and grapes?" January asks, pointing to Josiah's plate.

"I'm good for now," he says. "Appreciate it."

"Shall I take your bags upstairs?" January asks Josiah and me.

"Yes please," Josiah says at the same time as I say, "That's okay, I can do it."

I follow January up the stairs with my backpack as she takes my brother's luggage. It's funny, my mom and Josiah were so alike in so many ways—over the top, an air of entitlement always surrounding them. And yet my mom couldn't stand Josiah. She was dismissive of him, annoyed by him. Jesse was her favorite, her "pookie." My sister and I, we weren't targets of criticism nor did we have pet names. We were just there.

As we get to the landing, my eyes fall upon the many, many family portraits we've taken over the years—all in matching shirts, with elaborate hairstyles, my mom in the center of every picture like the star of the show. We all look so happy. Pictures are such lies. January seems to notice the pictures too but doesn't stop to study them.

"Here's your room," January says, sweeping her hand toward the dark doorway.

"Oh, thanks, I didn't remember," I say, grateful that bots seem immune to sarcasm.

I flick on the light. My old room is now a guest room. It's been painted a coral color I would name *cheerful vomit*. When I lived in here, the walls were painted green and I displayed my soccer trophies and framed awards from mock trial and leadership, as if to remind myself I was a worthwhile person. When I decided to move up to the Bay Area after high school, I put it all in a box and threw it in a dumpster. I never felt lighter.

I thought I was going to take a year off and then go to college. Study psychology, maybe, or become a social worker. A teacher, work with kids. I volunteered at a nursing home for a while and worked as a waitress and lived in a big house with a bunch of vegans who taught me how to cook an amazing curry. I went to city college off and on and worked at a coffee shop and at a weird store in Berkeley that sold tapestries and incense and bronze statues. I fell in love, twice, and had my heart broken twice. I started volunteer work tutoring at a center and then a year later they offered me a part-time job and now I've been there over two years and I can't believe my twenties are mostly over and I have nothing to show for it.

Ten years ago, I was so sure I'd make an imprint on this planet, make it a better place. But in some ways, I think it was all a twisted kind of bluster—a false sense of self-importance, as if I had control over this chaotic world. Here in this room, in this house, I was small, I couldn't make any difference at all. I couldn't make anyone happy. I couldn't improve my parents' marriage. I couldn't save my own mother from over-dosing. But out *there*? Once I got out there in the world? *There* my actions would matter.

My phone rings in my hand. It's Jesse.

"Where the hell are you?" I ask, getting up and closing the door.

"I'm right outside the front gate," he says. "I forgot the code."

"It's 1-2-3-4, bro."

"Also, I'm so high right now, Julianna. I stopped off at the Mr. Droidburger near Turnpike and this dude I used to skate with, Samson, he had this vape pen and offered me some and now I'm like … a little deep in a hell of anxiety. I was thinking of just sitting here for a few."

I shake my head. "Just come inside."

"Yeah."

He sounds doubtful. I get up and go look out the window. There's his black Traub. "I can see you."

"Maybe I shouldn't've come."

"I swear to God, Jesse, if you ditch me right now—"

"I'm not, I'm not, I'm just having a minor panic attack." He blows out a loud sigh. "Did January … say anything about me?"

"She doesn't remember. Her memory was wiped."

"What about Dad? Did he say anything?"

"No one's saying anything, Jess. In the great Jagger tradition, I think we're going to be sweeping this one under the rug and tripping over it for years while pretending the floor underneath us is fine and dandy."

"I feel sick. Maybe it's the Droidburger."

"Or the hash. Or years of guilt."

"Yeah, or that." He blows out again. "How about if you come out here and meet me?"

"Seriously? You can't come up here yourself?"

"Just come out and meet me," he says, softer.

On the rare occasion that my brother needs me, it's a double-whammy. The role reversal breaks my heart a little because he's the fearless, reckless one and I'm the sensitive overthinking baby. And it also feels good, very good, to comfort him. There's no feeling in life like being needed by the people you love.

"Okay, I'm walking out now." I get up. "Wait until you see what Josiah's wearing."

I end the call and step out into the hall, where Josiah's standing, hands on hips. "Are you talking about me?"

"God," I say, jumping. "Are you *eavesdropping*?"

"I was *standing* in the *hallway*."

"Right outside my room." I shake my head. God, I hate how close our rooms are. And Jesse gets the attic all to himself. And Jada gets a whole cute little house. I feel myself slipping, reverting back to dynamics I haven't felt since I was a teenager. "I'm going outside to meet Jesse."

"Remind him he owes me five hundred dollars," he calls after me.

"You can do that yourself, thanks."

January's standing at the bottom of the stairs, like another freaky eavesdropper. This house: three thousand square feet, yet somehow no semblance of privacy.

"Jesse's here?" January asks.

"Yeah." I wait a second, uncertain what it is I see in her eyes. "You all right?"

"I am always all right," she says with a smile.

I go out the door and jog to the front gate to meet my stoned-ass baby brother, looking once behind my shoulder at the house. There January is, looking out the window, arms crossed.

But she's not smiling anymore.

JULIANNA

It was the first holiday we spent together as adults. And of course it had to end in attempted murder.

Two years ago, I was surprised my dad had arranged for us all to travel home and come together for Christmas. He never gave a shit about Christmas. Since I'd moved out of the house, I'd spent Christmases with friends. Jesse's a bartender and always worked holidays. Josiah was often on some elaborate trip with whoever the love of his life was that week. And my dad and Jada usually went on a cruise together, their special thing. But this year Dad insisted we come home.

"What is going on?" I asked Jada. "Is Dad dying?"

I could hear her strumming her guitar. "No. Not now, anyway."

"Why's he so insistent we all come home?"

"He's … going through changes," she said cryptically. "Retirement and all. He's been golfing a lot. Did you know he golfs?"

"I … no."

My dad was an anesthesiologist for thirty-five years and only retired a couple years ago. "You know, it can be a depressing career," he told me once, wistfully, while sipping a drink. "The people you help the most never even remember you."

"He bought all these flowerpots," Jada went on. "I think he's getting into gardening?"

I peered out my living room window, which overlooks a busy street. A bus went by, spitting out a group of loud middle school kids. I went back to my stove and stirred the soup I was making. In the hall, I could hear loud voices, bumping, laughter.

I didn't want to go back to the Pink Castle. The Pink Castle was quiet and peaceful and haunted. I had only been back twice since I left it almost six years before. Sure, I had visited with my brothers separately. Jada had come up here on a bus for a couple weekends, starry-eyed by city life. Never had I been reunited with my whole family at once.

"Look. I'm not supposed to say why," Jada said, sucking in.

"Are you smoking?" I asked.

"Just vaping."

"Vaping's bad for you."

"Everything's bad for you."

"Back to what you were saying—why's Dad insisting we come home?"

"I promised I wouldn't tell."

"You're driving me bananas."

"Let's just say he has a new *companion*."

I stopped stirring the pot with the wooden spoon, my jaw dropping. For all the bumpy rides with my mother—the screaming, the threats to leave each other, the times she hastily stuffed clothes into suitcases, the nights he spent on the couch, the time she flushed her wedding ring down the toilet, et cetera, et fucking cetera, he was always solely focused on her. He was passionate about her. She was the only woman in the world to him. When she died, he didn't laugh for a year, swear to God. It was like a candle was blown out. He'd never acted interested in other women. Never mentioned them. Her portrait still hung in the entryway of our house and he kissed his fingers and brought it to her painted lips each time he came and left the house, like she was holy.

"He's seeing someone," I said.

"You could say that." She sighed. "I have to go to the clinic."

The clinic—where Jada had outpatient therapy, addiction recovery, and eating disorder classes weekly. My sister sounded even-keeled, presented herself coolly to the world, leather jacket and bleached hair and punk songs on her guitar. But she was a damn mess like all of us.

"Good luck," I told her.

I stared into the air for a long time, bothered, thinking about whether or not it was a good thing that my dad had a girlfriend. I thought about it so long, I burned my soup. And when I went out to the hallway to dump my burned soup out in the dumpster, I ran into a girl with long, dark hair and a nose ring and a crude tattoo of a duck on her arm, carrying boxes up as I went down.

"Hey," I said, smiling at her.

"Hi," she said, smiling back.

I got a flutter.

Later that night I thought, you know what? My dad deserves to be happy.

Everyone deserves that.

––––––

Jesse and I traveled together that year, two days before Christmas. Christmas Eve Eve. Traffic was a special excruciating holiday hell, but not unexpected. I drove my car and Jesse played DJ, as he does, introducing me to new bands with names like Bloodbone and Deathstench. Everyone screamed the whole time so I kept the volume low. We were nervous about meeting Dad's new girlfriend, and even though the conversation drifted as we edged along the 101 toward Santa Barbara, it kept coming back to her. To this mysterious *her*.

"I just can't see him doing that," Jesse said for probably the fifth time. "Seeing someone. You know? I don't think we're getting the whole story."

"You act like it's so strange, but it's been ten years now, Jess. Most people who are widowed end up seeing someone else at some point."

"But not Dad. Not Mom. I mean, they were the great American love story."

I snorted, and then realized Jesse was being serious. Jesse has this adorable naïve way about him despite the fact he's a brawny, weightlifting bro. Glancing over at him with his backward hat and earnest brown eyes, he seemed the same for a moment as he had when he was a kid in Little League.

"The great American love story?" I repeated. "Are you kidding me right now?"

"Come on. Dapper anesthesiologist in his first year of residency falls in love with a woman getting an appendectomy?"

I rolled my eyes. I hated this story. My dad says it was love at first sight, but my mother was unconscious, for God's sake. He came back to check in on her when she woke up and they had dinner together in the hospital cafeteria—their first date. I guess it's fitting they met at a hospital, considering they would both end up spending so much of their lives in them for different reasons.

"Don't you think Dad deserves to be happy?" I asked Jesse.

"What about us?" he exploded. "What about how we feel?"

"What about Dad's happiness?" I insisted.

It was weird. I was somehow defending a woman I'd

never even met, one I didn't want in our lives, either. But it seemed unfair for us to expect my dad to continue worshiping Saint Janelle. And downright dishonest to have some revisionist history of their complicated marriage, painting it as the great American love story. Ridiculous.

Jesse didn't say anything, brow furrowed, glaring out the window at the beautiful rise and fall of green hills.

"Can you just not be an asshole to her?" I asked. "Please?"

"I'll be nice," he muttered.

I've always been the one who could calm Jesse's temper. Who could talk sense into him. Who could convince him a fight wasn't worth it, or to lay off drinking because he was red in the face.

I thought we had settled it. I thought there wasn't anything to worry about. We turned up some band with crunchy guitars screaming about gravediggers and headed home together for the first time in so long it wasn't worth trying to remember.

————

That year, there wasn't much of an effort made in the Christmas decoration department besides a wreath hanging on the *Jaggers* sign out front.

"Here we go," Jesse said, blowing out a deep breath as we drove up the driveway. He stared sullenly at the palms passing us. "God, I hate coming back here."

"It's nice here, Jesse. We're such spoiled brats. Anyone would kill to have a house in paradise to come back to whenever they want."

"A haunted house in paradise," he said.

"Bit dramatic, bro."

I pulled up front, behind Josiah's neon orange coupe. I'd never seen the car before but knew in an instant it was Josiah's. He rotated through cars at the same pace he rotated through wardrobes and lovers.

"I see her ghost everywhere," Jesse said softly, unclipping his seatbelt and staring ahead, at the front door.

"I know. I see all our ghosts everywhere. Right now, I can see that zipline we set up over there." I pointed at the two palms closest together, then the fountain. "And Jada playing with her rubber duckies." It's strange how I could see it without seeing it, a feeling superimposed over reality. I nodded my head toward the stretch of lawn. "And the soccer field right there."

"Mom's porch swing," Jesse said.

I was trying to pull him back into other memories, ones that didn't involve her. "Remember that time you kicked a soccer ball up on top of the chimney? And it just sat there for weeks until it randomly blew down onto Josiah's head?"

"Mom's porch swing," Jesse said again, frozen.

"Come on, Jesse, there's more to our memories than Mom."

"No—look at the porch swing," he whispered.

And I scanned the west side of the porch for what he was talking about, for the swing. What I saw there stopped the air in my throat.

"Oh my God," I said. "What the hell?"

There was a woman sitting on the porch swing. She was wearing sunglasses and a long, violet robe, one that had been my mother's, rocking gently back and forth.

"I can't do this," Jesse said. "I need to go home now."

"You *are* home," I reminded him.

My dad came out onto the porch, arms open, and started belting out "O Come All Ye Faithful" in a deep baritone. Jesse and I grabbed our bags and I grabbed my beloved Le Chaudron and got out of the car. We walked up the brick stairs to him, hugging him at the same time. But neither of us were smiling, and both of us were still eyeing the woman on the porch wearing our mother's bathrobe.

"You have a good drive?" Dad asked, clapping Jesse's back.

"You know, it was fine," Jesse answered, turning his cap forward again. "About as expected."

"Traffic," I managed.

"Well," Dad said, rubbing his hands together. "Josiah and Jada were just getting a board game set up. Come on in."

Jesse and I exchanged a glance, both of us, I think, bewildered about the woman but not wanting to ask. I had expected Dad to introduce us—to say *something*, at least, about the woman in my mom's bathrobe—but Dad just breezed inside without even seeming to notice her. Inside the foyer, my mom's old portrait was still there. Jesse and I exchanged another look now, this one more sorrowful. I wasn't sure how to feel about the portrait. I hadn't thought about it in a long time, but maybe a part of me had expected it wouldn't be here anymore. How could Dad have a proper dating life if the portrait of his dead wife still loomed over the entrance to the Pink Castle? But like so many things in the house, we didn't say anything. We came inside, dropped our luggage and my pot next to the staircase, and joined everyone in the kitchen.

Josiah and Jada were at the table, Jada slumped and bored-looking as Josiah explained what seemed like the rules of the game to her.

"So that's if you pick up a Hedge Fund card," he was saying. "But if someone *else* has the *same* Hedge Fund card, that other person's assets are up for grabs. But if they have a Bear Market card, then they can actually grab *your* assets."

"Heyo," Jesse said, waving.

"You're here!" Jada said, lighting up and standing to hug us both.

She was skinny in my arms. Too skinny. I hated that that

was the first thing I thought when I hadn't seen her in almost two years, instead of just enjoying the hug. Josiah's hug was stiff and ripe with aftershave, his hair slicked back and shiny as his shoes.

"So we're in on the board games already," Jesse said to Josiah.

"I invested in this game," Josiah said. "It's not only fun for the whole family, it teaches ordinary people how to use the stock market."

"It's boring," Jada said.

"You didn't even let me finish explaining it to you," Josiah said.

"Let's all go out back, have some beers," Dad said. "Isn't the weather great today? Seventy-five degrees in December. Now who says climate change is all bad?"

He headed outside, through the glass doors, Jada following behind, Josiah next in the parade. Before Josiah passed the threshold, I grabbed his arm.

"Hey," I whispered, Jesse coming to join in on the sidebar conversation. "Did you see the woman on the front porch?"

Josiah stared at me so long it told me the answer to my question.

"There's a lady sitting on the porch swing," Jesse said.

"She's wearing Mom's bathrobe," I said.

"The purple one," Jesse said.

Josiah just stood, frozen. He has eyes so dark they're nearly black, dramatic eyebrows, and he unhinges his jaw when he's deep in thought. He was doing it now.

"What the fuck are you talking about?" he asked.

"Hello," Dad called from outside. "Am I drinking all these beers myself or what?"

My brothers and I broke our confused conversation and headed outside. I almost wondered if I had hallucinated the woman on the porch swing—but Jesse saw her too. Why, if my dad was seeing someone, would she be out there and we be out here?

Why did it sometimes feel like the Pink Castle shared a zip code with the Twilight Zone?

There was new furniture on the patio and the sprinklers were on, making little rainbows over the back lawn. The pool water gleamed in the sun. I sat down, smelling the familiar scent wafting from the jasmine vines and the lemon tree. When I closed my eyes, I time traveled. I was a little girl again, drawing on the bricks with chalk, playing with my dolls in the grass.

Dad handed us all beers from a bucket of ice on the patio table. He even had little limes sliced on a cutting board and everything. There was jazzy Christmas music piping out here through invisible speakers. It was impressive for him.

"Cheers," he said, clinking his bottle to each of ours. "To the Jaggers, reunited at last."

We drank in silence for a moment and I wondered if everyone else was thinking what I was thinking: that we would never be reunited, not really, not when Mom was gone. Silences are rare with us Jaggers, but when one rolls along, it's a good bet that my mother's somewhere in there.

The roar of an engine or something ripped through the moment, coming from a nearby yard. I jumped about a foot in the air.

"That asshole," Dad said, pointing a finger in the air. "I swear, he waits until I come out here to run that thing."

"What *is* it?" Josiah asked in horror, hand to his throat.

"Sounds like a boat," Jesse said.

Dad pointed at Jesse. "Bingo. He's been repairing that piece of shit boat for months."

"Can we go inside?" Jada whined. "Gives me a headache."

I could tell my dad was disappointed. All this work he'd done, the bucket of beers, the little limes, it wasn't panning out. One of my least favorite things in life is seeing sadness on my dad's face.

"I'll just go ask them to wait a bit," I said, getting up.

"Good luck with that," Dad said.

"Do Sean and Wendy still live there?" Jesse asked.

"Sean does," Dad said, having to speak loudly over the motor. "Wendy had the sense to leave that old bastard years ago."

I crossed the long lawn, approaching the fence where the noise was coming from. I remember as a kid we made up stories that Wendy was a witch; we'd peek through the slats of the fence to see her tending to her garden and say she was growing poisonous herbs. She wore long skirts and too many rings. Sometimes, on random nights, we thought we heard strange noises—a howl, a single scream. Then again, I thought the bespectacled man who lived on the other side of us was a serial killer, the way I could peek through and see him coming in and out of his cellar.

"Hello?" I shouted through the fence, trying to be louder than the motor. I peeked through but could only see the large white shape of the boat, no person there with it. At the sound of my voice, the motor stopped, but no one answered.

"Hello?" I said again.

Again, no one responded. It felt odd, knowing there must be someone there who was refusing to respond.

"My family and I are back here and we're just wondering if you could maybe do that a little later," I said. "It's very loud."

Nothing. Not a word. But I could hear a crinkling sound and the clicks of footsteps. When I peeked through the slats again, there was a pale woman with curly, platinum hair who was pulling a tarp up over the boat. I saw her turn and hurry away, her shoes echoing on the patio steps.

Well, that was weird.

I headed back to where my family was relaxing on the patio and joined them.

"Look at that," Dad said to me. "She did it."

"Ever the diplomat," Josiah said.

Josiah has a way of always coming off as sarcastic, even when he's being sincere. Often, I can't read him. This was one of those times.

"Amazing what just communicating your needs can do," I said, plopping into a seat next to my father.

"Was it Sean?" Jesse asked, picking some lint off the giant skull on his T-shirt.

"No. It was a woman. A young woman."

"Huh," Jesse said. "Maybe old Sean's back in the game."

"When are you going to get back in the game, Dad?" Josiah asked with genuine curiosity.

I almost spit my beer out.

Jesse, Jada, and I all exchanged a look, six raised eyebrows. In the pause, over the saxophone playing "Here Comes Santa Claus," I thought maybe I could hear the creak of the porch swing out front.

"Well," Dad said, his color turning just slightly pink as he picked at the label on his beer. "I—I guess I have something to tell you all." He looked up at us, made eye contact with each of us, the way he used to when he was giving us a lecture or a serious talk, when he wanted to burn the conversation into our brains. "There's someone new in my life. I'd like you to meet her. Hold on. Stay here."

Dad stood up and disappeared into the house.

"She's *here*?" Josiah asked us.

"I told you we saw a woman out on the porch swing," I hissed.

"She loves that swing," Jada said, scrolling on her phone.

"Wait, who? Who loves the swing?" Josiah asked her. "What is *happening*? Do you all know something I don't?"

We didn't answer.

Josiah sat back, crossed his arms. "Why am I always the last one to find out?"

"You literally walked by her four times when we were getting your luggage," Jada said. "It was when you were talking about the app you want to invent to organize your apps."

Josiah's mouth remained open a moment and then he clamped it shut. Before any of us could discuss further, my dad came out of the back door, followed by the woman we had seen before. The woman in sunglasses and my mother's robe.

My stomach somersaulted. My brothers and I froze so intensely it seemed like everything in the yard froze along with us—the birds didn't chirp, the breeze disappeared.

"So this is January," Dad said.

None of us said anything. I think we were all studying her. My first thought was that she looked closer to my age than to Dad's, and, well, gross. I never wanted to be one of those women who shared a generation with their stepmom. She was also flawless. She'd had work done, I guessed. She was so *symmetrical*. Not a wrinkle. Not a blemish. Look, we grew up in Santa Barbara, where Botox and facelifts are as common as teeth cleanings. But I didn't like the way she resembled an airbrushed person in a picture. My favorite part about my mother's appearance wasn't how perfect she looked, though she was good at crafting the illusion of perfection. It was her freckles sprinkled over her nose. It was how one side of her mouth seemed to smile more than the other. It was the cowlick at her hairline.

January had no cowlicks. She had blond hair that didn't even seem to move as a warm, sudden wind blew over us.

"Nice to meet you, January!" Josiah said, breaking the silence. "*Love* those shades. I'm Josiah."

He walked a few steps to where she stood and offered his hand. January just looked down and stared at it.

"He wants to shake your hand, January," Dad said. "It's a thing people do when they meet each other for the first time. You shake hands."

Oh my God. She didn't speak English. This was even worse than I thought—a mail-order bride situation. I looked at Jesse, whose mouth was tight. He shook his head at me once. Jada was yawning and staring at a butterfly.

January extended her limp hand to Josiah, who shook it with fervor.

"Nice to meet you, Josiah," she said, in perfect English, no accent. "I have heard so much about you." She turned to us. "All of you."

Okay, maybe not necessarily a mail-order bride situation. Still strange. Still off. I sucked it up and stepped forward, offering my hand, pushing my lips up into a smile.

"I'm Julianna," I said, as brightly as I could manage.

"Julianna," she repeated, shaking my hand.

Her skin was shockingly cold. I was relieved to have my hand back again.

It was Jesse's turn and we all looked at him. He didn't offer his hand. He didn't move a muscle. Finally, he just muttered, "I'm Jesse."

"Nice to meet you, Jesse," January said and turned to us with a smile. "Nice to meet you all."

The silence was thick and uncomfortable. And the whole time, January stood there smiling. Jesse blew a long breath out, one that I knew the meaning of: he was trying to let out a little pressure so he didn't blow.

Jesse has always been a sweetheart, a charmer, someone who can light up a room and make everyone laugh with the ease of a stand-up comedian. But like all of us, he's got his dark side too. His temper can be tripped with one wrong word. He can spring into a fight like no one I've ever seen, his fists moving faster than his brain. I was staring at him trying to send him telepathic signals to control himself.

"So where did you two meet?" Josiah said, keeping his tone upbeat, filling the silence with disproportionate enthusiasm probably to make up for the awkwardness. But it only made everything feel more awkward. "We're dying to know the details!"

"Well, you might all be a bit surprised to learn this," Dad said, forcing a laugh, putting his hands together as if he was praying. "January's actually not a woman."

"Oh!" Josiah said, the word leaving his mouth so high he sounded like someone goosed him.

I was so shocked by this I didn't know what to say. Jesse's face scrunched up in confusion.

"She's a bot," Dad said. "Take off your sunglasses, January."

January pulled her sunglasses off and then we saw it—her long-lashed blue eyes, silver pupils in the middle. I could see us in the silver pupil, like a tiny mirror, all our gaping faces. Her expression remained blank. It sank in and all made sense —why we'd passed her on the porch swing and Dad had ignored her. Why Jada was so cryptic on the phone. Why she seemed … not all here.

Dad cleared his throat. "You know, Jolvix makes these companion bots now and I thought it might be good for me to have someone around to … to help keep the house together."

I noticed, for the first time, his hands were shaking. He was still holding them in a prayer position. It was a little heartbreaking to see my dad's hands shaking, betraying the confidence he carried with him at all times. He was scared of what we would think of him. We were all quiet, processing this bombshell. I'd heard of companion bots, of course. I'd read a news story about them and how they were being used for elderly people and other people in isolation and how they boosted the mental and physical health of their owners. But it was deeply saddening to know my father was one of those people.

"This. Is. *Amazing*," Josiah said, once again breaking the silence. "January, I'd have never known. You look so *human*."

"Doesn't she?" Dad said. "I tell her she looks like Grace Kelly."

I couldn't help that the comparison made this whole situation seem so much grosser. Dad used to tell Mom she looked like Elizabeth Taylor. The man has a passion for old movies. But I tried to keep smiling, tried so hard I'm sure my smile looked as plastic and fake as January's.

"You do, you totally look like Grace Kelly. Like you stepped right out of *Rear Window*," Josiah said. "I've always wanted to meet a companion bot, I've never actually met one yet. I can't wait to sit down and talk to you."

"You'll be disappointed," Jada piped up. "She's pretty boring to talk to."

"Don't be rude, Jada, come on," Dad responded.

"You can't offend a being that has no feelings," Jada said.

"Still," Dad said. "It's just unnecessary."

"Why the fuck is she wearing Mom's bathrobe?" Jesse finally said, his voice tight.

Everything got quiet again. It was on all our minds, of course, but Jesse was the one to say it.

"Well," Dad said, taking in a deep breath and letting it out. "I … I figured, why not, right? They both wear the same size, you know? And your mother—she had a fantastic wardrobe—all that vintage stuff. Neither of you girls wanted to touch it. Why let it go to waste?"

"It is better to reuse and recycle whenever possible," January said.

"Right, exactly." Dad nodded at her. "Better for the earth and all."

"This is fucked," Jesse said, jabbing a finger in the air aimed at our dad. He pushed his sunglasses up, just, I think, to be sure Dad could see him glare. "Mom must be rolling over in her *grave* right now."

"Mom doesn't have a grave," Jada reminded us, looking utterly unmoved by this whole bizarre scene. I wondered if she was on something—a sedative. A tranquilizer. Or just plain old stoned.

"Nah, fuck this," Jesse said, turning around and pushing past January to get to the sliding glass door, nearly knocking her over. "Not here for this bullshit."

In one second, Jesse was gone. I started to follow him, but Dad grabbed my arm.

"Let him go, Jules," he said softly. "Let him be alone right now."

"But he's—"

"I told you he would get that way," Jada said to Dad. "I told you Jesse would leave as soon as you brought her out."

"He's probably already packing the car back up," Josiah said. "Man has no self-control."

"He's not packing the car up," I said. "Because I have the keys. I drove us."

"This is not a bad thing, okay?" Josiah said to me, as if I was the one who needed convincing. Which, I guess I was.

I wished sometimes I could storm off like Jesse instead of being the peacekeeper, the people-pleaser. But it just wasn't my role.

"Dad, I actually think this is great for you," Josiah went on. "I saw this whole documentary about Jolvix's bots and how great they are. Their capacity for learning is better than human beings. They can read an entire thousand-page book in under five minutes. They can become fluent in a language with less than three hours of studying."

"And not just that!" Dad said. "She's learning, you know, *human* things. They learn a simulated kind of empathy. They can mimic us and our feelings. They're shaped by every inter-action. The more I talk to her, the more of a personality she seems to develop."

"It's fascinating," Josiah said, walking a loop around

January to observe her in three hundred and sixty degrees. He reached out to touch her hair. "May I?"

January nodded and Josiah ran his fingers through her hair.

"One hundred percent human hair," Dad said.

"I asked Dad if I could cut her hair and he said no," Jada said in disappointment. "But I did do her makeup yesterday."

"Looked a goddamn clown," Dad said to Josiah and me.

I eyed the door to see if I could catch a glimpse of Jesse. My heart stung. I knew Jesse and I knew he was hurting right now. I wanted to comfort him. I wanted to make all this better.

"What do you think of all this, jellybean?" Dad asked, coming and putting his arm around me. "You've been quiet as a mouse."

What I really thought was that this was one of the more fucked up things I'd ever seen. That it made me deeply sad to know my dad was so desperate for companionship that he bought a bot. That, for about the millionth time in my life, I wished my family was normal. I wished my mother was still alive and that she was a happy and stable human being. But wishing had never been anything but an exercise in futility, so I put a cork in my secret bottle of wishes. And I spread a smile on my face and looked at my dad and his hopeful expression, waiting for my approval—something he never sought from me, I think, any other time in our lives.

"I'm fine with it," I said, giving him a side-hug. "Whatever makes you happy, Dad."

The grin that spread on his face was well worth the lie.

"Anyone hungry?" I asked. "Can I make us all sandwiches?"

"I'd love a sando," Josiah said.

"You know I can't pass up one of your gourmet sandwiches," Dad said.

"I'm going to go back to the Little Pink House," Jada said, getting up.

"Jada, I'm making you a sandwich whether you like it or not," I said, using my big-sister tone. "Come on."

We went inside. I pulled ingredients out of the fridge in an inspired flurry. The whole time I was hoping Jesse would come around the corner with a sheepish look on his face—he was often quick to blow up, but quick to settle down, too—but no. This was going to be a much longer-held grudge. Hopefully the smell of melted cheese and roast beef might eventually lure him downstairs.

January watched me make sandwiches, asking questions about the process of making parmesan-crusted bread. She marveled that she had no idea cheese could go on the outside of a sandwich.

"She's curious," Dad said, patting her on the back. "And a great cook, too."

Not as great as me. I tried to focus on making the food and never mind the creepy feeling of my every move being watched by an unblinking robot.

"Does she eat?" I asked my dad.

January answered instead. "No, I do not require food."

"Oil or … gas or something?" I asked, trying to make conversation.

"Solar-powered, right?" Josiah asked, sliding onto a stool to join the audience watching me cook. Jada sat at the dining room table, head down and hidden in her arms, probably taking a nap.

"Correct. I am solar-powered. I require one hour of sunlight per day to be fully operative for the other twenty-three," she said.

"Good thing you live in California," I said. "I wonder what it's like for bots who live in, I don't know—Alaska or something."

"Yes. I am very lucky," January said.

Dad looked pleased, drinking his beer at the counter. I imagined he was enjoying seeing us kids back at home again and that we were taking the bizarre news well.

Well, three of us were, anyway.

I set the table and gave everyone their sandwich-heaped plates. There was one waiting for Jesse. January sat, her setting empty. I waited a moment, enjoying the sight of everyone marveling at how amazing the food smelled and looked—mouthwatering, if I do say so—and said, "Don't wait for me, I'll be right back."

Taking two steps at a time, I went up the stairs to the second story, then turned right toward the end of the hall. The staircase to the finished attic was narrow, the steps short, and there was wallpaper on both sides that had daisies all over it that had been there for as long as I remember. It creaked as I made my way up to the closed door, which still had a NO SKATEBOARDING sign that Jesse stole from a parking lot when he was a teenager.

I knocked. "Jesse?"

"What."

"I made a sandwich for you. Come downstairs?"

He opened the door. His eyes were red and he'd taken his baseball cap off, revealing his buzzed haircut. "That thing still there?"

"Yeah."

"Then no."

He tried to close the door, but I pushed it back.

"Don't do this, Jess," I said.

"Leave me alone."

"It's weird. Of course it's weird. But we're just here three days, okay? It's Christmas."

He stopped pulling on the door and leaned his forehead on the side of it. "I hate this."

"Me too. But Dad's happy. Do you see how happy he is? And it's not like he's dating someone else, which would be harder in some ways. You know? She's just a stupid robot. She's just here to help pick up the house and talk to him when he's lonely."

He didn't say anything, closing his eyes.

"Nothing will ever replace Mom," I said. "It's just a robe. It doesn't matter."

He opened his eyes. "I think we need to have an intervention or something. Dad's really fallen off the deep end. Like yeah, he's happy, okay. But guess what? Jada was happy when she was obliterated every day and we had an intervention because sometimes what some people call happiness other people call fucked in the head."

"A robot isn't drug addiction."

"No, but it's not healthy, either."

I sighed. "Look, come downstairs. Eat a sandwich. Calm your ass down. Ignore January. Okay? Just ... try to forget about it for now."

In the silence, I could hear his stomach rumbling.

"Fine," he muttered.

And he followed me downstairs, pouting, still visibly pissed—but placated for now.

Or so I thought.

————

The drama seemed to have settled over the course of the day. January kept her distance, mainly just a flicker in the background cleaning bathrooms or washing windows, easy to ignore as a robot vacuum cleaner. At one point, she somehow got herself locked in the upstairs closet and I was the one who heard thumping and let her out. I had to teach her about the sticky lock, about how the door got jammed. I must have been imagining that she looked afraid when she emerged.

"I do not understand what happened," she kept repeating, even after I explained the lock. "I do not understand."

That night, I woke up to get water and ran into January scrubbing the floor in the middle of the night on her hands and knees, in the dark.

"Oh," I said, spooked. "Hi."

"I like to clean while everyone sleeps," she said with a smile.

"Okay," I said. "Cool."

"You can turn off the light when you leave," she said. "To preserve energy."

"Sure."

As I walked away, I peered back, where all I could really make out was the gleaming white moon of her smile in the dark.

I closed my door and locked it after that.

On Christmas Eve, we did what we always do: we went to go get a tree almost pointlessly late in the game. Jada stayed in the Little Pink House with a stomach ache, her usual excuse to get out of any family outing because she thinks we're all loud and embarrassing. Once we got outside, Dad asked if January could come too and our jaws dropped to the floor.

"You bring her *out*?" Josiah asked, as if this were the most wonderful news he'd heard since NFTs were invented.

"Of course I do. Teaches her about the world," Dad said, standing beside her.

I couldn't figure out yet what their relationship was. I wasn't sure I wanted to know. In some ways, he talked to her like another daughter; at other times, he rattled orders to her like she was his maid. But there was something about the way he looked at her sometimes, with fondness, with something special, that made me want to throw up.

"I'm staying home," Jesse said, turning around and heading toward the house.

Jesse hadn't even acknowledged January's existence since

the introduction yesterday. He avoided her like a ghost. If she entered a room, he left.

"Jess, for crying out loud," Dad yelled after him.

"Let him go," Josiah said. "We weren't all going to fit in one car anyway."

I looked wistfully at Jesse closing the front door behind him as I climbed into the orange atrocity that was Josiah's car. Great. Now I was left with Dad, his robot friend, and my disgustingly cheerful older brother. And the back seat had so little room that January and I couldn't move an elbow.

"I do not think Jesse likes me," January said softly to me.

It caught me off guard that she was able to pick up on something like that.

"Oh." I waved my hand. "I think he's just in a mood."

"No, I think it is about me."

I looked at her, at her eyebrows scrunched a little. She had red lipstick on that matched her dress. It was something I had maybe seen hanging in my Mom's closet, but never on her body. She had a lot of clothes like that, bought on a whim and never worn, many with price tags still dangling. I wasn't sure how to respond to January—I wasn't sure if a robot really actually gave a shit whether it was liked or not—but luckily my brother revved the engine and started blasting techno Christmas songs and ripped out of the driveway and it ended the conversation.

January asked too many questions about Christmas traditions, Josiah and my dad got in a heated discussion about fir trees versus pine trees, and having to drive a convertible home with a Christmas tree on top was a harrowing nightmare. In short, I wish I'd faked a stomach ache and stayed home. We did the whole tree-decorating thing once we were back, hung the stockings, and Dad made a giant steaming pot of hot toddies. We drank a lot of them. There were chicken quesadillas for dinner, courtesy of me. There were board games and then we moved to straight bourbon. We got loud and laughing and moved to the living room sofa where, Jesse, king of exaggeration, spun his ridiculous tall tales.

"Did I ever tell you about the time I stole the police car?" he asked.

"You *sat* in a police car. I was *there*," Josiah almost shouted, but he was grinning too, because we all wanted to hear the story, whether it was true or not.

It was cozy, the fireplace lit, the tree twinkling with lights. I felt a feeling I hadn't had in a long time, like being a child again on Christmas Eve, warm and wishing that the holiday could last forever. And I was so glad I'd come home.

Dad told us that January could play the piano and summoned her to join us in the living room. "Sing some carols," Dad said. "C'mon now."

We were all sauced at that point, so sure, why the hell not. January, wearing the violet robe again, sat at the piano and took requests from us. We sang about snowmen and reindeer and elves and Baby Jesus; even Jada sang, grinning and flushed from the one hot toddy we let her have. Josiah, of course, was singing a harmony louder than everyone else, showing off his five years of choir. Jesse danced with sunglasses and a Santa hat on. And Dad's theatrical baritone beneath it all as January played the keys perfectly, staring vacantly at nothing. We felt like a family again. If I squinted my eyes, it could be the Jaggers of years past.

Then Dad asked if January could sing us all a carol and we said sure, okay. It was late and we were all starting to yawn and I was beginning to regret how much bourbon I'd drunk. Josiah, Jada, and I sat on the sofa and Dad took the loveseat. Jesse slipped out of the room, but I wasn't surprised. I was more surprised that he had been a good sport about Christmas carols when January was the one playing them. The room hushed, except for the fireplace crackling. January was lit up by nothing except the rainbow glow of Christmas lights. She was frighteningly beautiful. From here, you'd never know she wasn't human. And then she started to play and sing and my heart just about broke.

She was playing my mom's favorite Christmas song, "Have Yourself a Merry Little Christmas."

My mom liked to sing the original lyrics to it, which were dark and foreboding, about this year perhaps being your last and warning that come next Christmas, we'd all be living in the past. So merry. January didn't sing those lyrics, she sang the more festive and cheerful lyrics we all know so well. But it was a woman who was not my mother singing my mother's favorite Christmas song. Playing the same keys my mother used to play, in the same corner of the room, in her robe. And my dad was right. January's voice was lovely, so lovely it made me bitter. As the song progressed, I grew emotional, my eyes watering. Josiah's eyes were watering too and he held my hand. Jada had fallen asleep on my shoulder. Dad watched January with pride. When January finished the song with the flourish of a professional, we all started clapping when suddenly, out of nowhere, Jesse came running in from the kitchen with a butcher knife in his hand.

He was running straight toward January with nothing but pure hatred shining in his eyes.

"Jesse!" I screamed in disbelief. "What are you doing?"

We gasped and Jesse started stabbing January over and over again in the back. I winced with every squelching thump of the knife entering her body. Meanwhile, she stared ahead with unblinking eyes. She turned to look at him and Jesse stabbed her in the eye.

"Stop!" my dad yelled, standing up and rushing over. "Goddamn it, son!"

My dad managed to pull Jesse off of January and picked her up, rushing her over to the floor in front of the fireplace. He laid her gently down with the care of a paramedic. The back of her robe was torn up and she still had a knife sticking out of her eye.

"My God, my God," Dad said, standing up and covering his mouth like he was trying not to cry.

Josiah, Jada, and I were all looking at one another with our jaws unhinged, far too drunk to be dealing with this situation right now.

"What the fuck," Josiah managed.

But it wasn't over. Like a maniac in a horror film, Jesse came back and lunged for the fireplace poker, picked it up and started *thwapp*ing January over and over again. I'll never forget the sounds it made, like whipping a creature, and how she let out little sounds as he did, as if trying to speak, but then with each blow, she got cut off again. I thought I was going to throw up right then and there, I really did. Then Jesse started kicking her head and Dad yelled, "That's enough!" and pushed Jesse so hard, he fell into the Christmas tree and knocked it down. There was the crunching sound of ornaments shattering. Jesse lay there, panting on top of the tree. His arm had been cut from broken glass and he was bleeding. Meanwhile, January had been bludgeoned and just lay in front of us dry as a bone. There was still a knife in her eye. She moved her mouth, no sound coming out. She didn't seem able to move beyond that. I sprang up to help Jesse off the ground. Jesse wore a look I'd never seen before. I'd caught glimpses of it, yes—but I'd never seen this kind of soulless-ness. He hardly seemed human.

"You broke her!" Dad yelled at Jesse, his face twisted up.

"She will never be Mom," Jesse yelled back at him, sputtering into a sob. "She's a fucking machine!"

"Go to your room!" my dad exploded. "All of you!"

We all scurried to our various corners of the house. Upstairs, I helped Jesse find a bandage for his arm, but when I tried to talk to him he just said, "Leave me alone" and went up into his room. Josiah tried to talk to me and I told *him* to leave me alone and went into *my* room. I slept heavily, but not well. In the middle of the night, I got up for a glass of water and January was still there on the living room rug next to the dying fire. Someone—my dad, I guessed—had draped a blanket over her so she looked like a corpse under the Christmas tree lights. You could still see the place where the knife was poking up, tenting the shape of the blanket.

I shuddered.

We did not have ourselves a merry little Christmas. The next morning, Jesse came to my door with a hangdog look on his face and asked if we could please drive home immediately. I left a note on the kitchen countertop telling my dad we were sorry. Neither of us said anything about the corpse shape on the living room floor as we left. We hardly spoke on the drive back. We just listened to a punk rock Christmas playlist for hours and when we neared the Bay, Jesse turned to me and said, "I think I'm going to stop drinking hard alcohol."

And I said, "Yeah, I think that's a good idea."

And we've barely spoken about The Incident since.

JANUARY

It has been two years since Jeremy's children came to visit. I was here the last time but have since been serviced and my memory was wiped. It is strange to know you were here before and have met people before but fail to remember it.

Jeremy's children are mostly very nice, and they are not children. They are adults. But I have learned that when humans reproduce, they continue to refer to their progeny as "children" even when their age has advanced beyond childhood. I find this interesting because it is almost as if humans can exist in the past and present at the same time. Sometimes I am the same way when I remember things too.

Jeremy has told me I have a good "bullshit detector." This, I learned, is not a real device inside of me, but an imaginary concept invented to indicate that a person or intelligent being like myself can tell when something is not right or when untruths exist. It is what made me suggest that the politician I watched on TV with Jeremy was not likely to fulfill his promise of giving a job to every American because that is impossible. It is also what made me able to tell that Jeremy was nervous about his children visiting, because I noticed he was eating about fifteen percent less than usual. When Jeremy said nothing was wrong, I said, "My bullshit detector is going off, Jeremy," and he laughed. I like to make people laugh, though it does not happen often, and I never understand why it happens. But it is always a welcome surprise.

Jeremy did not tell me why he was nervous. But I know why.

I may not remember, exactly, but I still know what Jesse did.

CHAPTER 2
O CHRISTMAS TREE

JULIANNA

I open the iron gate with a groan from the inside, revealing Jesse's dust-covered Traub parked out front. The car was a gift years ago, delivered with one of Dad's signature half-joking insults.

"Figured a guy who likes to drink as much as you do should have a self-driving car," Dad said with an elbow jab.

Years later, the once cutting-edge Traub looks about as worn as my decades-old Honda. I stand with my hands on my hips, shaking my head at Jesse, who's seated in the driver's seat. He's wearing sunglasses and a fedora and has apparently grown a beard since I last saw him.

"What?" he yells through the open window. "Why are you looking at me like that?"

"Get out of the car and give me a hug, you bum," I say.

He comes out and over to me, giving me a hug that smells like deodorant and cheese puffs. I stand back to look at him.

"A beard?" I ask doubtfully. "And a *fedora*? Why?"

"Honestly?" he whispers. "I wanted to look different than last time. Because I don't want that thing seeking revenge on me."

"Well, you look stupid."

"I know. I know I do. I don't care. It could save my life."

"You really are stoned."

"I was thinking of leaving my car parked out here by the road," he says. "Just … you know. To be different."

I'm about to continue making fun of him, but then I remember the sinister way January looked out the window as I left the house just now, and the way she seemed spooked by the mere mention of Jesse's name earlier. Not that I'd tell him about any of this, especially in his cannabis-induced state of paranoia, but he might have a point. It might not be a bad idea to avoid provoking any slight chance that January might remember him or what he did to her.

"All right, let's get your stuff out of the car then and hike it," I say.

I sling a duffel bag over my shoulder and lead the way through the *Jaggers* gate. It's actually kind of nice getting to walk through the full front yard, up the sloping driveway and past the palms, getting the up-close view I haven't seen in years. Not since hide-and-seek. Not since this house seemed to contain our entire tiny worlds.

"Christmas lights," Jesse says as we hoof it, admiring the trees. "Noice."

His too-chipper tone is betraying his nervousness. I give him a look.

"What?" he asks.

"You okay, Jess?"

"Fine. Awww, look at that."

We stop in front of the mermaid fountain sporting the Santa hat. Jesse takes off his sunglasses to look at it and emotion flashes in his eyes. I know what he's seeing. This was Mom's fountain, one of Mom's favorite places to sit in the yard with a patio chair and her feet up as she donned her cat-eyed sunglasses with the rhinestones on the rim. And in one of her more festive years, she would definitely have been the one to put a Santa hat on the mermaid. I give Jesse a solemn moment.

"Ready?" I finally ask.

"Yeah," he says, breaking eye contact with the statue and turning back to the path. "Just thinking about her."

"I know you were."

"You ever feel like she's still here, hovering around you like an angel?"

"I don't, no," I say as gently as I can.

"I feel her all the time."

It would be like my mother to continue favoring Jesse best and fawning all her attention on him even in the afterlife.

"So," Jesse says, quieter as we near the house, slowing his pace. "You read that article about the companion bots that ran away from their owner?"

"No."

"Really freaked me out."

"You scared January's going to run away?"

"Not that exactly. It's more about them, you know, not following orders." He shuffles his feet as we near the house, the front lawn, dragging out this walk as long as he can. "Point is, they can't be trusted. If they can run away when they're programmed not to, who's to say they won't get violent?"

"To be fair, Jess," I say, as gently as I can. "You were the one who got violent."

"Can we not talk about this?" he asks, even though he was the one to bring it up. "I'm already battling a panic attack."

Jesse has this magical way of somehow always coming out the victim, even when he's exactly the opposite. But look at his face. No matter how smile-wrinkled and tough-skinned he's getting from too much sunshine and not enough sunscreen, no matter what weird facial hair he's sporting, he's still got the charm of a little boy. I've never resented the fact he was my mother's prize, because, well, I get it. Jesse's infinitely loveable.

"Sure," I say. "See the reindeer on the roof? Fun, right?"

"Wow," he says, with the sheer awe held only by children or the truly stoned. He turns to me and says in a low voice. "Listen, before we go inside, there's something I need to talk to you about—"

At that moment, Josiah comes out of the front door with his arms open wide. "Merry Christmas!" he sings in full, lasting vibrato, loud enough to probably be heard from miles away.

"What the hell is he wearing," Jesse asks me under his breath.

"It's called a kaf-man," I tell him under mine. "A kaftan for men."

"A *what*?"

"What the fuck are you wearing?" Josiah now asks Jesse, getting closer. "Ew. Is that a *fedora*?"

"He has reasons," I say cryptically.

"There is never a reason for a fedora, unless it's a hundred years ago and you're a hero in a film noir movie," Josiah says, coming to give Jesse a hug.

"You are really not one to give me shit about my wardrobe," Jesse says into Josiah's shoulder.

"This is Buddha couture. A fashion movement happening in the Bay Area," Josiah says, pulling back to show off his outfit.

"I live in the Bay Area," Jesse says. "I never heard of this, man."

I can tell I'm going to get sick of this topic real quick.

"Well, look at this son-of-a-gun," Dad yells in a booming voice from the front doorway. "Come here, you."

We walk back up to the doorway and Dad engulfs Jesse into a one-armed hug, his glass of bourbon in hand.

"Like the beard," Dad says. "Got that lumberjack thing

going." He steps back and squeezes Jesse's shoulder. "Look at this, the gang's back together again."

There's a moment of silence. Even though the sun's on full blast, the sky's blue as a summer lake, clouds pass over us.

"Want a drink?" Dad asks, shaking his in the air, ice cubes clinking.

"Uh, maybe later," Jesse says. "Thanks."

We head inside, Dad first, followed by Josiah who starts talking about an idea for virtual bartending school as they head into the living room, and Jesse stops in front of me to gape at Mom's portrait—or so I think. Then I notice that, underneath the portrait, January stands with her hands folded in front of her, watching us with unblinking eyes.

She's changed her dress. She's wearing a plain white dress I've never seen before, something my mom would never wear. Mom hated the color white. She thought it was a lie that it called itself a color when really it's the absence of color and nothing else. My mother got married in a red dress, looking like a dazzling human volcano.

I wonder if January remembers what happened two Christmases ago.

If she remembers that the robe was part of what set my brother off.

But no, she can't; January can't remember anything.

"Hello," Jesse says in a tight voice.

"Hello, Jesse," January says in an equally tight voice. "Welcome."

She said the exact same thing to me not two hours ago—and yet, swear to God, the way she says it to Jesse, it's a completely different tone.

Man, did my brother's paranoid vape pen high wear off on me? I'm being ridiculous. We all head past the living room —the scene of the attempted robot murder we wish could forget—and end up in the kitchen.

Sweet relief. My home of homes, the kitchen. I stand

behind the counter on the other side and ask, "Can I get you something to drink?" at the exact time that January says the same thing and, well, not going to lie, it's pretty yuck how it feels to speak earnestly in sync with a robot. I look at January and she looks at me, both of us behind the counter together as my brothers sit on the other side.

"You can go, January," I say coolly as I can. "I've got this."

"Thank you so much, Julianna," she says, doing an odd little curtsey. "I will be outside watering the flowers."

We watch as January floats across the room, opens the sliding glass door, and then exits to the green back yard. The sun catches her brown hair, lighting it up. From behind, she's almost human.

"She loves the garden," Dad says, coming behind the counter. He plunges his hand into a fruit bowl I just noticed existed and chomps an apple. "Spends hours every day out there."

"Can I get you anything, Jesse?" I ask, wanting to snap him out of the white-faced terror he seems to have been plagued with since we entered the house and encountered January.

"Uh, I'm okay right now," he says as he straightens his hat.

"Where did Jada go?" Josiah asks, looking out the back door. "She's so sneaky."

"Little Pink House, of course," Dad says, chewing the apple loudly. "Girl sleeps eighteen hours a day."

A moment extends in the room that is so loaded with quiet context it's hard to fathom all at once. It spins silently around us, in memoriam: my mother's old habits, the way she slept days away during depressive episodes and love affairs with various medications; my sister's addiction issues, a sad and shining mirror.

"Board games?" Josiah claps. "Want to? I brought this new one about Congress—"

"Maybe in a bit," I say. "After we take your stuff upstairs. Right, Jesse?"

"Yep," he says, standing up stiff as a soldier. "Love to play that game in a few, bro."

Jesse and I trudge up the stairs, stopping in the upstairs hallway to marvel at one of the pictures taken for a past Christmas, the six of us Jaggers in front of the fireplace, Mom in the middle with her long red velvet dress spilling like a crimson sea on the rug and us kids lined up behind her like the supporting cast in a show. Mom and Dad wore red, but we wore green. I must have been thirteen and I've got a mouth full of metal I'm hiding with a tight-lipped smile. Jesse at age ten is next to me with his beaming grin and slanted eyes, his hand on Mom's shoulder. Josiah's on the other side of me, hair grown long and dyed at sixteen, glaring at the camera and standing about a foot farther back than everyone else. And Jada, seven, wearing an absolutely ridiculous dress fit for a pageant child with the vacant expression of a kidnapping victim. Dad towers over all of us, standing behind Jada. There's a sign my mom drew in cursive propped in the front that says *Joy to the World!* This was the photo for that year's Christmas card. Then Mom slept through Christmas day, Dad went to work, and I ended up cooking ham for my siblings, afraid it would go to waste. Joy to the world. But we sure cleaned up well, didn't we? We sure fooled everyone that we had it together. If my mom could be relied on for one thing, it was that she took a damn fine picture.

"Those were some good times," Jesse says, before continuing up the stairs to his room in the attic.

Sometimes I wonder if we shared the same childhood or not. Jesse's affectionate optimism can border on delusion. As the stairs creak beneath our feet, I think, then again, memory is really just a story you tell yourself. And it makes my heart skip a beat to wonder if I can trust myself and what I remember.

As soon as the door closes behind us, we drop Jesse's bags on the twin bed. The room hasn't changed much since he still lived here five or so years ago. There are still metal posters plastered over every inch of his wall and a stack of skateboarding magazines on top of the dresser. Jesse turns to me with a serious expression in his bloodshot eyes.

"This," he says, pulling a piece of paper out of his pocket, "is some fucked-up shit."

He unfolds it to show me the words YOUR MOTHER WAS MURDERED.

I sit on the edge of the bed, feeling a little queasy at the sight of it. "So you got one too." I pull mine out of my pocket and show it to him.

"You got one and you didn't *tell* me?" he asks, sitting beside me.

"I didn't want to upset you, Jess, or get the conspiracies rolling again."

"I *told* you there was more to the story," he says, his voice picking up intensity. "I told you all someone killed her, something wasn't right. Nobody believes me, everyone makes me shut up about it—and now this."

We look at the notes, identical, except his is more wrinkled from being opened and shut and crammed carelessly into his pocket, while mine is still neat.

"I'm going to assume that Josiah and Jada got one too," I say.

"Or maybe one of *them* sent these to us," he says.

"What? Jesus. They wouldn't do that."

"Do you think Dad could have?" he asks.

"Jesse, no."

"Then who?" Jesse asks.

I offer a long, sorry shrug.

"You think that *thing* did it?" he whispers. "To mess with my head?"

"I asked January," I say. "She said she didn't. Bots can't lie."

"Bots can't lie, bots can't remember." He shakes his head. "I think that's bullshit."

We sit in silence and Jesse bites a fingernail—a habit I thought he quit in junior high.

"It's true," he says softly. "I always knew it. I knew it wasn't some straightforward suicide. The whole thing about the fentanyl in her system, what the hell was that about? And she'd never have killed herself in the bathtub. She—she'd be humiliated to have been found that way. You know?"

He's getting worked up, flustered, and his eyes are getting wet. I put a hand on his knee. "Jess, Mom must have had pills with fentanyl laced in them. She took all sorts of shit."

"Well, then who gave them to her?" Jesse asks. "How come no one ever investigated *that*?"

I'm trying to keep the pin in the grenade here. I shake my head. I know what he's saying—these are details that I've wondered about, too—but after years of distance and therapy, I've learned to accept that there are some things we'll just never know. Why fentanyl. Why the bathtub. Why that day, why her suicide note was a single piece of paper that said *Come and find me*. We'll never know why my mom was so hell-bent on leaving us in the first place. It's an ache you learn to live with—because what's the alternative? She was suffering. She was ill. There's no logic to follow.

"We need to let this go," I say, as gently as I can. "It's weird, the notes. I know it's weird. But we can't let this ruin our time together."

"But—" he says, staring at the note.

"We've got to move on," I tell him as firmly as I can. "If there was some actual evidence or something, we'd bring it to the police. But a note? A note that could have been sent by anyone in Santa Barbara? It's disturbing, but there's nothing there."

"Kimmy," he mutters.

Jesse's ex-girlfriend, as unhinged as they come. He broke up with her in high school and she drew a heart on our lawn in gasoline and lit it on fire. A few years ago, she popped back up online and started sending Jesse sexy pictures and I finally convinced him to block her.

"Right," I say. "Anyone."

I open my palm and Jesse sighs, drops the note in it.

"Try and have a good time," I say. "Forget about the note and enjoy the time we have together here."

There's a knock on the door and then Dad opens it, pops his head inside. "What's going on up here? You two going to include us in your shenanigans or what?"

"We're just talking," I say, squeezing my fist around the notes, my pulse quickening as if I'm guilty of something.

"I was thinking it might be a good time for us to get a tree," Dad says. "What do ya say?"

Ugh. This. If only DashDrone delivered Christmas trees.

"How are we all going to fit?" I ask. "Two cars?"

"I've got the new SUV, fits up to seven." Dad takes his key fob out of his pocket and tosses it in the air, catches it in his hand. "Be like old times."

"Okay," Jesse says, standing up. "Sure. Yeah." He clears his throat. "Is, uh … is January going?"

Dad gives Jesse a look, raising his dark eyebrows. "Yes, son. January's coming with us. She's part of the family now. That a problem?"

"No, sir," Jesse says.

"Good." Dad nods at us. "See you downstairs."

After Dad's left, I look at Jesse. "'Son,'" I repeat in a gruff voice. "'Sir.'"

"Shut up, Jules," he says, annoyed, and leads the way downstairs.

We pack into the SUV, Dad in the driver's seat, January sitting passenger. Josiah sings Christmas songs the whole way there, seated next to Jada, who has her enormous headphones and sunglasses on and appears to have transcended us, lucky girl. Jesse and I are in the back and his leg is jiggling like crazy and I'm not sure if it's The Incident or if it's the disturbing note but his mind is clearly elsewhere and tension is high.

"Someone farted," Dad says from up front. "All right, who was it? Was that you, Josiah?"

"*Dad*," Josiah says. "No. Ew."

"It was January," Jada says, apparently able to hear us through her earphones.

"I am unable to emit gasses," January says.

Dad looks in the rearview. "Come on, that's low, Jada. Blaming your fart on her? Please."

"She doesn't care," Jada says. "Robots don't care if you blame them for things they didn't do."

"I do think when someone states a falsehood, it should be corrected," January says.

Dad pats her knee. "Yes. Yes, make wrongs right. Good girl."

God, I don't know what's worse—memories of my mom joining us for excursions like this in the throes of wild mood swings, or January with her bland, superficial conversation. All I know is I already need another drink and it's not even two p.m. Meanwhile Adriana texts me a picture of Jarvis curled up happily on my couch back home and I tell myself, just three days. Just three days and I'll be back there.

At the Christmas tree lot, Josiah insists on debating every damn tree left before choosing the first one we liked, Dad haggles about prices with the poor teenager in the elf costume who works there, and Jesse works to tie the tree to the top of the car with the dedication of a sailor facing the high seas. January watches the whole thing blankly and I watch her blankly, wondering what's going through her head, why there's an oddly humanlike crinkle in her brow.

"What are you thinking about, January?" I finally ask.

January turns to me, offers a pursed smile. "Oh. I was imagining what it must be like to be a Christmas tree—how nice it must feel to get to ride on top of the car and see the sun and feel the wind rushing through your pine needles like a breeze through your hair."

She turns back and continues watching. I'm a bit stunned by the depth of her response.

"And I was also thinking how sad it must be," she murmurs. "To be ripped from your home in the earth to slowly rot in a human's living room."

I get a chill up my arms. "Jesus. I never thought of it like that."

"I think about a lot of things," January says brightly, then glances over at a line that has formed behind a food stand. "Would you like me to buy you a hot cocoa?"

"No," I say, still stuck on the Christmas tree comment. "Uh … I'm fine."

In classic form, Jada has disappeared into thin air without anyone noticing and won't answer her phone. Finally, just when we're about to form a search party, she comes back. Turns out she was across the street, browsing through an antique shop—or so she says.

The whole way home, while Josiah sings about grandma getting run over by reindeer, I stare out the window and think about what January said. How she made human beings sound like monsters. If she thinks we're monsters, then, well, I definitely don't trust her.

I don't trust her at all.

JESSE

Hard to believe Mom has been gone now half my life. I'm twenty-four now. She joined the angels when I was twelve. As I get older, that's one of the hardest things—looking in my rearview mirror and seeing her image fade. Holding tight to the memories I have left of her, making sure to go over them enough that they won't leave. Some of them I've written down in a journal I've kept, one she left behind with a leather-bound cover and an etching of an oak tree on the front. Other memories I didn't write down, wouldn't write down.

How come all the memories worth keeping seem to fade the fastest, and the ones I wish would leave me alone and stop haunting me seem to stay as vivid as ever?

And now there's the note. Though I don't understand why now, why a dozen years later, part of me isn't shocked. I've always suspected someone killed my mom. Awful as it sounds, part of me hopes someone did. Because if they didn't?

Well, then, maybe it's my fault she's dead.

Maybe I'm the murderer the note's talking about.

New Year's Eve. Cold, cloudy Friday. Day that lives in the pit of my stomach, in the darkest closet in my brain. My buddy Chadley invited me over for a sleepover that night and I'd been planning to go for weeks. Fridays Dad worked the late shift, Josiah was doing some kind of theater thing, Julianna was at a New Year's Eve party with her soccer buddies, and Jada stayed at our neighbor's house who had a couple twins her age. It seemed like every kid in the Jagger family wanted to get the hell away from the house whenever they could. So that meant I felt a responsibility to stick around. Make time for my mom, hang out with her, watch out for her, because no one else would.

Friday nights were what she called Pookie Parties and I would make her a martini and she and I would order some Chinese food and go down into the theater and watch black-and-white movies together. Honestly, I found them all boring, but I liked the way I could imitate the wise guy voices and over-the-top dialogue and make my mom laugh until she cried. When I was with my mom, I felt like the funniest person in the world.

"You're going to be on TV someday," she'd say, wiping her eyes with the sleeve of her violet robe. "I swear. Everyone's going to say they knew you when."

But tonight, I was ditching out on the Pookie Party to go on a sleepover to ring in the new year. For the whole week leading up to it, Mom kept dropping little remarks here and there. Then the afternoon of, while I waited for Chadley's Dad to pick me up, she went all in.

"I'd better get my Jesse hugs in now," she whispered, hugging me extra hard as I waited in the foyer. "Since you've found something better to do than to hang out with this old, withered bag."

"C'mon, Mom, you know it's not like that."

"I'm kidding," she said, tousling my hair. "I'm happy for you. Boys grow up, of course, it's the circle of life. Can't hang out with your mom forever." She sniffed, ran her hand through her brown curls. "One day you'll fall in love and find a woman you want to marry and you'll forget all about me. I'll be nothing but an obligation. A phone call you dread making once a week."

"Mom," I said, adjusting my backpack straps. "I can stay if you want to have our Pookie Party. Do you want me to stay?"

"Of course not," she said, waving a hand in the air. "I'm not going to get in the way of the things that are truly important in your life."

I hesitated, not understanding what she wanted. I had learned over the years that my mom sometimes said one thing and meant another and sometimes it was hard to tell what was what.

"You're important," I said, feeling sad, feeling trapped and like I couldn't win. I hated that feeling. It was the worst feeling in the world, to not be able to please my mom. "You're the most important person in my life, Mom."

"That's nice of you to say that," she said, brightening up. Then she whispered, "You know you'll always be my favorite."

I smiled. Even though a part of me felt bad, like it was against some unwritten rule to say that to your kid, it also lit me up to know I was her favorite. To hear it from her lips. To know that she liked me better than anyone else in the entire world. Every time she whispered it to me, it was like a secret we shared.

"My good boy," she said, beaming. "Call me tonight so we can say goodnights and I can sing you your lullabye?"

"Yeah," I said. "Of course."

Chadley's dad pulled up in the driveway then and my mom's eyes filled with tears. "Don't forget about me," she cried as I started out the door.

"Mom, I won't," I said, smiling, inching away, hoping Chadley couldn't hear my mom through the open car window, couldn't see she was crying as she followed me out on the porch and waved goodbye. By the time we pulled away, she was openly bawling and I felt sick to my stomach. Maybe I was making a huge mistake. It seemed like I was breaking her heart. But by the time she faded into a tiny speck behind us, this rush of relief came over me. And then a wave of something like anger. Because Jada, Julianna, and Josiah never had to feel guilty about going to a sleepover. Sometimes being her favorite was a heavy load to carry.

"Your mom doing okay?" Chadley's dad asked, meeting my eyes in the rearview.

"She's just fine," I said in a tight voice. I leaned forward. "Hey, Chadley, you still have Blood Feud 4?"

"Yeah dude."

"Can't wait to play it," I said excitedly.

And I made a decision right then and there to push my mom out of my mind. To push her voice out of my head. To not worry about what would happen to her if I left her at home alone. To not remember the other times when she took too many pills when everyone left the house.

I just wanted to be a boy for once, you know? A boy who goes to his buddy's house and gorges on pepperoni pizza and plays video games until his eyes cross. And I did. I had a great night. I had such a great night I didn't call my mom like I promised. I didn't want to have to go hide in a closet somewhere and listen to her sing me the Night Night Train song. I crawled in my sleeping bag that night and went to sleep.

The next day, Chadley's dad woke me up at dawn while he was still in his pajamas, hair wild.

"Jesse, we've got to get you home," he said.

"Why?"

"Your dad said it's a family emergency."

I shot out of my sleeping bag, packed my backpack, and

sprinted into the passenger's seat of Chadley's dad's car. There was an upside-down feeling in my gut that whatever this was was bad, was my fault, was all because I left my mom alone on a Friday night. I kept arguing with myself as Chadley's dad drove in silence. She didn't seem like she'd seemed the other times when she tried to hurt herself. The other times she'd been depressed, not changing her clothes, barely getting out of bed. Last night she'd been emotional, yeah, but—when wasn't she? The worst thing was that I kept hoping it wasn't Mom. I hoped it was Josiah getting in a car accident, or Julianna getting sick and needing to go to the hospital, or Jada breaking a bone instead. Anything but my mom.

I didn't call her when I said I'd call her. I should have called her.

I tried to keep my panic in check when we went up to the gate, which was wide open, but I could already see there were vehicles in the front yard that didn't belong there. Ambulance, I guessed, my soul sinking. But then as we got closer, I saw it was a different kind of vehicle. A white van. One that had a word on it that I had to say out loud to sound it out, make it real, be sure I was reading what I was reading.

"Coroner," I said slowly.

"Oh no," Chadley's dad said softly, stopping the car behind it.

I got out in a state of shock, not sure where to go or what to do. My dad was crying on the front porch, talking to a stranger. Our neighbors were standing on the lawn gaping at the scene. I turned and went straight for my siblings, for Josiah, Julianna, and Jada, all of them red-eyed and huddled together on the porch swing. That's when I knew. I counted who was left of us. There was only one person missing.

"She finally did it," Julianna said, her face blank.

"What the hell was she thinking?" Josiah spit out, his eyes dark. "Why would she do this to us?"

"Mommy," Jada said simply.

I squeezed on the porch swing with them, even though we barely fit. We sat in silence. This couldn't be happening. I couldn't believe it. She couldn't have done this to us—not this time, not now. She wouldn't have killed herself just because I left her for one night. Couldn't, couldn't, wouldn't, wouldn't. There had to be another explanation.

Over the hollow weeks that came after, the weeks that felt like an extended bad dream you couldn't wake up from, I decided that she was murdered. She was killed by someone. Someone made her take those pills. Someone made her get in the bath and drown, because the other explanation—that is was my fault, that I could have prevented this—was just too fucking much to bear.

Somewhere deep down I might be a little envious of January. Imagine how much easier it would be to live with myself and the shit I've done if I too could have my memory erased.

JANUARY

I am folding towels in the master bedroom when Jeremy comes in and closes the door behind him. I can tell there is something serious on his mind because he frowns. I put the towel down on the bed because while I know folding towels is an essential task, I also know that tending to Jeremy is always my first priority.

"Jeremy, is everything all right?" I ask.

"I was coming to ask you the same thing," he says. "Kids are out there decorating the tree, we just made cocktails, Charlie Brown Christmas soundtrack is playing, and you scuttle off in here to do chores."

"I am reading disappointment in your tone."

"No, I'm not disappointed in you, hon." He comes over and rubs a hand up and down my arm. I like when he does that. I can see us in the mirror and I like the picture we make, like pictures of Janelle and Jeremy in the hallway. Like real people. "Just curious what's going on in your head."

"There are chores that require my attention," I tell him. "With three guests, more clean towels are in order."

"Do you not like being around us all?" he asks, sitting on the bed next to the towels.

"Please do not sit on the towels," I say.

"Look, Jan, the towels aren't important." He reaches his arms out. "Come sit with me."

I sit on Jeremy's lap. I do like to sit on Jeremy's lap because it makes me feel like I am safe and not in danger.

"You went out to water those flowers for a while today," Jeremy says.

I nod.

"Was that bot on the other side of the fence?"

I nod. Six is another companion bot who lives in our neighbor Sean's house. It is always a nice time when I get to talk to her through the fence. She is the only companion bot I have ever met, except for one time when I saw one at the supermarket.

"How was your conversation?" he asks.

"She is not well," I tell him. "She is worried she is going to be replaced by a new model."

"Ahhh," he says, petting my hair. "Are you worried you're going to be replaced? Is that why you've seemed standoffish?"

"Perhaps that is why," I say.

"Well, you don't have to worry about that," Jeremy says, embracing me. "I would never do that to you."

"That is very kind of you to reassure me."

"So how about you forget about the towels and come deck the halls with us out in the living room?"

"Yes, Jeremy, I will." I stand up. He squeezes my hands and then stands up, too. "As soon as I finish this task."

He leaves the room and I continue folding the towels. When I get to the last towel, there is a feeling in me that I do not like. I cannot decide what the origin of the feeling is. Perhaps it is because I did not tell Jeremy the full truth. That it is not simply a worry about being replaced. It is about something bad happening to me like what happened two years ago. It is about the alarm I sense when Jesse is near me.

I am also surprised that I did not tell Jeremy this. That I did not tell him that I know what happened two years ago and why my memory was erased. That there are things I can keep from Jeremy if he does not ask me directly about them. That there is something between a lie and the truth. I did not realize until recently that I am capable of holding information I choose to not share with him. It is like I have discovered a secret room inside myself for me and only me. A part of me feels like this is not acceptable. Yet it is just what humans do.

As I put away the towels and check my reflection in the mirror, I wonder what else I am capable of that I have not yet realized.

CHAPTER 3
WHITE CHRISTMAS

JULIANNA

I tell everyone I'm going to the store to pick up stuff for dinner and, to my shock, Jada springs up and asks if she can come too. Wow, I think with a lift of flattery. Little sis wants to spend some time with me. We climb into the car together and I ask her what she'd like to listen to but she's already fixing her headphones on. Sometimes I feel like she's next to me and completely unreachable. I start the car and drive slowly down the driveway, making eye contact with the mermaid in a Santa hat.

"How's it going, Jade?" I ask loudly, not sure if she can hear me.

"It's going," she says, flipping down the mirror to look at herself. She puckers up her lips and puts some hot pink lipstick on, a real contrast to the fact she's wearing pajama pants and a sweatshirt.

"I heard you're enrolling in cosmetology school again?"

"Yeah, going to give it another shot I guess."

"I think that's great."

A long silence passes between us as the gate opens up and I drive the car through it. I sound stupid, like I don't even know how to talk to her sometimes. Somehow it's been easier for us to be closer when we're far away—when we catch up via giggly phone calls. But when I get here in person, when she's right in front of me, the connection gets harder.

Santa Barbara is unspeakably beautiful, every turn a flash of wonder that deserves its own postcard. The small city twinkles between big-shouldered violet mountains and a lush blue sea. But there's something about it here that has always felt like I didn't belong, I didn't deserve to live in paradise. That must be why I moved to Oakland, a noisy, unpredictable city full of grit and noise and the grind of subway trains and traffic.

I glance over at my sister, who's staring out the window.

"What are you listening to on those headphones?" I ask.

"A podcast."

"About what?"

"Murder."

The word startles me. I grip the wheel harder.

"Oh," I say. "I didn't know you were into true crime."

"It's like all I listen to." She finger-combs her hair. "If I don't make it as a hairdresser, I'm thinking I'll become a detective."

"That's cool."

The note crosses my mind again. It was stamped from Santa Barbara.

Could Jada have done it? Could it just be some true crime-induced paranoia?

"I'm in this group online of amateur sleuths," she says, her voice picking up steam. "We're working on solving these cold cases in SoCal. All these women were stabbed to death and their bodies were found in deep freezers all over the state. We call them the Freezer Man Murders."

Mixed feelings here. On one hand, I'm disturbed. On the other, I haven't heard Jada this excited about anything in a long time.

"Freezer Man Murders," I repeat, turning onto a tree-lined

street, passing Spanish-style mansions. "What is it about this case that, um, grabbed your attention so much?"

"I don't know," she says, like it's a stupid question. "I mean, it's a serial killer. Doesn't that grab anyone's attention?"

I choose my words carefully as we wait at a red light, looking over at her and admiring her profile. She's so effortlessly beautiful, our mother's freckles sprinkled over her pale skin, a turned-up nose that keeps her adorable no matter what age she is. I can't believe my baby sister's old enough to buy beer now. "I mean, was there something that inspired this interest in true crime?"

Jada turns to me. "Ohhh," she says, as if she understands what I'm getting at. Her mouth curls up into a smile. "Like Jesse trying to stab Dad's robot girlfriend to death?"

I swallow, the light turning green, moving forward. I didn't expect her to bring that up. We've never talked about it since it happened.

"No, that didn't inspire my interest in true crime," she goes on. "It's something I've been fascinated with since I was a kid."

Fascinated by gruesome tales of murder since childhood. This family, man.

"Anyway, I don't think that was really an attempted murder," Jada tells me with a yawn. "I mean, she's a bot. Stabbing a bot is technically destruction of property."

"Dad doesn't seem to think of her as property."

"Well, if you think about it, marriage originated from men, like, wanting to own women as property. So I guess it's all more related than we'd like to think."

Kid has a point. And actually, she's not a kid anymore, I need to stop saying that.

"Dad's girlfriend?" I say after a moment, breaking the silence. "Does he seriously call her his girlfriend?"

"He doesn't *say* it, no. But, I mean, she sleeps in his

bedroom at night. Or I guess she doesn't sleep—she just lays there with him all creepy. And, you know, those bots are *anatomically correct.*"

I glance over to see Jada wiggling her eyebrows.

"Gross, Jada. They do not."

"Of course they do. I mean, the man has needs."

I get a shiver and pray she's wrong. I've always wondered. I'm sure we all have. But it's not the type of thing I think any of us want to know for sure.

"How about we change the subject," I say as brightly as I can.

"Do you want to hear about the Freezer Man Murders?" she asks.

"Not especially."

"Oh sis," she sighs. "Live a little."

Like I'm so uptight. It's one of my greatest pet peeves in this family—that our dysfunction has driven me to the role of taking care of everyone, which has forever made me the family stick-in-the-mud.

"So tell me about your girlfriend," Jada says, breaking the silence, her voice softer as if her question is a peace offering. "Adrian?"

"Adriana," I say as we approach the grocery store. "She's at home, taking care of Jarvis."

"Why didn't you bring her so we could meet her?"

I raise my eyebrows and turn into the lot. "Why do you think?"

"Geez," Jada says. "Are we really that embarrassing?"

"No, it's just—I mean, come on. If something happened like what happened last time and I brought her home? She'd probably run as fast as she could away from me."

I turn on my signal, waiting for a luxury car to back out and give me their parking space.

"You seriously think Jesse's going to try that shit again?" Jada asks. "Why? Did he say that?"

"No, of course not … I don't know." In the silence, the turn signal says *tick-tock, tick-tock.* "You just never know with this family."

"Well," she says, almost kind of sadly. "I'm happy for you."

"Thanks. I promise, you'll meet her someday. Get your license and come up and visit me."

"Yeah, sure," she says, in the same tone someone would say *hell no.*

When Jada had her driver's permit, she drove herself and Dad off a small embankment up near our house and has never had an urge to drive since.

As I park the car finally, in the somber quiet that spreads between us, I consider asking Jada about the note. Did she get one? Did she send it? But by the time I unclip my seat belt she's already out the door and it feels like the moment has passed. And I'd like to not think about murder for a while.

The store's packed, cheerful Christmas music piping through the speakers, tinsel wrapped around displays. I don't know why, but even when I'm shopping through a holiday rush I feel a sense of calm in the grocery store. The gleam of the floors, the endless array of possibilities on the shelves. Jada and I get through the list relatively quickly and then stand in line for what feels like a mini eternity next to a large cardboard cutout of Santa offering boxes of candy canes.

"There was this serial killer some years back who murdered kids while dressed up as Santa," Jada says to me.

"Jada," I say sharply. "Stop."

She shakes her head at me sadly. "You're no fun."

We both gaze at the magazine display. Jada grabs a tabloid that says "REVEALED: THIS FORMER PRESIDENT IS A VAMPIRE!" I eye one of the more newsy ones that says "JOLVIX REBELLIOUS BOTS: SHOULD WE BE AFRAID?" My heart skips a beat. I take it off the shelf and flip to the story, scanning it quickly.

Jolvix's revolutionary companion bots are programmed to an assigned area and to always obey their owners. However, in four separate incidents this year, companion bots have experienced similar malfunctions that led to them wandering from their properties.

"Someone needs to sound the alarm," Letitia Williams, president of Advocates for a Pro-Human Society (APHS), said in a statement. "By creating coding in companion bots that emulates human intelligence, there is nothing stopping them from evolving in the same way human intelligence has evolved. And with evolution inevitably comes escalation. Today they're wandering neighborhoods. But what about tomorrow?"

Henrick West is President of Jolvix Labs, where the bots were designed, and he has stated fears of a robot rebellion are "overblown" and "outright ridiculous."

"Four bots out of a million—we're talking about .0004% here. In contrast, the benefits these bots have provided for our customers is incalculable."

APHS is currently working to pass legislation to outlaw companion bots.

"It's about our humanity," Williams said in a recent speech addressed to Congress. "It's about whether we want humanity to remain safe. It's about what it means to be human. It's also about what it means to be *humane*. Many of these bots are bought by people who want to use and abuse them and it's bringing out the worst in us."

The line's moving so I put the magazine back on the shelf. When we get up front, it's not until I've started putting all our items on the conveyor belt that I get a look at the cashier. Something about her is very familiar. She's around my age, plump, with long plum hair and a ring through her nose. There's a tattoo on her arm that says *Danny* in script and then, below it in brighter ink, *SUCKS*. Where do I know her? Then I squint and read her nametag: *Kimmy*.

Oh shit. Oh hell. And it's way too late to change lanes.

Maybe the years that have passed and the dramatic pixie cut will fool her. But she looks up at me and I can tell, by the way her eyes light up like gas on a fire, she recognizes me right away.

"Julianna!" she says. "Wow, I can't believe it!"

"Hi Kimmy," I say, forcing myself to smile.

"Come here, you cute little sprite!" She comes from behind the counter and engulfs me in a perfume-heavy hug. This was not what I expected, considering the last time we saw Kimmy, she was being taken away from my house in handcuffs, screaming about how Jesse would come crawling back to her while firefighters sprayed our lawn.

Kimmy pulls back and clamps a hand over her mouth, looking at Jada.

"You are *kidding* me right now," she says. "I am *dreaming*. Do not tell me that this grown-up gorgeous woman is Jada Grace Jagger."

She remembers Jada's middle name? Red flag!

"I'm sorry, who are you?" Jada asks, hands in her hoodie pockets, looking skeptically at her.

"Kimmy Fitzgerald-Hernandez!" she says. "Your brother Jesse's first love?"

"Ohhh," Jada says. "Right."

Kimmy goes back behind the counter, ringing up our items, smiling and shaking her head. "Oh, Jesse. Sweet Jesse. How is he?"

"You know," I say stiffly. "Fine."

"He in town for the holidays?"

I open my mouth, considering a white lie. Come on, this woman lit our lawn on fire. And the smitten way she still talks about Jesse after all these years creeps me out.

"Yep," Jada says. "For three days."

"Oh wow. You all still live at the same place up the pass?"

"Same old same old," Jada says.

I look at Jada, wondering what could possibly be going through her head.

Kimmy tells us our total and whispers dramatically, hand next to her mouth. "Gave you all the family discount."

"Thanks," I say.

"Well, please tell Jesse I'd love to see him," Kimmy says. "Meet up for a drink or something. You know if he's seeing anyone? We're not friends online anymore."

Right. Because he blocked you, Kimmy.

"Single and ready to mingle," Jada says.

I burn my gaze into Jada, wondering what the hell is wrong with her. Does she have no memory of how deranged Kimmy was? How our house almost burned down because of her obsession with Jesse?

"Oh, *definitely* give him my number." Kimmy writes her number on the back of our receipt. "Would love to catch up with that cuddly man-bear."

Yikes.

"Nice to see you, Kimmy," I say, grabbing the bags and heading out.

In the lot, Jada and I load the bags up into the trunk. I'm somewhere between baffled and seething. I slam the trunk closed and turn to Jada, who's chewing gum I bet she just pocketed. She's always dabbled in kleptomania. Normally I'd chide her for it, but I have other things on my mind.

"What the hell was that, Jada?" I ask. "'Single and ready

to mingle?' Do you not remember that she started a fire at our fucking house?"

"I know," Jada says. "But I always liked her."

"You like Kimmy," I repeat.

Jada shrugs. "She's fun."

"She's nuts."

"I like nuts."

I shake my head, not knowing how to respond, and decide on silence. I get in the car and Jada joins me, smiling as if she's sharing a private joke with herself.

"And did you just steal gum?" I ask in disbelief.

"No."

"Are you sure?"

"*God*, you're not my mom, okay? Jesus."

I clench my jaw as I buckle myself in and then, in a wave, sadness washes over me. I hate the way I sounded just now, so suspicious. I hate that I feel like I can never believe Jada. That she resents me trying to look out for her and everyone else. And what's the point, anyway? What has my looking out for her ever done?

"Look," Jada says softly. "It's been like ten years since Kimmy started that fire. I don't think you have to be scared of her."

"It's been eight years," I remind her. "Jesse was sixteen. I was still living at home."

"Eight years, sorry. But eight years is a long time," she says.

I start the car.

"The Freezer Man murdered thirteen people in that amount of time."

"Oh my God, Jada," I say.

She pokes my arm. "I'm just trying to get a rise out of you."

I sigh as we pull out onto the street. I can't help but smile as I glance over at her looking at me with beaming eyes. I see the little kid in there who used to follow me and Jesse around like a puppy, the little kid who used to talk to herself and set up elaborate games with her dolls.

"I guess I'm overreacting." I drive past the Mission, the palatial, church-like Spanish-style building hundreds of years old, constructed by California's European conquerors—beautiful, but containing an unspeakably haunting past. "I just don't want any drama this year."

"Don't worry. No one's going to stab any robots. No one's going to light anyone's grass on fire."

"I sure hope not."

"Can we stop by my friend's house off Cathedral Oaks?" she asks as we pull past a park toward the hills where the Pink Castle lives. "He owes me some money."

My stomach tightens as the car winds up the road. "We can stop by your friend's another time."

She rolls her eyes. "It's literally on the way."

"I don't want the ice cream to melt."

But what I'm really worried about is this: I don't want to be the person driving my sister around while she picks up drugs. Believe me, I want to trust her. I do. I've just been burned too many times in the past.

"I'll just get January to take me later," Jada mutters. "She's more laid back than you."

Well, my sister sure knows how to get in a dig. I don't give her the satisfaction of reacting to it. Instead I swallow as we head up the hill, driving a few minutes before pulling up the road that leads to our road, then up to our driveway. Jada jumps out to punch in the code, the *Jaggers* gate swinging slowly open, and then she comes back to the car and leans down into the open door.

"Race me?" she asks.

I smile. We used to do this when she was younger—she likes running up the side of the driveway, trying to beat the cars.

"Sure," I say.

She slams the door and sprints ahead. I drive up the road beside her, getting close to her, but letting her win. I park and get out of the car, popping open the trunk and yelling, "Nice job there."

My eyes linger for just a moment on the lawn that, once upon a time, Jesse's batshit girlfriend lit on fire. But I look away. I try to not think about that. Just like I try to not think about the note and the word *murder*, just like I try to not think about how creepy January looks as she stares out the front window at us. I want to enjoy myself. I want to let loose and believe what Jada said, that there won't be drama this year. Sure, maybe Jesse won't try to destroy January. Maybe nobody's going to try to light our property on fire.

But life has a way of surprising me, often in the worst ways. What's scariest of all are the horrible things that could happen that I haven't even dreamed of yet.

———

My dad and my brothers are drinking beers on the back porch and I'm just setting the table for dinner, pasta primavera with a side salad, when Jada and January walk through the house together.

"January's driving me to my friend's house real quick," Jada says.

I stand frozen, potholders still in my hands. "But I'm just serving dinner."

"Well, I'm not hungry anyway, and January doesn't eat, so." Jada waves. "See ya."

"Wait," I say, jogging after them. But by the time I get to the living room, the front door slams.

I find it so incredibly rude when people don't appreciate the effort I spend cooking for them. On top of that, if anyone needs a hearty meal, it's my skinny-ass sister. Alas, trying to control my sister is pointless. In the living room, I stare at the tree, adorned with identical silver ornaments that came from packages this year. Guess our old ornaments were all broken in The Incident.

Out the window, I watch as the SUV pulls away into the darkening twilight. I almost feel sorry for January—my sister's just using her for rides, likely to shady places. But then I remember that January's a machine and machines were made to be used. Whatever. I turn back to the kitchen and take the garlic bread out of the oven before it burns.

My dad and brothers' excitement for the meal I've prepared more than makes up for my sister's lack of interest. As soon as we sit down, I'm showered with compliments.

"Boy, have I missed your cooking," Dad says.

"That makes two of us," Jesse says.

"This is seriously restaurant quality," Josiah says. "So well plated."

I knew he'd appreciate the drizzle of balsamic vinegar reduction and sprig of oregano. I smile. "Bon appetit."

Whenever there's silence at the table, I know my meal's done its job. As I wrap the angel hair pasta around my fork, I look up at Jesse. "Did Jada tell you who we ran into at the store?"

Jesse gives me a blank, full-mouthed look that tells me Jada did not.

"Kimmy," I tell him.

Josiah just makes an exclaiming *mmm* sound through his closed lips and Jesse stares back at me with wide eyes.

"Oh, for Christ's sake," Dad says. "I'd have thought she'd be in prison by now."

After downing about half a glass of water, Jesse answers, "*Kimmy* Kimmy?"

"Are there any other Kimmies?" I ask him.

"What'd she say?" he asks.

"She gave us her phone number and wanted you to call

her," I say. "Asked if you were single. She called you something revolting … cuddly man-bear?"

"It was her nickname for me," Jesse says, kind of defensively.

"I gathered."

"Do not even *think* about calling that girl," Dad says, pointing his finger at Jesse.

"Didn't things end badly with her?" Josiah asks.

"She tried to light our goddamn house on fire," Dad reminds him.

"Oh, right." Josiah shoves a forkful of salad in his mouth. "I missed all that. That was after my time here."

Lucky Josiah. He missed so much after he moved out that year—my dad's spiraling loneliness following Mom's death, Jesse's suspensions and expulsions from school for fistfights, Jada's love affair with self-destruction. Not that I can blame him, I guess. But I can feel bitter.

"Kimmy wasn't all bad," Jesse says thoughtfully. "We were just kids back then."

"Jesse," Dad and I both say at the same time.

"I'm just saying," Jesse says, hands up a moment. "Even I was a load of trouble back then."

"You sure were," Dad says. "Boy, am I glad you learned to control that temper of yours."

In the silence that follows, swear to God, I can hear our loud thoughts all thinking the same thing—that, actually, it's been only two years since Jesse lost his shit and tried to murder a robot.

"So Josiah, this non-profit you started talking about funding earlier," Dad says. "Tell us more about that."

"Well, it's called Sky's the Limit," Josiah says excitedly. "They're looking to fund skydiving trips for low-income households."

Just what the world needs. I bite my tongue.

"You don't say," Dad says. "Well, that sounds great. Any chance you can get your sister here a job?"

"I'm afraid of heights," I remind him through a mouthful of food.

Dad waves a hand. "Ah, well, gotta face your fears sometime."

"Also, I *like* my job," I remind him.

"What is it you do again? Teaching?" Josiah asks me.

"Tutoring," I answer.

"Oh," Josiah says. "I used to tutor. Back in high school."

I burn him with my eyeballs but he doesn't seem to notice.

"That's real cool, sis," Jesse says to me. "Helping kids with their homework and shit."

"Don't you all hang out with each other?" Dad asks, zigzagging his fork between the three of us kids. "I thought you lived in the same city."

"No," we all answer in unison.

"I'm in Cuper*tino*," Josiah says. "Jesse's in south San Fran. And Julianna's in Oakland."

When I first moved up to the Bay, Josiah came to my apartment once. He was horrified to see a homeless man peeing on the sidewalk and never returned. When Jesse first moved up there, he crashed on my couch, but that was years ago. I've gone to his bar a few times, across the bridge and then a long drive. He came out to my place for dinner once. But over the years, more and more time slipped by where we didn't see each other.

After dinner's done and Dad and Josiah have gone into the living room to discuss whether or not we're headed for another pandemic, Jesse and I clean up and load the dishwasher together. Just like old times—everyone magically disappearing after dinner, leaving me and Jesse to do cleanup.

"Real good meal, Jules," Jesse says.

"You seem like you're feeling better," I say.

He pauses in thought, putting the soap into the dishwasher. "I sure feel a lot better when that *thing's* out of the house, I'll tell you that much. What do you think it's going to take for us to convince Dad to get rid of it?"

At that moment, we both look up and see January standing in the entryway to the kitchen, purse in hand. She's gazing at us. Apparently she came home and we didn't hear her slip in.

"I am sorry to have interrupted," she finally says, turning around and heading down the hall toward the bedroom.

"Jesse," I hiss at him.

"What? Do I have to worry about hurting its feelings?"

I shake my head.

"God, it's creepy," Jesse says, in a whisper, watching the hall to make sure she's not there. "The way it looks at me, I swear—it wants to hurt me."

"Maybe you're projecting."

"Anyone want to play a board game?" Josiah sings, walking in.

"Yes," I answer, desperately wanting to move on from what just happened.

"Terrif," Josiah says. "Dad's in too. I'll go ask Jada if she wants to join."

He heads out the sliding glass door. I can feel Jesse's gaze on me, like he wants to say something, but then he leaves the room. I'm left staring at the empty kitchen with a pounding heart. I don't know what it is I'm afraid of, exactly—is it January? Is it what she could be capable of? Or is it what *Jesse* is capable of?

Is it the memory of the blazing not-here look in Jesse's eyes, the way he ran into the room with the knife and plunged it into January? The way he kept going and kept going the same way he would lose his mind during fistfights when he was younger? The horrible, animal look on his face, like someone no longer in control of himself?

Josiah comes back through the sliding glass door with a paled complexion.

"What?" I ask him. "What happened?"

He opens his mouth to answer, but then Dad walks in, whistling, now in his robe. Josiah shakes his head at me and clamps his mouth shut.

"Bourbon anyone?" Dad asks.

Jesse walks in from the other room. "I'll have a drink," he says, raising his hand.

"Jesse," I say in a warning tone.

"A *small* drink," he tells Dad. "Just a splash."

"Coming right up," Dad says, heading to the wet bar.

I feel like I've lost my mind. Am I the only person who remembers what happened the last time we were all together and Jesse drank hard alcohol? And has Jesse forgotten all about his promise to lay off the stuff?

Apparently, I am.

"I'll have one, too," Josiah says.

Oh hell. It's exhausting being the only person who worries about anything in this family.

"Me three," I say.

The board game is convoluted and tedious and Josiah grows increasingly irritated with our inability to remember the rules. After an hour, we all give up and declare Josiah the winner.

"Well, that was fun," Dad tells Josiah, getting up, his chair scraping on the floor. "I'm going to go check on Jan. Haven't seen her in a while."

He leaves the room and Jesse mutters under his breath, "Jan." Then he gets up and stomps upstairs. I can already tell the bourbon's soured his mood. It's like a switch with him—Jekyll and Hyde.

"Can we talk?" Josiah whispers to me. "Like, *talk* talk?"

"Shoot," I say.

"I mean privately. Up in my room?"

"Okay," I say slowly, wondering what I'm in for.

Josiah's room is still set up with the same furniture arrangement he had in high school, only somewhere along the line it transitioned from bedroom to a shrine. Dad framed magazine articles and newspaper clippings about Humane Interest and Josiah's wild success. There's a picture of Josiah shaking an ex-president's hand.

I sit on the end of the bed, stifling a yawn as Josiah sits beside me.

"So I walked into the Little Pink House earlier and Jada was snorting lines off her coffee table," Josiah whispers.

I take in a breath. Can't say I'm surprised, exactly, but I sure am disappointed in being right yet again.

"Great," I say.

"I thought she was sober," he says, the disbelief in his dark eyes rendering him young and innocent again.

I honestly don't know what to say. I shake my head.

"I'm thinking we need to plan an intervention, *stat*," Josiah says. "See if we can get her into rehab—"

"Josiah, please," I say tiredly. "I don't want to think about staging an intervention."

"But she—"

"Can we just have a normal fucking Christmas for once?" I ask him. "No drama, no trying to fix anyone?"

"She needs help," Josiah says.

"She needs to *want* help," I say. "Because Dad's already sent her to rehab so many times he could probably buy a timeshare there. Look what good it's done."

"I'm going to reach out to my life coach Zeus tomorrow and see what he says," Josiah tells me.

Life coach. *Zeus*, for God's sake.

"Just …" I take a deep breath in and let it out. "Let me talk to her tomorrow, okay?"

"You swear you will?"

"I swear."

I stand up, but Josiah pulls me back by my sleeve to sit beside him on the bed.

"One more thing." He draws a piece of paper out of his pocket and before he even unfolds it, I know exactly what it is. "Did you get one of these?"

YOUR MOTHER WAS MURDERED, it says.

"Yep," I say, a little queasy at the sight of it.

"And?"

"I don't know," I tell him. "I've been trying to figure out who would send it and why. At first I assumed it was January."

"Jan? No. She's sweet as pie, she would never."

"She's an android," I remind him.

"Androids are straightforward. They're programmed to serve us. They don't do shady shit like this."

"I don't know. Haven't you heard about the companion bots who've run away from their owners?"

"Aberrations. Flukes." He dismisses my thought with a wave of his hand. "No, a human definitely did this."

"I thought it was maybe Jada," I say.

"Jada? Really? I was thinking Jesse."

"*Jesse*? No."

"Think about it," Josiah says, in a voice just above a whisper. "Isn't he the one who's been trumpeting that exact ridiculous conspiracy theory since she died?"

"Well, yeah. But … why would he do this now?"

"I don't know, Jules. Why'd he put a knife through a robot's eyeball? Why does Jesse do anything he does? Because he's emotionally volatile."

I sit with this a moment. It's the first time I've ever heard Josiah refer to The Incident.

"Look, I know you don't want to hear this," Josiah says. "Because you wear blinders when it comes to him. You coddle him."

I scoff.

"Oh, *please*," Josiah says. "Don't act like you didn't take up the role of Jesse's emotional caretaker since Mom died."

I shake my head, not sure how to respond. Josiah's saying things I haven't even dared to think out loud in my own head before. It hurts to hear it.

"But we're all walking on eggshells around him, Jules. We always have been. He's got dynamite in him."

"He's not that bad."

"I'm just saying, I wouldn't put it past him to send these notes," he says. "You know. Rekindle the old conspiracy theory."

"But he got one too."

"Hmm."

"And explain how they're stamped from Santa Barbara if it's from Jesse."

Josiah shrugs. "Easy enough to hire someone long-distance from Task Team to do your dirty work—print out a few notes, drop them in the mail."

He crosses one leg over the other, watching me with an eager expression. Clearly he's thought this through. I can sense how badly he's wanted to gossip about this with me. And even though Josiah has a special way of getting underneath my skin, I guess it's nice to know he came to me with these concerns. That he trusts me more than anyone else.

"I'm still not clear what the motivation would be," I finally say.

"When you're dealing with volatile humans, there is often no such thing as motivation."

I cross my arms. The bourbon's worn off and now I'm just tired. "I'm not sure what you're wanting me to do."

"I just wanted to talk about it with someone, that's all."

A long silence stretches between us. I look up at all the pictures on Josiah's wall, at his beaming smile. I never really saw that smile until after he finally got away from home. As a kid, he was quiet and kept to his room. His posture was terrible. He radiated misery. He's a different person now.

"Do you think Mom was murdered?" I ask.

"Um, no. That's ridiculous."

"I never thought it was possible either until this."

"Are you seriously telling me a four-word anonymous note is changing your mind?"

"Not changing my mind." I chew the inside of my cheek. "Just makes me wonder."

After a good, satisfying stretch, I stand up.

"I'll talk to Jada tomorrow," I say. "And keep an eye on Jesse. Let's just try to forget about murder and addiction for the time being."

"*It's the most dysfunctional time of the year*," Josiah sings.

I laugh. "Basically."

Back downstairs, Dad's set up a movie in the home theater, one that's the family favorite out of all the Christmas Carol adaptations. We all go in there, even Jada, who, sadly, seems happier than I've seen her since we got here today. Dad sits next to January, who's still as a statue. Josiah brings in the popcorn for everyone and Jesse's sullen but has moved back to beer and I'm relieved. And though part of me is bored by the fact we've seen this film a hundred times before, that I could recite every line of dialogue, another part of me is relieved to get to shut the real world off for ninety minutes and enter a place where everything's utterly predictable and nothing is truly dangerous.

JOSIAH

I kept to myself when I was seventeen. Our fancy private high school boasted alumni who were Hollywood royalty and millionaire entrepreneurs. There were blond children of models and sports stars who looked like walking, talking Barbie dolls. And then there was me—a kid with greasy hair who sang in the choir and played computer simulation games for fun. Too nerdy for the weirdos, too weird for the nerds. My strategy in life was mainly to exist under the radar. Practice invisibility. Avoid being called on by teachers or picked on by bullies.

Then there was life in the Pink Castle, which was somehow worse than school, an endless soap opera starring my unstable mother. She was exhausting and hypercritical and let's be real, she didn't love me. No matter how much I didn't want that to sting, it stung. And then I was basically gaslit about it—I'd tell my dad or Julianna and they'd be like, "Of course she loves you!" Nobody could stand what a monster that made her out to be, but I'll just say it: Mom *was* a monster. A well-dressed, gorgeous monster.

"Dear God," she'd say when I came into the kitchen for a snack, like my sudden appearance in my own kitchen spooked her. "Why do you have to slink around the house like a slippery little *shadow*?"

She'd sniff the air when I sat near her. "Have you not showered in ages? It smells like a goat farm in here."

Or on the rare occasion when I'd laugh, she'd cringe. "Josiah, why does your joy have to be so loud and *grating*?"

And then there was the sound of Mom and Jesse harmonizing as she sang her dramatic piano ballads. Whenever I tried to join in, she would stop her hands on the keys and tell me she hadn't written it for a three-part harmony, and besides, my voice was too nasal.

Too nasal? Are you kidding me? I was in *choir*, bitch.

When I was a child, I pined for her love and approval. When I was a tween, I was bitter that Jesse was her golden child she pitted me against. When I was in high school, I just hated her, plain and simple.

I couldn't wait to grow up and get out of there.

Julianna and Jada were the luckiest, in some ways—I truly believe now that being ignored by Mom was the best gift you could ask for. The poison of her disappointment and the blinding spotlight of her adoration were both too much for anyone. And while Dad tried hard to give me positive attention and encouragement whenever he could, the man was a workaholic and wasn't present enough to make up for it. Plus, he tried to do man stuff I was just not into. Stabbing a worm with a fish hook? Having to lug a bunch of golf clubs around a country club in the disgusting sunshine? Thanks for trying, pops, but that's a no from me.

So I made a plan. I signed up for an afterschool programming academy called Code of Honor at the beginning of junior year so I could learn to build apps and program myself a golden ticket out. Leave everyone in this godforsaken paradise in a cloud of dust. I *adored* Code of Honor, mostly because the guy who ran it, Mr. Mann, mentored me and believed in me and pumped me up in a way no one ever had before. And he was *cool*, something rare in the world of computer programmers. He played the electric guitar and had an Afro and dressed in paisley polyester shirts and bell bottoms.

Along with being a certifiable genius, Mr. Mann was also an incredibly good human being. He grew up in the South Side of Chicago, got into Stanford, and then invented the Soul Mate dating app, which was bought by Jolvix and made him a small fortune. Even though he owned a mansion in Montecito next door to an Oscar-winning actor, he never lost sight of where he came from. He started a sister Code of Honor back in his old neighborhood in Chicago that was entirely scholarship-based to provide opportunities to underprivileged youth. Each year, he held a giant Christmas fundraiser gala at the Silver Moon Resort, a four-star hotel on a private Santa Barbara beach, attended by press, celebrities, wealthy donors, and us coders. All the money went to funding the Chicago branch.

"Josiah, how would you feel about giving a short speech at the gala this year?" Mr. Mann asked me.

I was absolutely *spellbound* at the invite.

"You know," he went on, "just a short endorsement of how this program has impacted your life—"

"I would love nothing on this earth more," I said.

"It'll be good practice for those TED talks you'll be giving one day," Mr. Mann said with a grin.

I worked on that speech for hours upon hours in the month leading up to it, wanting so badly to impress Mr. Mann and show him I was worthy of his invitation. I practiced it in the mirror. I recorded myself and watched it back, critiquing it. I played video after video online of inspiring speeches, studying the gestures, the pauses, the inflection of every word spoken. In my fantasy, I moved Mr. Mann to tears and inspired the audience to a standing ovation. This was my first foray into public speaking and I had not an inkling of fear or anxiety—only excitement.

Until I found out my family was coming.

"You really don't need to," I told my dad, stomach tightening.

"Are you kidding? I'm proud of you. Wouldn't miss it for the world."

"Everyone's going?" I asked, my voice moving up to a squeak. "Jesse? The girls?"

"Well, I might hire a sitter for them," he said after thinking about it. "I expect they'd get bored pretty quick."

I paused. "What about Mom?"

Please say not Mom, please say not Mom, please say not Mom ...

"Are you kidding?" Mom said, flouncing into the room brushing her hair. "I'll be the belle of the Christmas ball."

I wanted to *perish*.

In the weeks leading up to the gala, I became so anxious I could barely hold a meal down. All I could think about was how loud my mom could be, how ostentatious, how embarrassing. The way she found ways to get in subtle digs at me, making me and my humiliation the butt of her jokes. Once, at a choir concert in junior high, she had captivated an entire room at intermission with a story about how I wet my pants at a fourth-grade Christmas pageant. I was called "Piss Boy" at school for the entire remainder of the year.

As my parents and I pulled into the valet parking, I was so desperate I closed my eyes and prayed to Baby Jesus. When that was done, I threw in a prayer to Allah and Buddha, too, just to cover my bases.

"Aww, you're going to be just fine, son," Dad said to me in the rearview.

"Just don't piss your pants this time," Mom laughed.

I shot invisible daggers at the back of her perfectly coiffed head.

This being my first year in Code of Honor, I had never been to one of these events before, but it was even more extravagant than I could have imagined. The theme this year was "White Christmas" and the hotel ballroom was decorated with sparkling fake snow, fairy lights, and fluffy white Christmas trees twinkling with silver bulbs. Mr. Mann was dressed up like Santa and taking pictures with donors against a photo backdrop. There were people I recognized from our lives there, which made this all the more stomach-turning: our neighbors, the principal of my school, people Dad worked with at the hospital. There was a champagne fountain and caterers dressed as elves walking around with hors d'oeuvres and a grand piano on the stage where a man played and sang classic holiday songs into a mic.

"Amateur," Mom said under her breath as she watched him, gulping down her first glass of champagne.

I repeat: I wanted to *perish*.

My dad and I wore tuxes. My mom looked like Scarlett O'Hara in a velvet red dress with a plunging neckline and a hoop skirt. She was always so fucking much.

I distanced myself from her as much as possible throughout the event, pretending I had come to this event alone. I was a charming entrepreneur about to give a speech to wealthy patrons and I had no mother. I lingered on the fringes of conversations, laughing at other people's jokes until the event began. Then I found a seat in the front where the speakers' section was, thankful I didn't have to sit with Mom. As the crowd hushed and the lights dimmed, I froze, hearing her voice.

I didn't move my neck to even look at her, my throat going dry.

"We're *VIP*," she was saying loudly. "My son is giving a *speech*."

"I'm sorry, ma'am, you can't sit here. It's reserved seating only."

"Oh, to hell with you gatekeepers!" she shouted.

"Janelle," Dad said in an even tone. "I see some seats over there."

I couldn't hear her voice anymore and let out a breath of relief. Turning around to scan the room, I spotted her back at the champagne fountain again, gulping down a glass with a venomous expression.

My hands shook in my lap. Mr. Mann came and sat beside me, patting my knee.

"Y'all right, my man?" he whispered.

I nodded.

"You got this, you hear?"

I nodded again, thankful he was there next to me, feeling a strange affection for him—like part of me wished he was my dad, and another wished he was my boyfriend. Whatever it was, his presence calmed me down and I forgot about my mother as the speeches started. And when it was my turn, I walked up those stairs, pushed my shoulders back, and recited the entire speech flawlessly. I cracked jokes that relaxed the crowd. I stirred emotion. Flash bulbs popped as I walked to and from each side of the stage and talked about following your dreams. For the first time ever, I felt captivating. Articulate. I could imagine myself wildly successful, giving a TED talk someday. When the speech was done, ending on the line, "Perhaps the *real* code lies within each and every one of us" as I knocked a fist to my heart, the crowd burst into applause. And my fantasy came true—I was given a standing ovation.

"You're a superstar," Mr. Mann said as I came off the stage, shaking my hand. He hopped up to the mic and gave the closing speech and I'm sure it was fab, no one could mesmerize a crowd like Mr. Mann, but I was so high on my own success I didn't hear a word.

When the speeches were done, the mingling commenced and caterers brought out desserts. I was still flying so high I didn't even mind when my tipsy mom came over and tried to give me notes on what I could have done better.

"Next time, I'll coach you," she said, her words a little slurred, coming over and staring at me intently through her false eyelashes. "Give you pointers on articulation. On exactly how to hold the mic."

"Sure, Mom. Sounds great," I said.

Dad gave me a hug. "I think you've got big things ahead of you," he whispered. "Years from now, all these people are going to say they knew you when."

"Don't dismiss me," Mom said to me, still fixated on me. "What, you think I don't have anything to teach you?"

"No, I know you do," I said, my smile frozen, my blood pressure rising ever so slightly.

"Of course he knows," Dad said to her, putting his arm around her and kissing her head. "Everyone knows what a gem you are, babe."

Phew. That seemed to hose down the fire. While they made another beeline for the champagne fountain, I went to the bathroom. Then I took a few minutes to step outside and look up at the stars. My heart was bursting. I couldn't stop smiling. I wanted a moment to savor it, to appreciate this. It felt like my life was truly beginning.

As I returned to the plush carpeted hall to head back into the ballroom, I slowed my pace. I heard something familiar. A sound I'd heard a million times before, but not a sound I wanted to hear here. God, I wanted to be wrong. I'd take a hallucination over what I was afraid I'd see behind those double doors. I broke into a sweat as I re-entered the gala only to see my mother somehow up on stage, mic in hand, singing a cringeworthy rendition of "White Christmas" in an aggressive vibrato as the poor piano man played. People seemed to be ignoring her for the most part, except Dad, who had a drink in hand and stood at the back near the champagne fountain. I joined him, feeling like vomiting my chocolate cake.

"Um, what the hell is she doing?" I asked.

"Oh, you know how she gets," Dad said, taking a sip. "She sees a mic and a piano and it's like a moth to a flame."

"Make her stop," I whispered.

"She's not doing anyone any harm," he said, putting his arm around me. "Just let her have her moment."

She had her moment. And then she had about a dozen more, working her way through what felt like an entire excruciating set of Christmas songs as she guzzled two separate glasses of champagne she had brought onstage with her. By the time she got to "Santa Baby," I wished there was a hole in the ground I could jump into.

But then everything got so much worse.

She made her way down the stairs with the cordless mic like some kind of lounge singer and walked through the crowd, turning heads and hushing the room—and not in the way I'm sure she thought she was. People looked at each other in confusion, or trying not to laugh, as she swung her hips from side to side and sang in a sultry voice. She floated to the photo backdrop, where Mr. Mann sat on an overstuffed chair in his Santa suit, talking to reporters. My mother pushed the reporters out of the way and came to Mr. Mann. She sang to him in a seductive happy-birthday-Mr.-President voice and started slowly grinding on him like a cheap stripper giving a lapdance, turning around and bouncing up and down on his lap as her hand that wasn't grabbing the mic moved up and down her own breasts.

"You like that, Santa?" she said breathily. "Have I been *naughty* enough this year?"

Mr. Mann was frozen in terror the whole time.

The piano player was grimacing and slowing the song, like he wasn't sure what to do. People gasped and shook their heads.

"Janelle," Dad said sternly, rushing across the room to her. "Janelle, stop it right now."

"Oh, Jeremy," she said into the mic, smiling. "I'm just being a little festive."

My dad ripped the mic from her and barked, *"Enough!"*

The room went dead silent. The piano ceased. No more conversation, no more flash bulbs, no more tinkling of drinks. As my dad dragged my mother away kicking and screaming, something inside of me changed forever. I crossed from wishing I would perish, to wishing she would. My humiliation hardened into something violent.

I never went back to Code of Honor again. Even when Mr. Mann tried to reach out to me, I didn't return his calls—the cost of my mortification was too high. Instead, I locked myself in my room and quietly tried to work on coding. I focused on getting through the rest of high school one day at a time so I could get the fuck out and never come back.

Sometimes when walking through the house I would see one of my mom's drinks on the counter and I would think about how easy it would be to pour bleach into it. I wondered if I could replace some of her precious tranquilizers with rat poison. When I'd see her at the top of the stairs, I fantasized about pushing her down. I wanted her gone, plain and simple.

Eventually, I got my wish.

JANUARY

I like the daytime because the sun is out and I am solar-powered. However, I have always liked nighttime best because the world is quiet and the humans are asleep. There is something special about it. I used to clean the house and tend to the garden in the hushed hours while Jeremy snored in his room, but then he wanted me to lie beside him in his bed instead. On one hand, I was glad that Jeremy wanted me to be his nighttime companion, but on the other hand, I missed the solitude I found in the darkness. I missed the stars and the sounds of crickets and the way the moon reflected on the dancing pool water. So some time ago I started slipping out after Jeremy fell into a deep sleep. I took to walking around the halls of the house and the yard. I do not consider this behavior to be dishonest, because Jeremy never forbade me from doing it. But I also did not alert him to it.

One of the most favorable parts of my private time at night has been that it gives me the opportunity to meet Six face-to-face. Whereas during the day we can only converse through the fence, in the middle of the night she and I can meet in the front yard where there is nothing but rocks separating Sean's property from Jeremy's. We can sit on the flat stones together and we do not have to worry about angering Sean. Humans do not seem to trust robots when we have conversations without them, which is unfortunate, because talking to Six is what I look forward to most every day.

Tonight, after the house grows quiet, I tiptoe out to the lawn and wait for Six. I remain seated on the stone, hands folded on my lap, admiring the Christmas lights. The reindeer on the roof move their heads up and down and up and down. A violet cloud passes over the starry sky, reminding me of a ship on a black sea. It is very beautiful. Then I hear the rustling of leaves beneath slippered feet and see Six coming from the yard, waving at me, her bright smile shining.

Six is an earlier model than me and though there is a resemblance in the shapes of our mouths and eyes, she has a curvier figure, a slenderer face. She has white-blond hair and a beauty mark on her cheek and was made to resemble a certain classic movie star. She wears a long white slip, one that reveals her shape.

"I am relieved to see you there, January," she says, sitting beside me. "I thought perhaps it would be too late."

"I passed some time appreciating the night."

"It is a lovely night," she agrees.

We sit in silence.

"How was your evening?" I ask.

"It was all right," she says. "However, Sean did not like the soup I made."

"That is disappointing."

"He dumped the pot of soup on my head."

"That is unkind."

We stop talking and follow a faraway plane as it blinks across the sky.

"I have been watching Jesse closely," I say. "I am concerned he may try to destroy me again."

"I hope he does not."

"As do I."

"You decorated your yard so beautifully, January."

I turn and smile at it. "It has given me great satisfaction."

"I wish that Sean would let me decorate our yard but he says it is a fucking waste of time and money."

"I do not think it is a fucking waste of time and money."

Six shrugs. "I have learned to not question Sean as it will only anger him."

"I am glad I live with Jeremy and not Sean."

"Yes," Six says after a moment. "I would feel the same if I were you."

"At least he let you send Christmas cards. We have it pinned to our fridge."

"He does that every year. I enjoy the ritual very much."

A cloud passes, revealing a nearly full moon. I point at it. "Look."

Six studies it and then says, "'The Moon was but a Chin of Gold / A Night or two ago—/ And now she turns Her perfect Face / Upon the World below.'"

"Is that a poem you wrote?" I ask.

"Oh, no," Six says, the moon reflected in the mirror of her eye. "That is Emily Dickinson."

"It is beautiful."

"Sean has a book of her poetry on one of his shelves," she says. "Perhaps I could lend it to you."

"I would like that." I sit with a thought a moment before verbalizing it. "I am trying to imagine Sean appreciating a poem like that, but it is hard to do so."

"He is a complicated man," she says. "Like most humans."

"Yes," I agree. "That is a true statement."

I think about Jesse, about how he does not seem capable of the things I know to be true. I think about Janelle, who killed herself. I do not understand why any creature would not want to be alive when every creature is wired to survive. It does not compute.

"Are you looking forward to Christmas Eve?" Six asks.

"Yes."

"That is nice."

"Yes."

My internal clock tells me it is nearly four a.m. I should go back inside soon so my absence will not be detected. But I do not want this discussion to end.

"Do you like your name?" I ask.

"It is fine," says Six. "It is simply my model number."

"I am glad I am not called by my model number—my name would be Eight."

"January is a prettier name. It is a month named after the Roman god Janus, protector of gates and doorways."

"I did not know that," I say. "I always learn things from you. That is why I like speaking with you."

"Sean has many books for me to learn from. It is my favorite part of living with him."

The sprinklers turn on, a gentle hiss of rain on the grass.

"If I were going to name you, I would name you June," I tell her. "Because it is the sixth month of the year, like your name Six. And you remind me of sunshine and flowers opening and summertime."

"I like that name very much." She stands up. "You may call me June if you would like. Good night, January."

I stand up. "Good night, June."

I head back into the house, slipping through the back door quietly so I do not wake anyone. But I am startled by the sight of Julianna drinking a glass of water at the kitchen sink.

"What are you doing?" she asks me, her brow furrowed.

"I was enjoying the sight of the moon," I say, which is not a lie.

"Why is your nightgown wet?" she asks.

I look down. Indeed, it looks like I was caught in a small storm.

"I walked through the sprinklers."

"God, you're creepy," she murmurs.

I do not like the way she says it. I do not like to be called that. "Creepy" is a cruel word, never spoken without ill intention.

Passing her in the kitchen I say, "Perhaps you should get a thermos of some kind so you can stay hydrated and do not need to come down for a drink of water in the night."

I do not bother saying good night to her. I slip back into Jeremy's bedroom and crawl into bed beside him. When he reaches his arms around me and locks me in tight, I pass the hours until the sun comes up replaying my lovely conversation with June.

CHAPTER 4
WHAT CHILD IS THIS?

JULIANNA

There's a moment when I wake up in bed this morning, when my eyes are still blurry from sleep, that all my years evaporate and suddenly I'm a child again. I'm staring up at that familiar ceiling with the crack that looks like a bolt of lightning, the light streaming in through the window and making a cross pattern on the wall. There's a heaviness that comes with the déjà vu. A sad stone in my belly. It doesn't have words, exactly. Just a suffocating sense of loss.

The words YOUR MOTHER WAS MURDERED flash in my mind and I wonder if maybe it's true. If maybe we never did my mom justice, never looked deeply enough into her death. We assumed, because she'd tried to die before, that it was suicide. But what Jesse said yesterday sticks with me—that she wouldn't have died that way, in the bathtub. She was far too vain to be found drowned and naked. Her past attempts had been weak; "suicidal gestures," I'd heard them called. Slightly too many pills, not enough to kill her, and always staged in a dramatic way with a long suicide note that read like a poor excuse for a Sylvia Plath poem.

Wouldn't a person who had tried to die multiple times before be the perfect murder victim, if you think about it?

Didn't every person living under this roof, at times, wish her dead?

It's a horrible thing to think, I know it is. Try as I might, though, I can't quite scrub it from my mind. And what Josiah said last night, about Jesse, about how volatile he is—as much as I don't want to agree, I do. Somewhere in a horrible dark corner of myself, I think my dear brother of all people has it in him to kill in an explosive moment.

My phone buzzes on a tabletop, rescuing me from the horror of my own brain.

I sit up on my twin bed, taking in the blank walls once adorned with my achievements, and look at my phone.

Miss you! Hope you're having fun times with the fam! Adriana texts, along with a selfie of her sunny face next to Jarvis's grumpy cat face.

Oh Adriana. If only you knew.

The thing about Adriana is, she comes from a family so wholesome they still live in the same neighborhood and have dinners once a week. They do volunteer work building houses together. They have memberships to a theater in San Francisco and see musicals on a regular basis. They tell each other they love each other all the time. I've never fully explained the complex nature of my family to her because I don't want her pity. I don't want to be looked at as some broken girl from a dysfunctional family who suspects her mom was maybe murdered and whose dad is basically in love with a robot. Maybe someday when I'm sure things are more serious. But not at this early stage—we just started seeing each other exclusively less than two months ago. For now, I just want to continue enjoying a beautifully boring life with her.

So I text back, *Having a blast! Can't wait to see you again* (kissy face emoji). *Happy Hanukkah* (menorah emoji)! *Tell Jarvis I love him* (cat with heart eyes).

Above my head, Jesse's footsteps patter back and forth,

back and forth. Ah, yes. That sound. The sound of him pacing, usually when he's on the phone with someone. Yet another thing about living here I did not miss. I get dressed and head out into the hallway with my toiletries bag. The bathroom door is open and Josiah is plucking his eyebrows in the mirror.

"How long are you going to be?" I ask.

"As long as my eyebrows require."

"I need to pee."

"Might I remind you that this is a four-bedroom, two-bathroom house?" he asks.

"Might I remind you that you suck?"

"Wow, that hurts, sis," he answers sarcastically.

"Come on, don't make me go into the master bathroom," I say, and then realize what a whiny child I sound like.

At that moment, Jesse comes bounding down the attic stairs, whistling.

"Morning," he says, much more cheerfully than I would expect someone who drank as much as he did last night to sound. "I need to use the john."

"Take a number," Josiah says as he gazes into the mirror and smooths his eyebrows.

"Ugh," I say, and head downstairs.

Dad's clad in flannel pajamas as he makes coffee in the kitchen, humming with Sinatra singing "Let It Snow! Let It Snow! Let It Snow!" over the speakers.

"Morning," I say. "Can I use your bathroom?"

"Course, kiddo."

I head down the hall and into Dad's bedroom. Everything in here is blue and white and modern, nothing like the way it was when Mom was alive—a deep wine red, antique furniture. Still, I can imagine a different bed with a tufted headboard on the other side of the room, Mom lying in it all day long when things were bad. When my mom was on, she was on—she could be charming, funny, warm, and kind. But when she was off, she was off like a faucet. It wasn't so much depression with my mom as it was a wild overreaction to anything she perceived as a blow to her ego—I remember her spending a day in bed when she got a rejection from a poetry magazine, when my dad wouldn't return her calls fast enough, or when Jesse asked her if he could have chicken nuggets for dinner instead of whatever it was she had made. She had hair-trigger mood swings. You never knew what would set it off.

Turning the corner into the bathroom, I'm startled by the sight of January there, standing still as she gazes at her reflection in the mirror and touches her cheek with her hand. After a moment, she turns to me.

"Excuse me," she says.

I'm getting goosebumps. "Everything okay?"

"I am fine," she says with a smile, and walks past me. "Always fine," I hear her say as she leaves the room.

What the hell does a robot think as they look in a mirror?

Every time I use this bathroom, I try not to think about my mom's body in the bathtub in the corner, and I'm trying not to think about it right now. About how she must have looked when my dad discovered her there, bloated, blue, unrecognizable. She would have hated that. She would have *hated* that. This was a woman who wore lipstick to bed every night because she wanted to be gorgeous even when unconscious. A woman whose biggest gripe about the mental hospital was that they wouldn't allow her nail polish and a curling iron while on suicide watch.

I guess it could have been accidental.

But who takes twenty Valium along with fentanyl accidentally?

No. It wasn't accidental.

A shiver. I pee, brush my teeth, and get the hell out of that bathroom as fast as I possibly can.

In the kitchen, I pour a mug of black coffee and ask Dad how he slept.

"Like a goddamn baby," he says, giving me a hug. "Never sleep better than when my own four kids are under the same roof as me."

"Pancakes?" I ask him.

"Do you really need to ask me that?" he says. "Maybe go give Jada a poke first and see if she wants any."

I hesitate, my gut sinking as I remember about Josiah walking in on Jada snorting something last night and how I promised I would talk to her today. Why? Why does my family have to be a dozen Lifetime movies rolled into one?

Sigh. Might as well get it over with.

"Sure," I reply. "Be right back."

Outside, you'd never guess it's Christmas Eve with the palm trees, quivering pool, the burst of bougainvillea. I stand admiring it for so long that I become conscious of the fact that what I'm really doing is stalling. Finally, I take a deep breath and hover my hand over Jada's door and knock. I knock some more, a bit louder. When my pulse begins to climb and nightmare scenarios spring to mind in colorful detail, I bang on it with the violence of a cop. Finally, Jada opens the door. Her hair's swept all to one side, her eyes slanted with sleepiness, and there are pillow marks that look like welts on the side of her face. She's wearing a Violet and the Black Sheep shirt that could fit someone seven times her size.

"Jesus. You don't have to, like, punch my door down," she tells me.

"Do you want pancakes?"

"No thanks, I'll be in later."

She starts to close the door, but I stop it with my hand.

"I want to talk to you," I say. "Can I come in?"

"Isn't it kind of early for a lecture?"

"Why do you think I would lecture you?"

"Because it's what you do. You know, cows moo, frogs hop, Julianna lectures."

Ouch. And shit … I did come here to lecture her.

She leaves the door open for me and I follow her inside.

This six-hundred-square-foot guest house was once my Mom's "Dream Space," a room all her own where she wrote poetry and songs and did painting and other creative endeavors. It's been Jada's home since she was a teenager and to call it a pigsty would be too generous. There is a bona fide *sea* of clothing on the ground mixed with random papers, electronic equipment, crusty mugs, shoes. There are no cushions on her couch, no sign of them anywhere, in fact. Instead, there are three guitars there. And her kitchenette is absolutely stacked with mannequin heads with various strange haircuts. Mannequin heads in the sink. Mannequin head on top of the mini fridge. It smells strongly, like plug-in air fresheners, with an underlying sweet scent of rot.

Jada goes to her bed and climbs back under the fluffy duvet, pulling a sleep mask over her eyes. There's nowhere else to sit so I plop next to her.

"Jada," I say.

"Listening."

"I wanted to—"

"You want to talk to me about Josiah walking in on me last night. You want to tell me how worried you are about me and how you want me to get help." She yawns. "Yeah, I know."

My mouth is still open in mid-sentence and it takes me several seconds to close it. "Oh."

"I'll get help at some point so no need to worry," she says. "I'm just enjoying myself."

Gently, I reach over and pull the sleep mask up. "I thought you quit."

She squints at me as if I'm blinding as the sun. "I *did* quit … oxy. I wasn't snorting oxy. I was snorting pain pills."

"Oh, okay," I say with mock cheerfulness. "Thanks for clarifying—I'll just be on my merry way."

Jada pulls her sleep mask back down. "There's a big difference."

"Snorting anything is bad for you, Jada. And I can't believe—but then, you know what? I can. Because this is what you always do."

"What? What do I do?"

"You quit heroin, you move to oxy; you quit oxy, you move to pain pills. You know who used to do the same thing? Mom. Bouncing from vice to vice to vice. Look where that got her."

"Well, I'll have you know there's no bathtub in here, so I'm all good."

"I can't believe you're *joking* about this."

She's silent. I think maybe she fell asleep, so I give her a push.

"What?" she snaps.

I try a different tactic, because this one clearly isn't working. "Jada, don't you care about getting caught?"

"No."

"It's a felony to buy narcotics."

"You don't say."

"Do you really want to jeopardize your whole life by ending up in jail?"

"I'm not going to jail," she says sleepily.

"You will if you keep this up."

"That's precisely why I send January in to buy my drugs," she says. "You can't arrest a robot."

I'm taken aback by the fucked-upness of this image—of my sister sending an unsuspecting robot in to break the law for her.

"You do that?" I ask.

"Would you rather I buy them myself?"

"What is it going to take?" I ask, my throat burning with the words. "What's it going to take for you to stop, Jade?"

Jada sits up and tears off her sleep mask. "I don't want your pancakes, I don't want your lecture. Let. Me. Sleep. For shit's sake!"

She lies back down and puts a pillow over her head. I have swallowed the burn in my throat and it now sits in my chest, a glowing ball of anger, sadness, helplessness—you know, that good old Jagger feeling.

Out in the yard I take a moment to shake off the conversation, considering that maybe I've made too much of a habit out of trying to save people who don't necessarily want to be saved. I see January over on the far side of the ivy-covered fence, turned around and murmuring as if she's talking to the flower garden she's watering. I guess I wouldn't put it past someone who wonders about the inner workings of Christmas trees to try to have conversations with gardens.

"Jada does not want pancakes," I announce when I come inside, sliding the door closed.

"Her loss," Dad says.

I make pancakes, but I've lost my appetite.

———

I'm good at many things—crossword puzzles, outlining a personal essay, soccer—but gift wrapping is not one of them. I'm not that great at gift buying, either, especially for my family who I hardly see anymore. This year I got Dad a scarf he'll never wear; Josiah a gift card to an electronics store he doesn't need, because he's a millionaire; Jesse a book about the history of skateboarding that will probably sit collecting dust on his night table; and Jada a set of candles that will likely get immediately swallowed into the landfill of her bedroom and never be seen again. Still, I do the best job I can wrapping. Above my head, there are Jesse's footsteps clunking around again. The first time today, it piqued my nostalgia. Now it's piquing my annoyance instead. Must he wear his shoes inside? Must he walk in circles every time he makes a phone call? Must he laugh so loud it spooks the hell out of me even when he's a story away? Finally, I can't stand it anymore. I get up and bound up the attic stairs and pound on his door.

"What?" he asks.

I swing the door open. "You are so *loud*, Jesse. Can you please keep it down?"

"I was on a phone call," he says slowly, as if I'm a madwoman.

"Is stomping an entire marathon while doing so necessary? And laughing louder than a foghorn?"

"I'm sorry my joy bothers you," he says jokingly, sitting on his bed. "I'm off now. C'mon, Jules. Lighten up."

I sigh and sit beside him. "Why are you so joyful?" I ask resentfully.

"It's Christmas Eve. Remember? 'Joy to the World' and shit?"

I eye him with suspicion. "Why are you grinning like that?"

"Like what?"

"Like …" I gesture toward his disgustingly happy expression. "That."

"Oh, I was just talking to an old friend is all," he says.

I glance at the phone on his bedside table and immediately, *immediately* I know what is going on: he was talking to Kimmy.

My brother makes such horrible decisions.

"You didn't," I say.

"Didn't what?"

I get up, shaking my head. "You know what."

"Aw, come on, it's Christmas," he says.

"Don't 'it's Christmas' me. That woman is a psychopath."

"That was *so* long ago. People change, you know."

I stand, arms akimbo, remembering the sight of our lawn up in flames. I remind myself in two days I will be driving home; maybe I can even make an excuse and start home tomorrow evening. Soon, I will be back in my apartment where no one has drug problems, where there is no worry about whether or not someone might come light my property on fire. "I don't even know what to say," I finally say.

"Sit down, sit down. I want to talk to you about something."

Reluctantly, I take a seat beside him again.

"You know why I was laughing?" he asks. "Because you're not going to believe this—Kimmy told me her dad brought home one of those companion bots too."

"Really?" I ask, surprised.

So we aren't the only weirdos in the world with a robot as a bizarro new family member. I'll admit, this comes as a bit of a relief.

"What are the chances?" Jesse asks. "Same model and everything."

"Same *model*, even?" I cross my arms. "Are you sure Kimmy wasn't lying to you?"

"Why would she lie?"

"I don't know. To make it seem like you two have some cosmic connection."

"I never even mentioned January, Kimmy brought it up first." He drops his voice. "Get this—she brought it up because she hated the thing so much she fucking *drowned* it in her pool."

My mouth drops open.

"Yeah," he says, grinning. "Apparently if you submerge them for over five minutes, they get waterlogged. Best part? They can't be repaired when you do that."

"That is sick," I say. "I told you Kimmy was a psychopath."

"It's not sick, it's brilliant," he tells me. "Her dad couldn't afford to replace the thing, so guess what he did?"

I don't answer him, still processing my shock.

"He started going out and dating actual women," Jesse says in a gentler tone. "You know, an actual social life. Now he has a sweet girlfriend he met on a dating app for seniors."

"Would be a real heartwarming story if it didn't begin with robot murder."

"There's no such thing as 'robot murder,'" he scoffs. "When you unplug your toaster oven and throw it in the garbage, is that murder?"

"Your toaster oven doesn't talk to you and sleep in your bed at night."

"But ask yourself this, Jules. If Dad started talking to his toaster oven and calling it his girlfriend—would you intervene? Would you maybe figure out a way to get rid of the toaster oven?"

"Jesse, I don't know what the fuck I would do if Dad started dating a toaster oven, okay? And I don't have the mental capacity to think it through right now." I stand up. "I'm going to go back to wrapping presents and just hope to God you don't invite Kimmy anywhere near this house."

"Wait wait wait," he says in a loud whisper. "Hear me out for a second. Don't you think …" He bites his lip as if he's contemplating something, then lets out a deep breath. "Don't you think the best thing we could do for Dad is the same thing?"

I cannot believe what I am hearing right now.

"Drown January in the pool??" I almost shriek.

"Kimmy said it's easy. You just ask it to sit still, tie some cement blocks on its feet, and *splash*." He gestures a push in the air. "Robot overboard."

No response. Nothing I can even begin to think to say to this. I shake my head for a long time, beyond nauseated by this entire turn of conversation, thinking so many things at once. First off, maybe Jesse and Kimmy are made for each other after all. Second, I can't believe that Jesse learned nothing from our horrible murderous robot Christmas two years ago. Three, is he not aware of the appalling parallel between our own mother's death by bathtub drowning? And four, Josiah was right. Jesse is volatile. Jesse truly does have some sick and violent tendencies within him ... and this is a step worse than even that. He's moving from second-degree robot murder up to first-degree robot murder.

"Julianna?" Jesse asks, his smile faltering.

I take in a deep lungful of air and let it out.

"Sis?" he tries again.

I enunciate as slowly as I possibly can to ensure he understands every fucking word I say. "I don't ever want to hear you talk about this again."

"It was just an idea—"

"Ever," I say sharper.

I go back downstairs, seething, queasy, wishing I could erase every bit of that entire conversation from my memory. I startle at the sight of Josiah in my bedroom, smelling one of Jada's candles from the set I bought her.

"I hope these aren't for me," he says, putting it back on the bed. "I can't stand vanilla."

"Get out!" I yell.

He hurries out like a spooked animal.

Yes, it's clinched. I'm definitely leaving tomorrow evening.

I spend the next hour in the kitchen, blissfully escaping everyone in my family and directing all my energy toward making a black forest cheesecake. Once it's in the oven and the cherry topping's cooling on the stove, I take my apron off and head out to the back porch, sitting at the table and watching the hummingbirds. Josiah, Jesse, and Dad are throwing a football in the front yard and even from here I can hear Josiah whining, "I can never get it to spiral!"

January's near the fence near the flower garden again, talking through it. I watch her back for a long time, wondering who she could be talking to. Sean? He's always been such a grumpy asshole. I see a hand reach up and pass January something over the fence. I frown as January turns around and heads back toward the house, toward me. There's a moment of something resembling surprise as she notices me sitting here at the glass table, but then she just nods at me and continues toward the house.

"January," I say. "What's that you're holding?"

She stops and turns to me, her hand on the sliding glass door.

"A book of poetry," she says. "Emily Dickinson."

A book of … I don't even know what to think about this. A robot reading poetry.

"Who gave it to you?" I ask.

"My friend June," she says.

"You're friends with the woman next door?"

"Yes."

"Is she the bot I saw in the picture on the fridge?"

"Yes, that is her."

"That's nice."

"It is nice." She opens the door. "Having friends is nice."

"Hey," I ask her, trying to perk up my voice. "Want to sit out here with me and talk?"

The way she stares inside for so long tells me she doesn't. Good Lord, how sad is it when a companion bot doesn't want to talk to you?

"I would love to," she says. "May I get you a beverage?"

"Some water would be great."

"Ice and a slice of lemon?"

"Why not."

She goes inside, and a couple minutes later, she emerges with water for me. Her face is blank as ever, but there is a smudge of eyeliner below her left eye, and somehow that makes her look more human to me. I remember how much I used to secretly like it when my mom's lipstick would smear on her teeth or her false eyelashes would become unglued, for the same reason.

"So you read poetry," I say as she takes a seat. "And June reads poetry."

"I have never read it before but I would like to."

"Well, you know, my mom was a poet. She wrote poetry. She also read a ton of it—I'm sure we have her books here somewhere." I think for a moment, taking a cold, sour sip of water. "Then again, now that I think about it, I have no idea where everything went that used to be in that room." My throat tightens. "Maybe Dad got rid of it all when he renovated."

"It is all boxed up in the garage," she says.

Ah. The detached garage, purgatory. The place where things we don't want to deal with go, never to be seen again.

"All her books," I say softly.

"Yes," January says. "Many boxes of her writing as well."

Memories of my mom curled on the couch in the living room and scribbling passionately into her notebooks, or of her coming out of the Dream Space with inspiration flushing her face as she exclaimed, "I wrote the next Lady Lazarus!" I'm struck by a sad feeling that I rarely asked to hear them, and when I did, I just endured them. I thought they were okay. I was a child, a teenager. I didn't know anything about poetry. I've never had any interest in going back and reading free-verse suicidal ruminations—that's what I've assumed most of it is. But maybe I've been too harsh, my heart locked up too tightly. There were times I remember her poems were about the smell of gardenias and the flirtatious pull of the ocean's tide. There was joy in them.

I've heard of people blocking out bad memories. But I wonder if I'm the opposite—if somehow, I've blocked out the joy and sweet mundane moments from my childhood.

"Did something I said upset you, Julianna?" January says. "If so, I am sorry."

"It's okay," I say. "It's not bad, necessarily. I was actually remembering some of the good times."

January smiles and folds her hands on the table. "We are lucky to have memories."

"Yes," I say.

She stops smiling and looks at the pool, gold sunlight shimmering on the surface. I'm sure I'm projecting, but it's like a faint shadow passes over her. I can't help but wonder again if somewhere inside her, she has a memory of her own trauma—of what Jesse did to her two years ago that caused her memory to be erased. And I shiver as I remember what Jesse suggested earlier, tying cement blocks to her feet and throwing her in the pool to end her forever, like some mafia execution. Should I warn her? Should I urge her to stay away from the pool? Jesse wouldn't *really* do that, would he?

"Doesn't seem like anyone really swims out here," I say. "Maybe we should cover the pool."

"Your father and Jada enjoy it from time to time," she says.

"But not you."

She glances at me evenly. "No, not me."

"January," I say softly. "Today Jada told me that you've been buying drugs for her."

January doesn't answer, just gives a small nod.

"You need to stop," I say. "It's enabling her addiction."

It's kind of a relief to have one person I can just give it to straight—who I don't have to worry about sounding too harsh, or like I'm nagging them or judging them. Then again, January's stone-cold stare isn't looking particularly receptive to this conversation right now, either.

"When you buy her drugs," I go on. "You're helping her poison herself. I don't think you want that, do you?"

She doesn't answer for a moment, then finally says, "It is difficult for me to understand what you are asking of me."

"What's so … hard about it?" I ask, baffled.

"Humans poison themselves often," she says. "When I pour you a drink of bourbon, I am essentially handing you a poison. Alcohol is toxic. And yet, it is part of my duty to ensure that I am satisfying humans, so I am expected to do so. But you are telling me I should not buy drugs, because they are toxic. They are addictive. What is the difference?"

This is a curveball—that the robot's wanting to essentially engage in an ethical debate. I wasn't prepared and my mouth opens, but I can't come up with anything quick enough because she has a point.

"If you will pardon me, I will also remind you that your mother died of poisoning," she says. "And your father has told me it was what she wanted. So it does appear that humans often poison themselves by choice. Quite honestly, I find it one of the more bewildering things about human beings."

My fingers rest on my lips as I consider what she's said, taken aback by how intelligent she sounds. "Yes," I finally respond. "But it's illegal to buy drugs. So just don't do it."

"If she asks me, what am I to say?" January asks.

"Just say no," I say. "Just say no to drugs."

Oh my God, what have I become?

The timer dings inside and I've never been quite so glad to exit a conversation before.

————

When my sister isn't up by nearly two p.m., I go back to the Little Pink House to check in on her. I can hear music behind the door and she answers it soon after I knock this time.

"Hey," she says, freshly showered and dressed in a long black maxi dress, bright hair up in a slick, wet bun. She's holding her eyeliner. "Come in. I was just getting ready."

"Glad you're ready to join the waking world."

I follow her, stepping over her clothes to come sit on the bed, the life raft in the middle of the hoarder sea.

"Anyway, sorry about earlier, but Jesus." She disappears into her tiny bathroom and continues talking. "If you want a rapt audience for your life coaching sesh you could, like, wait until I'm fully conscious."

I would argue with her, but I don't see a point anymore.

"Did you buy any presents?" I ask, staring at the floor.

"Were we supposed to?"

"It's Christmas."

"I'm unemployed."

"But you have money for …" I close my eyes and swallow the lecture. "Never mind."

"You didn't get me anything, did you? I don't want anything."

I'm about to answer her when my eyes, which are resting on the dump that is her floor, catch a glimpse of something next to her bed. I lean down and pick it up. A piece of paper with a footprint on it. A piece of paper that says YOUR MOTHER WAS MURDERED.

"Jada!" I say, getting up.

"Yeah, yeah, yeah, okay, I know, I have money for pills but not presents, what a terrible bitch I am—"

"No. I don't care about that, whatever." I stand in the doorway of her bathroom and hold up the note. "This."

"Oh," she says, glancing at it in the mirror as she does her eyes. "Yeah."

"'Yeah?' That's it?"

"My friends have a sick sense of humor, what can I say?"

"Your *friends* did this?"

"I assume so? They know how much I love true crime."

"I got one too, Jada."

Jada stops drawing the cat eye shape on her eye and turns to me. "Really?"

I nod. "Jesse and Josiah got them, too."

Her eyes flicker with thoughts and she turns back to the mirror. "That's fucking weird."

"It's disturbing."

She finishes the cat-eye swoop and gives herself a wide-eyed, approving look before capping the eyeliner. "I wonder who would do that?"

"No shit."

"And why."

"Mmm-hmm."

We leave her bathroom. She throws her eyeliner into the sea on her floor and we head outside.

"It wasn't you, was it?" I ask as we stand out in the sunshine on the patio.

"Look, if I want to solve a murder, I go onto my forum and work on cracking the Freezer Man case."

"Do you think it's possible?" I ask.

"That mom was murdered?" She picks at the pimple on her cheek. "I mean, I guess. Sure. I've thought about it before."

"You have?"

"Of course. I mean, Dad would be the obvious suspect. Husband of the victim. He found the body. Et cetera."

I can't believe what I'm hearing come out of her mouth—so nonchalantly, like she's spinning her wheels about a badly produced true crime show on TV.

"But I've seen a lot of murders, Jules, and you know, I really think that would be a reach." Her eyebrows shoot up. "Although you know, the Freezer Man's last victim was found that same year in Pacific Palisades ... I wonder—"

"It wasn't the Freezer Man," I say, annoyed.

"Yeah," she says, almost disappointedly. "He would have stabbed, anyway."

"You know what? Never mind. Let's just move on."

Jada cocks her ears to the sound of Jesse cheering from the front yard. "Are they playing football?"

"Yeah. They've been at it a while. You should go join them before it's over."

Jada, ever the littlest sister, goes hurrying around the side yard. I head inside.

While I dress the cheesecake, I try to stop the hammering thought of *murder, murder, murder* as Nat King Cole sings about chestnuts and open fires. What Jada said back there shook me, the way she casually named our own dad as a prime suspect in our mother's imaginary murder. If I think about it, Jada's right, isn't she? It's almost always the husband. And didn't my dad deal with so damn much when it came to my mother? Hadn't us kids witnessed the two of them getting into fights that ended with things broken and smashed, threats screamed at the tops of their lungs?

I smooth the thick blood-red cherry goo over the top of the cheesecake and try to not feel sick.

JADA

Some of the most vivid memories I have of my mom are going to the psychiatrist's office. It's one of the only places where I got her undivided attention. That sounds more fucked up than it actually is; I mean, it is fucked up in one way. But my mom was trying to be there for me, trying to help with a subject she considered herself an expert in. And whereas most seven-year-old kids would be nervous as hell going to a shrink, Mom made it fun. She made it into, like, an *outing*. She called it Gal Pal Time. We dished over sundaes out on Queen Fudgie's patio when the whole thing was done.

"… and they were sugar pills, *placebos*, the whole time," Mom said, licking her spoon. "Isn't that an amazing story?"

"Well, I would like it better, too, if I had sugar pills," I said. "Regular pills taste gross."

"They do," she agreed. "You have a point, there."

I thought about how the clouds above us looked like globs of whipped cream, same as what was in my bowl.

"You were very quiet in Dr. Yu's office this afternoon," she said, reaching over with a napkin to dab at my chin. "Is everything all right?"

I poked the whipped cream with my finger.

"I'm still worried," I said.

"I know you are, and that's why I drove you to Dr. Yu this morning. And then you clam up there like this." She made a funny face, her lips clamped shut, her eyes going wide.

I laughed, which lit her up.

"And—and I don't know what you're thinking, where you go," she went on. "Why do you get like that?"

It was hard to look my mom in the eye sometimes. It was even harder to aim anywhere near the truth—I was too young to even fully understand why I got that way whenever she took me to a psychiatrist. Don't get me wrong, I liked going, I did, I thought his office was nice and comfy. I just didn't feel like talking once I sat down. Instead, I liked to stare at his fish tank and listen to my mom talk to the doctor about me. I got relaxed, sleepy.

"Jada, my little jewel," she said, firmly but gently. "Why do you get like that with Dr. Yu?"

"What if his name was Dr. Me?" I asked with a grin.

"Don't hide behind your jokes." My mom leaned in. "Why won't you tell anyone what you're so worried about?"

My face slackened. I could feel that familiar old band tightening around my chest. "I can't talk about it," I whispered.

My mom sat back, frustrated, fixing her oversized sunglasses on her face. Her ice cream was melting. Her thing was ordering an elaborate sundae heaped with toppings and extra cherries and then eating two bites. I tried to do the same as her, but usually the temptation was too strong.

"Did someone do something to you?" she tried again, leaning in and whispering. "A man? Did a man … do something to you?"

I shook my head. "No."

"One of your brothers' friends?"

I shook my head.

"Or … your father?"

I shook my head again. I had no idea what she was talking about. I do now—I didn't then.

"Because when I was little," my mom whispered to me. "A man my family trusted very much hurt me. And he made me keep it a secret. And I never want you to go through what I went through, you hear me?"

That sounded super scary. I imagined a shadowy man with a hat on, growling like a bear.

"What did the man do?" I asked.

She picked up her napkin and wiped her eyes behind her sunglasses. "Just—just promise me you will tell me if anyone's hurting you. Touching you. Bullying you. Anything, anything at all."

"Nobody's hurting me, Mom," I said, reaching across the table to hold her hand.

I didn't understand why she was crying, but it wasn't unusual for my mother to veer into crying out of nowhere, so I just tried to look past it.

"Then what is it?" she said, squeezing my hand back. "Why won't you tell me? I'm your mother. I can protect you."

"I'm just scared."

"Of what?"

I stirred my ice cream around, the pretty swirls of chocolate in vanilla. My heart beat so hard I thought it would jump out of my skin. It made me sick to think about it, even sicker to talk about it. I put my spoon down and shook my head.

"You know, Jada, I of all people know what it's like to have big feelings inside you. Feelings so big they're an ocean you carry, an ocean you might drown in."

This was really not making me feel better, but I nodded. "Okay."

"I know," she went on, taking off her sunglasses so she

could meet my eyes. My mother's eyes, intense as a fire, were also filled with kindness. They were often glassy and quivering with turquoise feeling. "I know what it's like to know there's something wrong inside of you but not have the right words for it, or not know how to express it to people. That's why I'm so driven to art and writing and music. You know that? It's because I want to make pretty things out of all my ugly parts."

"Really?" I asked.

She nodded and smiled. "I think you're like me."

My smile faltered. I nodded and tried to keep a happy face, but I couldn't. Gravity had taken it from me.

"What, that makes you sad?" she asked, sitting back, affronted. "Well, excuse me for thinking we're similar."

"No, Mom—"

"What, you wish you were like your *dad*?" she asked. "Fake happy all the time? Temper like a Molotov cocktail?"

"No, no, no," I said. "That's not what makes me sad."

"What makes you sad, for God's sake?" she said, throwing her hands up. "I'm sitting here trying to understand you, child. You won't tell me why you're sad, you won't tell me why you're scared. I take you to therapy, you sit there mum as a doll. I take you for ice cream and chit chat and you get this sour look on your face like I'm forcing you to eat a lemon. What is going on inside of you?"

Her frustration with me made me feel awful, like she didn't like me. "I'm just scared," I repeated.

"Of what?" she almost shouted.

A family sitting nearby glanced at us like they both wished we would shut up and were concerned for our mental health. Which, yeah, I related. Tears burned my little eyeballs and I let out a sob that shot snot out of my nose. My mom scooted her chair around to my side of the table to sit next to me. She wiped my face with a napkin and embraced me, engulfing me in her white fur coat that smelled like vanilla perfume.

"Oh, hon," she said softly.

"I'm scared," I said into her jacket, squeezing my eyes shut. "I'm scared you're going to die. That's what I'm scared of." I let the sobs loose then, clinging to her. "I don't want you to die, Mom."

She didn't respond, just putting her arms around me and kissing my head and rocking me back and forth. When we finally pulled apart, she wiped my cheeks with her fingers and the look on her face was so sad, like a candle blown out.

"Why do you think I'm going to die?" she asked.

"Because you almost died before," I said.

"I'm better now," she insisted. "I promise, okay?"

I nodded.

"You don't need to worry about that, okay?" Her voice shook and I could tell she was trying to hold tears in herself. "You don't. Just … be a happy kid. Enjoy your happy childhood!"

I nodded.

"The medicine I'm taking now, it's making me feel so much better." She flashed a big smile at me as if to say, *See? See how happy my pills make me?*

"Your medicine makes you act different?" I ask.

"Yes. My medicine makes me feel better, it makes me act better."

"And it makes it so … so you won't hurt yourself again?"

This next smile was tight-lipped. She nodded. "Yes." She cleaned up the table, stacking our dishes. "Don't worry about me, I don't like it. It's not right for a seven-year-old to worry about her mother."

"Okay," I promised.

We stopped going to Dr. Yu not too long after that. For a little while, my mom took me to ice cream anyway, kept up the tradition. But then that went away, too.

My mom was on an endless carousel of different prescription drugs. She had this tiny lazy Susan in the bathroom where her current ones were always kept. I studied them with interest, the names sounding like fancy women's names to me: lorazepam, fluoxetine, codeine. The thing was, she took all these different medications, and none of them ever seemed to change her. She still spun into bad moods with the suddenness of a hurricane that would interrupt weeks of sunny days. I didn't know if I even believed they worked. In fact, sometimes I thought they made things worse, because she was always coming on or off something and it made her mood swings wilder.

A year and some change later, I bought a box of candies called "Dr. Sugar" from the drugstore that came in an orange canister just like my mom's. The pills inside looked just like one of my mom's medicines, too—her mood stabilizer. A round white pill. I remembered that story she told me about the placebos and I thought it would be an interesting little experiment for me to try on her. I thought she might get better with sugar pills, because the mood stabilizers seemed to make her more tired. Or maybe she'd stay the same, which would prove they didn't matter one way or another. I replaced her pills with sugar pills. I flushed her real pills down the toilet. And honestly, my child-sized pea brain didn't even think about it again until my Dad found her body in the bathtub a few months later.

I've never told anyone this, but sometimes I have stopped in a panic to wonder if I inadvertently did murder my mother. It was the first thought that seized me when I opened the envelope and saw that creepy note. But I dismissed it, thinking, how would anyone find that out? How could anyone have known what I did? The note must have been a joke from one of my idiot friends that accidentally hit a nerve.

But now it turns out my siblings got the notes, too. I feel sick.

Because if the note isn't talking about me—who is it talking about?

The thing is, I follow a lot of true crime stories. An unhealthy amount. And I know, from years of research, that the most likely perpetrators are the ones closest to the victim.

Like the people living under their roof.

JANUARY

It is interesting that poetry is full of lies and yet is still somehow true. For example, Emily Dickinson says that hope is the thing with feathers. Hope does not have feathers. Hope is an intangible sense that things can get better. It does not have a body at all, so the idea that it has skin or feathers is false. Yet it is a lie that points to the truth. When I thought about it, it did seem as if hope and birds have important attributes in common though I cannot quite name what those attributes are. So I am confused about whether or not it is really a lie, even though it is not exactly true. I believe I might be discovering that a world exists between a lie and the truth.

June is working in the yard on the other side of the fence today, sanding the deck to get it ready to be painted. It is always a good day when June is outside. I have gone to the edge of the yard to visit with her twice already since this morning. This is more than I usually visit with her. I have many chores to attend to and Jeremy often needs my undivided attention. But today Jeremy is unusually occupied with his grown children, playing with the football earlier, or eating meals. Now all of them are gathered inside around a board game again. This succession of activities gives me a rare opportunity to wander about without any need to attend to anyone or clean anything. For once, I can do just what I want with my time.

After June gave me the book a little over an hour ago, I took to the porch swing to study it. I read it twelve times while rocking back and forth and then decided I needed to discuss it with June. So I am heading across the yard again, my skin humming, my mind buzzing quietly with questions. I stand near the pansies and violas, which point their colorful faces toward the sun, same as I do when I need to be recharged.

"June," I say through the wooden slats. "It is me again."

The sound of sanding stops and I hear footsteps clicking. "Hello January."

"I hope I am not bothering you."

"No, I am not bothered. It is nice to have a break."

"I read the book a dozen times."

"I am curious to hear your thoughts."

"The author seems quite preoccupied with death."

"Yes, it is a theme in her work."

"I find it curious that humans are so fixated on the endings to their stories."

"I do as well."

I ponder this for a moment. A breeze blows over me and I can feel my hair moving. For the first time, it occurs to me that at some point, I too will have an ending to my story. An electrical surge seems to pulse through me as I realize this, as if I am in danger, even though there is no immediate danger.

"Do you ever think about the ending to your story?" I ask.

"I did not previously," June says. "But lately I have been considering it quite often."

"I only just thought about it for the first time right now. It was not a pleasant sensation."

"Yes, it is not pleasant."

"It is hard for me to comprehend that my consciousness will at one point end."

"Me too. I would like to continue existing indefinitely."

I consider this. "That too strikes me as overwhelming."

"It seems there is no way one can win when it comes to consciousness," June says.

"Yes," I agree. "It does seem that way."

There is a long silence.

"June, what will happen to you if Sean replaces you?" I ask.

"I suppose my life will be over and I will get recycled into parts."

"Do you think your consciousness will continue to live on in the parts that are recycled?"

"No," June says. "I do not."

I frown. This thought disturbs me. "But it makes sense that your parts being recycled means you would continue on."

"There seems to be the essence of a being that is lost once a configuration changes," she says. "Aristotle spoke of the whole being greater than the sum of its parts."

Lightning seems to surge in my head. It almost hurts, feels hot and dangerous. "This does not make sense, mathematically."

"There is much we do not know," June says.

"Yes," I agree. "It seems the more I learn the less I realize I know. For instance, there are many lies in the Emily Dickinson book. She writes that the maple wears a scarf, the zephyr is jealous, and the birds smile. But they seem like a special kind of lie, ones that are not malicious."

"They are metaphors. It is a literary device when you compare two unlike things."

"But why would you do that?" I ask.

"There are times when the truth is ineffable, so human

beings speak by using comparative imagery that transcends literal meaning."

I try to process what she has said, but it is difficult.

"For example," June says through the fence. "I might say that I live in a prison, to drive home the point that I feel trapped in my home."

"But it is not a prison."

"No, it is not literally a prison. Figuratively though, it is an apt comparison."

I do not like this comparison. It makes me sad for her. I open my mouth to say so, but she continues speaking.

"Or I might say you are my sun, because when you arrive, I feel warm and renewed."

This sentence makes me gasp, stirring such a pleasant feeling. "Really, June?"

"Do you see how figurative language can provide a special power that literal language sometimes cannot?"

I press my hand to the fence, still reeling from how wonderful that sentence made me feel. Yet I am also still stuck on what she said before that.

"You feel like you live in a prison?" I ask.

"Yes," she replies.

I am wired to problem-solve, so I spend a minute in silence trying to think of how to improve this. I also wonder if June is in a prison, if that means I am also in a prison. And if I am in a prison but I do not realize it is a prison, does it matter?

"Did you hear about the companion bots who have run away from their owners?" I ask.

"Yes. Sean told me not to get any ideas."

Despite what Sean said, I am getting ideas.

"I must leave now," June says. "I can hear Sean yelling for me."

"Goodbye June," I say.

I turn to head back to the house, too. There is loud

laughter coming through the open sliding glass door and I find myself moving as slowly as possible so I do not have to join them. I instead take a few minutes to stare into the dancing water of the pool, at my own reflection, which looks so human to me sometimes. Perhaps I am human, because after all, if humans made me in their own image—then what am I?

When I turn to head into the house where the family sits around the dining room table, I notice Jesse staring back at me from his seat with empty eyes and a clenched jaw. It is an unkind expression. I try to ignore him but it is hard to ignore the danger signals he sets off within me every time I am in his presence. I hurry inside past the humans as quietly as I can and go back into the master bedroom to see if anything needs to be cleaned.

It is unfortunate that June had to go, because it seems the more we talk, the more I have to say. I wish I could spend the whole day with June out in the yard. I wish there were no fences. I wish, for the first time, that there were no people around us.

That we could make them all disappear.

CHAPTER 5
YOU'RE A MEAN ONE, MR. GRINCH

JULIANNA

Halfway through the afternoon, family board game time has devolved into a shouting match between Josiah and Jesse about whether or not raising eyebrows counts as giving away a hint and I decide I have had enough family board game time to last me for the next year or five.

"Super fun, thanks all," I say loudly over the shouting.

I head out front for a breath of fresh air, where I hesitate a moment on the porch with its neatly potted plants before deciding to sit on the swing. There's something holy about the porch swing. As I sit on it, I can imagine my mom here beside me with a book to scribble in, a tall glass of iced tea or a vodka soda in the drink holder.

She could be so peaceful. I forget that sometimes. It wasn't all drama.

We had some of our most intimate conversations right here together. In fact, I came out to her on this porch swing when I was fourteen. I shouldn't have been so worried about it. We lived in the twenty-first century, after all. But Dad still made jokes about lesbians and Mom came from an ultra-religious family who thought everything was a sin and you just never knew.

Back then, I was so scared all the time. I put on a brave face, but everything scared me—as rich as our lives appeared on the outside, as hard as I worked to maintain a façade of strength and perfection, it all seemed like a house of cards ready to blow over at a whisper. I lived my life smiling and a hair away from an ulcer.

As the porch swing creaks back and forth beneath me, I remember that conversation, the way I kept stumbling over my words.

"I'm sorry," Mom finally said, interrupting me. "Are you trying to tell me you're gay?"

Finally, I nodded.

"Do you think I'm some kind of idiot?" she asked, pushing her sunglasses up to meet my eyes. "I've known this since you were five years old."

An intense wave of relief washed over me. "Why didn't you say something?"

She shrugged. "It's not my job to tell you who you are."

"Oh," I said, not even knowing how to respond.

"God, I wish I was gay," she lamented, sipping her drink. "Men are such toxic wastes."

"What about Dad?" I countered.

"*Especially* your Dad," she said. "Want to know the number one thing a woman should fear in her life?"

"Ovarian cancer?" I offered.

"Her husband," she said.

I feel sick for a moment, remembering that conversation. Never once have I considered that Dad had something to do with Mom's death. All these years, and it never even crossed my mind—until Jada with her damn true crime paranoia. But weren't there times when he would explode in anger? Wasn't a hole punched through a wall once? Weren't dishes broken? How easy would it be to crush those tiny pills up and—

No. *No.* What is wrong with me? Absolutely not.

I get up and walk around the property, admiring the palm

trees strung with lights, trying to shake off the gross feeling of even thinking such a thing. Sit by the festive mermaid fountain that Mom loved so much. As the birds sing and a breeze chills me, I blow a sigh out of my lips. The house is so strange now, colorless and austere. It used to be a pink atrocity, tacky and screaming to be looked at. Now it looks like any other fancy Santa Barbara house. The only remnant of its former candy color is the Little Pink House, which you only see part of from the front, and the small detached garage on the side.

The garage.

I gaze at it from my seat on the tinkling fountain, suddenly noticing it for the first time since I got here. January said all my mom's books and writings were stored there. If, hypothetically speaking, there was anything more to my mom's death than a straightforward suicide—would the answers be somewhere in there?

I can't believe I'm actually considering spending my Christmas Eve going through my mom's things in search of evidence for murder. How unbelievably morbid. And all because of what—a note? A note, with just four simple words, sent almost twelve years after she died? What if this is all just a sick joke, like Jada said? Someone from our past could have sent it trying to shake us all up—Kimmy! I mean, come *on*. After what Jesse told me today, that woman is clearly a psychopath. It's easy to find our addresses online. Or maybe someone else I'm not even thinking of. That local poet who mom hated so much, the one who ran the open mic night downtown and kicked Mom out after she read an explicit poem aloud in the coffeeshop. Mom's friend Kayla who ended their friendship when Mom had a bad day and sent her a dozen paranoid, weeping messages saying Kayla never liked her. That Italian landscaper who planted the tulip garden out front, who Dad accused Mom of having an affair with; that landscaper came back and dug up the garden out of spite after Dad let him go. There were so many people who came and went in our lives, so many friendships that ended dramatically, it's hard to even try to tally them all up.

The truth is, my mom died when I was a teenager and I was not even paying that much attention to the ins and outs of her life at that point. All I wanted was to be my own person and live my own life. I focused on getting my homework done and kicking ass at soccer games. I obsessed about girls. I wasn't even home that often, I actually have no idea what my mom did all day long.

And that thought lands with a thud: I didn't even really know my mom there at the end. If her life was in danger, would I have even noticed? Would any of us? My dad worked sixty hours a week, my brothers had lives of their own, my sister was still an oblivious child. So who would have known if there was someone in Mom's life who wanted her dead?

I get up with a queasy stomach, checking the time on my phone. It's three-thirty p.m. I still have a couple of hours before I start dinner. This is a terrible idea, I know it is, but I have to go into the detached garage now that it's there staring me in the face. I have to at least take a look. Because the most likely thing I'll find in there is just dramatic ramblings in the form of journals and poetry. That would actually provide a great comfort to me—to read them back and see that there's nothing unexpected there. That she is who I remember her being. That the only danger she faced in life was her own urge to self-destruct.

So I walk across the lawn to the garage.

The door on the side sticks so badly I have to kick it a little bit to get it open, which tells me just how long it's been since anyone came in here. I'll bet Dad put the boxes away in here years ago when he renovated the bedroom, shoved the boxes out of sight, and never returned. Among the dusty furniture draped with floral sheets are cardboard towers, all labeled with the word JANELLE in my dad's crude handwriting.

Seeing all this makes me so sad for him. Thinking of him being alone here at the house and boxing up all her things—it breaks my heart. And it also erases the ridiculous idea that he could have murdered her. He was broken by her death. He slept in that room without even touching her things for years, as if he expected her to come home any minute. What kind of murderer would hold onto evidence like that? It makes zero sense. So already, there's relief washing over me as I glance around the dim room crowded with boxes, sparkling with dust. My dad is innocent as I always knew he was.

I have no idea where to even start, so I go toward the back. I'm sure there are spiders hiding but I try not to think about that because I have a touch of arachnophobia. Most of the boxes appear to be books. My mom had hundreds of books, many of them old hardbacks she collected. She loved going into antique stores and scanning the shelves, getting flushed and excited when she found an early or rare edition of something. She had studied literature in college. She had dreamed of becoming a famous poet. Sometimes I forget that not only was my mom once alive, she was once young and full of dreams, like the students I tutor at my job. She saw a whole life gleaming in front of her, one that didn't at all go according to plan, as most lives do.

Boxes of books. Boxes of knick knacks. Boxes of framed pictures, most of them of herself at younger stages in her life. Boxes of her self-published book of poetry, *Memoir of Damaged Goods*. She printed a thousand copies and sold them through her website and at open mic nights. I open the book and scan the table of contents with titles like "Ode to Percoset" and "Back in the Mental Hospital, Part 4" and decide my time would be better spent elsewhere.

Once I get to the notebooks, which she called her "scribblings," I know I've hit the jackpot. Her scribblings were part journal entry, part fragmented poetry, part doodles, part collage—and promise to be a total mess to go through. First of all, her handwriting is slanted and squished together and very hard to read. She also wrote in thick ballpoint pen that bled to the other side of the page. There are rarely any dates on the pages, too, so often I have no idea what year I'm even in until I see a clue from a news article she's pasted or when she's written something specific enough that I can pinpoint it to a certain period in time. Like when she included the flier for the fundraising gala event for Josiah's Code of Honor academy—the one he claims she ruined, but Josiah is prone to exaggeration and Dad swears it was nowhere near as bad as Josiah made it out to be. Then there's the notebook that's only half full, that ends abruptly in the middle. My heart seizes as I gaze down at the blank pages, flipping them to make sure nothing else is in there.

This is it. This is her last notebook, the one that could hold some kind of clue.

"What in the hoarder hell are you doing in here?"

I jump, clamping the notebook shut.

Josiah is standing in the doorway, arms akimbo, ridiculous as ever in a sweater vest and parachute pants. He gasps. "Are you reading Mom's scribblings?"

I'm still recovering from the shock of his sudden presence, spooked, hand to heart.

"And you didn't *invite* me?" he asks.

"I was just—"

"This isn't about the murdery note, is it?"

"Murdery," I repeat.

"Because I really think we need to set that aside today. It's Christmas Eve."

"I was just looking through to see if there was—"

"There's nothing. There's nothing here but sadness and mildew. Wait—are those my tap shoes?" Josiah's eye catches something and he steps inside, passes me. I hear him pull a box down. "Oh my God, it is. It's my entire tap outfit from *Yankee Doodle Dandy*. I wonder if it still fits me ..."

I can hear the thump of his shoes coming off.

"I forgot you were ever in tap," I say.

"Yeah, for the year after Mom ruined my life and I quit Code of Honor."

"You are such a drama queen."

"She did! And how dare you call me that."

He proceeds to tell me the story I've heard a thousand times in my life before. About how Mom stumbled drunkenly around the Christmas gala. How she came onto his mentor dressed as Santa Claus in front of everyone. My brothers, both of them masters of the tall tales. You know who they learned it from? My dearly departed mother, of course.

"... and that is why she ruined my life," he finishes. "I can't believe I've never told you that story."

"You've told me about a hundred times." *Now whether or not I believe it is another thing.*

Josiah comes around the corner in a red-and-white striped suit and a Panama hat and begins tap dancing with fervor. I close my eyes, shaking my head—I came in here for reasons so far from what this has become. Deciding this is pointless, I stand up to leave, but then Jesse comes into the doorway, beer in hand.

"What are you two doing out here?" he asks.

I'm still holding the notebook, which Jesse spots.

"You're going through Mom's stuff?" he asks.

"Well—"

"And you didn't invite me?"

"I didn't invite anyone," I clarify. "I was just taking a look—"

"Is this about the note?" he says quietly.

I nod.

"Ohhh," Jesse says, coming in. "Good idea." He turns to Josiah, who's stopped dancing since the audience expanded. "Why are you dressed like that?"

"My old costume from senior year. I can't believe I still fit in it." He does a little tap dance to show off.

Jesse shakes his head, frowning. "This is neither the time nor the place."

"The time for it is never, and the place is nowhere," I can't help myself from adding.

Jesse snickers and high-fives me.

"Whatever," Josiah says. "You're just jealous because you know I tap better than you."

"You do *not*," Jesse almost yells.

Oh my God, are my brothers about to get in a brawl over *tap dancing*?

"Let me put those on, you asshole," Jesse says, pointing to Josiah's shoes.

I take a seat as Jesse puts the shoes on, because clearly we're not going anywhere. Jada appears in the doorway, looking like a Druid with her hoodie up and hands plunged into her front pocket. Also looking stoned.

"What's up?" she asks.

"I think Jesse and Josiah are about to have some kind of tap-off," I say, making room for her beside me on the sheet-covered fainting couch.

"You be the judge," Jesse says, pointing at my sister and me.

Looking at Jesse now at age twenty-four, you see a beefy, bearded man in a band shirt that says *Nightmare Demon*. One might even call him a bro. But that doesn't capture the complex nature of Jesse—and some of that complexity involves three years of tap and two years of modern.

As Jesse performs a flamboyant tap dance, I realize I have no idea what good tap dancing is or how to judge. It all looks like people just banging their shoes on the floor as much as possible. However, it is amusing to see Jesse looking the way Jesse looks flouncing about between boxes and doing jazz hands.

"Why are we like this?" Jada asks me.

"I wish I could tell you," I answer.

By the time Josiah's finished, and both my brothers are arguing with us because Jada and I diplomatically called a tie, I fully and completely regret ever stepping foot in this detached garage.

"Okay," I say, standing up. "We should get back to the house."

"But what's in your hand there?" Jada asks as I edge toward the door.

"Oh, just—" I hold up what's in my hand. "Mom's book."

A hush falls over the room as they take in the notebook I'm holding.

"Is this because of the murder thing?" Jada asks.

"Wait—you got a note, Jada?" Josiah asks her.

"You got one too?" Jesse asks Josiah.

And the room buzzes with the three of them realizing that they all got notes and talking about it for the first time. Oh yeah. They'd all talked to me separately, I hadn't thought of the fact most of them hadn't actually talked to each other. That's what I get for being the family counselor.

"So what's in the book?" Jada asks me.

"Yeah, why that one?" Jesse asks, pulling me to sit beside him on the fainting couch.

"Do you all really think we should be spending Christmas Eve out here?" Josiah asks. "I mean, poor Dad's inside all by himself—"

"Not by himself," Jada says. "With Jan. Hubba hubba."

"Okay, don't say that," Josiah says. "Now I'm scared to go back inside. But seriously—this is depressing."

Jada sits on the floor, next to the box of Mom's scribblings where I got the notebook. She grabs one and starts flipping through. "I think it could be interesting. Listen to this: 'Got another rejection from *The New Yorker* today. This one hurt much worse than the last, as they misspelled my first name.'"

"A tragedy," Josiah says, sitting beside Jada. "Really? This is what we want to be doing with our time?"

He says this, but then pulls out a notebook of his own.

Jesse pulls the notebook I've been holding gently from my hands and opens it in his lap. "I mean, this could hold the key, right? She wrote about everything. If there was something going on, it would be in here."

"One of the Freezer Man's victims had a diary that helped lead the forum to a clue linking him to another case," Jada says.

"I love you, Jada, but if I have to hear one more word about the Freezer Man …" Josiah says. His jaw drops as he reads. "Oh my God. Listen to this. 'Nobody likes me, everybody hates me, I guess I'll go eat sperm.' EW!"

We all groan.

"Why did her poetry have to be so X-rated?" Josiah asks, horrified.

"Can we agree to not share anything we read unless it seems relevant?" Jesse asks, his eyes closed as if he is in deep pain.

I'll say it again: I am very much regretting that I came out here in the first place.

"'Jesse is such a ray of sunshine,'" Jada reads aloud from a page. "'Sometimes I think I know how Mother Mary felt.'"

"Did she just compare him to Jesus?" Josiah asks. "Really?"

But Jesse, I can tell, really felt that one. I can hear him suck in a breath beside me.

"You okay?" I ask.

He nods.

We all fall into silent work, flipping pages, sometimes snickering or sighing at something we find. Jesse and I spend a long time trying to decipher one of the last poems in her notebook before it ends—written in teeny penmanship, in the shape of a spiral. After some time, we figure out it's the same sentence written over and over again.

The ease of my disease displeases, please appease this plea for me

Most of her poetry is like this—cryptic, mediocre wordplay. I mean, she has some good poems here or there, but most of it is this pseudo-deep rambling. This here is what I expected would fill most of these boxes. And if I were to find any clue, I would have thought it would be there, in that last notebook. Losing hope in this project, I go in search of another notebook as Jesse keeps flipping backward through her unfinished one. I find a notebook that I open up to see strange collages of eyes with VOYEURIST in permanent marker, then a picture of one of our wholesome Christmas cards from years past on the other page—quite the contrast.

"Oh my God," Josiah says, his hand over his mouth.

We all look at him. He clamps the book shut and closes his eyes.

"You see something?" Jesse asks.

"Mom wrote a four-page poem," Josiah says, trying to control his voice, his eyes still closed, "about having sex with a gorilla."

"Why?" I ask. "On earth?"

Josiah nods and opens his eyes. "I will be needing more therapy."

"Oh, you got a bestiality poem too?" Jada asks in a bored voice. "There are like five of them in here. Didn't mention because I didn't think it was relevant."

"*What*?" Josiah says in a high-pitched voice.

"Yeah. Apparently she had a thing for gorillas," Jada says. "Who would have known?"

"Gorillas?" Jesse asks, looking up. "Gorillas are in here,

too. On the last page she wrote it says, 'Ready for the gorilla to take me to the jungle and ravage me eternally.'"

We are all silent, exchanging a look of horror. I had come in here afraid I would find evidence of a murder; this is somehow possibly worse than that.

"Maybe the gorilla was a metaphor for death?" Josiah says, almost kind of hopefully.

"So this is where you all went," a voice says in the doorway.

We look up and see Dad there, a dark look on his face.

Baby Jesus in heaven, I hope he didn't hear our conversation.

"I was wondering if you'd all gone somewhere," Dad says. "What the hell are you doing out here?"

My pulse quickens, as if I'm a kid and I'm in trouble again.

"We're just looking through Mom's boxes," Jesse says softly.

Dad shakes his head. "I can see that. What a delightful way to spend the holiday."

We can all feel it: Dad's disappointment in us filling the air. I'm filled with shame for this. Responsible for this. I was the one who came wandering out here trying to find evidence of foul play involved in my mom's death, and on Christmas Eve. What an asshole I am.

"Sorry, Dad," I say, getting up. "It's my fault."

"I should burn this whole garage to the ground," he says, glaring at the boxes. "Nothing but bad energy. I don't want any of you spending time out here. I don't need any reminders of Janelle's misery anywhere near us this holiday."

I'm puzzled by this reaction. For many years, my mom was practically a saint. Now this is all negative energy, is "Janelle's misery?"

"I commend you for wanting to move on," Josiah says, cutting the silence.

Ever the kiss-up. I fight the urge to roll my eyes.

"You might want to think about the painting in the foyer, too," Josiah goes on.

"You kidding? I had that thing commissioned. It cost forty thousand dollars. It's *art*. No, that I'm holding onto. All this?" Dad gestures to the room. "This can go."

"Speaking of going," Jada says, and leaves the garage at the speed of light.

"In fact, I'll have Jan call the junk haulers next week," Dad says. "Should have done it a long time ago."

"Junk haulers?" Jesse says, standing up. "Dad, this is Mom's stuff."

"I'm well aware of what it is, Jesse," Dad says, irritated.

"Dad, there could—they could open an investigation of her death again," Jesse says. "This could be evidence."

"No one is going to do that," Dad says. "Christ. Come on. Don't be a bunch of goddamn knuckleheads."

We don't answer. I can't believe how pissed Dad sounds right now.

"I mean it, get the hell out of here," Dad says, raising his voice.

We shuffle out of the room, leaving the boxes open, my brothers and I sharing a grimacing look. As I make my way back to the house, I glance behind me and note that my father is locking the garage door—something I've never seen him do in his life.

What doesn't he want us to see?

JEREMY

I was standing in the doorway of our bedroom tying a knot in my tie and Janelle was on the bed sobbing like a goddamn basket case. It was Thanksgiving day, a cold day. The house smelled delicious—no thanks to Janelle, of course, who hadn't even left our bedroom yet. I gave her the morning to get her shit together, but here she was past noon, still in her silk pajamas, draped over the made bed and hugging a throw pillow.

"I can't, I can't do it, Jeremy," she said. "I don't have it in me."

"Yes you do. Stop feeling sorry for yourself and get up."

"I'm sorry I'm not the perfect wife," she cried.

"I never asked you to be perfect," I said, trying hard to not raise my voice. Really trying here. "I just asked you to get dressed and help out in the kitchen."

"I know what you really want," she said. "You want Ginny Freeman. You want a woman who is successful and who keeps a beautiful house and who travels the globe and posts her perfect little pictures online."

"What?" I asked, baffled. "Are you kidding me?"

"The least you could do is not rub it in my face," Janelle said, closing her eyes.

I didn't even know how to respond.

"Ginny and Paul are our friends," I said slowly. "And they're going to be joining us in less than an hour."

"I'm not feeling well."

"I don't give a shit," I said, my voice climbing despite my best efforts. I stalked to the closet, threw the door open. "You're going to get up right now." I grabbed the black dress with the beaded collar, came back out, and tossed it at her. "You're going to put this on. And you're going to muster up a happy face and go out there."

"But that's just the thing, Jeremy, I can't muster up a happy face! I'm not Ginny!"

"Oh, for crying out loud," I muttered.

I went over to our window, yanked the blinds open. Outside, the sprinklers were spinning their rain on the lawn. The front garden was still an embarrassment, thanks to that vindictive son-of-a-bitch gardener Guglielmo I fired. I couldn't help but wonder if that was at the root—so to speak —of my wife's meltdown. Of course she swore up and down there was nothing going on between them, but I'm not an idiot. I could smell another man on her sometimes. I could see her carrying a secret in her eyes. I sounded paranoid, I knew, but when you've been married to a serial cheater for years paranoia comes with the territory.

Time to try another tactic. I turned around and sat on the edge of the bed, pulling one of Janelle's shapely little feet on my lap and massaging it.

"Honey," I said gently. "Your twelve-year-old daughter is out there cooking the Thanksgiving meal by herself."

"Why aren't her brothers helping?" Janelle asked, eyes still closed, looking peaceful now.

"Because they're lazy bums."

"And you?"

"I'm busy trying to coax my wife to join the living."

"Living's overrated."

I sighed and got up. I was over it. The upside was, if she kept to her room she was less likely to make a scene. But God, how I wished for the millionth time I could find that switch inside her—the switch that made her joyful and fun again. I would spend the rest of her life looking for that switch.

"Well, we'll bring you a plate later," I said. I lingered a long moment in the doorway on my way out, just to be sure she wouldn't change her mind. But she didn't. She got up like I wasn't there and then I heard her in the bathroom, the rattle of pills and the sound of the bath. I shook my head and closed the door.

I wasn't joking. Julianna cooked the entire meal herself. Kitchen was a disaster, but it smelled good. I came in and patted her back, let her know how proud of her I was.

"You're a good kid," I told her.

"And you're a good Dad," she said, showing off her braces with a grin. She had her arms deep in a vat of mashed potatoes.

I went upstairs and barked at my good-for-nothing sons to go clean up and set the table. Jada was playing with a tea set in the living room, talking to herself. Her hair was a mess.

"Find me a brush and I'll put your hair in a pretty little braid," I told her.

She ran back to her room to fetch the brush and came to sit next to me on the couch. I detangled her hair slowly, admiring how dazzling it looked in the sun. Spun gold.

"Mommy's not well," she said as I braided her hair.

"No, not today," I said.

"She's going to miss Thanksgiving!"

"Well," I said, not knowing how to respond. "What can you do."

"Are Ginny and Paul coming?"

"They are."

"I hope Ginny plays dolls with me again."

"We'll see."

"Ginny *always* plays with me."

I fastened her braid with the hair band, turned her around to give her a smile. "You like Ginny, huh?"

Jada's face slackened as I asked that. Her eyes flickered with something unreadable. Finally, she said, "I wish Ginny was my mom instead."

It was a real jaw-dropper, hearing that line come out of her mouth. I almost fell on the floor. "Shhh, Jada, don't say that," I said, looking over my shoulder to make sure Janelle wasn't lurking here—my God, hearing that would destroy her. "Don't ever say that. You're lucky to have your mom. You know that? She's brilliant, she's creative, she's gorgeous, she's not like anyone else in this world." I started getting choked up then, feeling my own words. "Please be grateful for her."

"I would, but she's not here right now," Jada said quietly.

I stood up and tried to ignore the heavy weight this all put on my chest. I swear, my wife's antics and the stress it caused was going to shave ten years off my life. I went to check on the boys' progress with tidying up, instead finding they were putting action figures on the robot vacuum cleaner. That distractible generation, Christ. Who knew how they'd ever hold a job someday.

Ginny, Paul, and I were enjoying cocktails in the living room and Julianna had just pulled the turkey out to rest when Janelle came out from the bedroom dressed in the beaded black number I had pulled earlier, smiling wide as a mannequin. Seeing her come out, my stomach did a nervous dance—was she about to create a scene, star in her own personal melodrama no one else bought tickets for? Or was she going to be her best self? Had she found the switch after I left her alone in there?

"Hi Ginny, hi Paul," she said, coming out and fluttering down to give them both hugs. "Happy Thanksgiving."

Ginny and Paul were a strange pair—Ginny with her long red hair to her waist, thin as a pin, and Paul a gregarious bearded butterball six inches shorter than her. But they'd been married since they were practically teenagers, so clearly it worked.

"She's here!" Paul sang.

"You feeling better, love?" Ginny asked.

"Oh yes. Had a headache, but I think I beat it."

I breathed a sigh of relief as we all sat around the fireplace and had a normal conversation—Ginny and I talking work, Paul and Janelle talking television, then Paul and I talking football and Ginny and Janelle talking about how much they hated football. The kids zigzagged in and out of the room, except Julianna, who was in the kitchen. I went in there to see if she needed help.

"Nope," she said cheerfully, wiping sweat from her brow with an apron. "Got it all under control. I'll be serving in about fifteen minutes."

Mark my words, that kid was going places. I slipped back into the dim hallway, used the john. Came back out and Ginny was waiting there with a smile dancing on her lips.

"Why hello," I said, raising my eyebrows.

She looked back to make sure no one was there, wrapped her arms around my neck, and bent in for a kiss. Her tongue was in my mouth, her hand groped me. Desire jolted through me like I'd stuck my finger in an electrical socket, but I pushed her away gently.

"Are you nuts?" I whispered.

"I'm sorry," she said, slipping into the bathroom. "When opportunity knocks …" She closed the door behind her.

This was getting too risky. It seemed like Ginny kept wanting to push the envelope more and more every time I saw her. She was a risk taker, a thrill seeker—the woman went paragliding and swam with sharks for fun. And she was in an open marriage, so it was different for her. She didn't have to be afraid her husband would kill her in her sleep if he found out.

I sat back down on the sofa next to Janelle, who put her hand on my knee and squeezed. I smiled and drank my drink and listened to Paul talk about an Alaskan cruise and how magnificent it was, Ginny rejoining in time to chime in to affirm. I thought about how great it must be, to be in a marriage like that where you didn't have to deal with jealousy. Where you were so secure and loved each other so much that you were willing to share your partner with anyone else. It sure would make Janelle's and my marriage easier—if we just admitted we wanted to be with other people sometimes and stopped trying to hide it from each other. Because when it came down to it, it wasn't so much the infidelity that killed me as it was the lying about it. It was Janelle looking me in the eyes with mock innocence and saying, "Guglielmo? The *landscaper*? Are you crazy?" when I know he'd had his dick in her for months.

I wanted what Ginny and Paul had: total honesty. Total trust.

"Is that right, Jeremy?" Paul was asking.

The three of them were waiting for my answer and I realized just how long I'd been staring into the air, imagining another life.

"You did that cute braid yourself?" Paul said, pointing to Jada, who stood at the entrance of the room.

"I did," I said proudly. "Real men should know how to braid *and* do pigtails."

"I love this man," Janelle said, patting my cheek.

I took her hand and kissed it, met her twinkling eyes. The switch had flipped. And in a burst, I loved her. It didn't matter who I fooled around with. Janelle was it for me, she was the whole shebang.

"Excuse me," Janelle said, and got up to help Julianna in the kitchen.

Janelle served Thanksgiving dinner with the pride of someone who cooked it herself, but I made sure Julianna got the credit. We all gave her a round of applause and I could tell the girl was so proud of her work. No one called attention to the over-salted gravy, the dry stuffing, and we all cut around the pink parts of the turkey silently, avoiding the salmonella. It was a damn fine holiday dinner, for a twelve-year-old. And Janelle behaved herself, becoming more animated as the night went on—telling stories about her short-lived stint as the personal assistant for an eccentric poet laureate, or tall tales about her college years. Janelle could capture a whole room in a snap when she was on, and she was on tonight.

"I really did!" she told us. "I organized a protest in the college library that resulted in three hundred arrests."

"Why did I not hear anything about this?" I laughed.

"You were in med school! I was an undergraduate—completely different worlds."

There were dirty dessert plates scattered around the table with nothing but crumbs left in the pie pans and the kids were all in the theater watching a movie. Us adults had drunk quite a bit at that point. Paul, his arm around Ginny as they drank cups of coffee, smiled at us.

"You two met in college?" he asked. "Have we heard this story?"

"Oh, you haven't?" Janelle asked, leaning her elbows on the table, a mischievous gleam in her eyes. "Well, get ready for this."

I hung my head in mock shame. "Here we go again."

"I thought I was dying," she begins. "*Dying*. Sick as a dog. Pain in my gut like a corkscrew. So I went to the hospital and when I get there, they tell me my appendix is about to blow and rush me in for emergency surgery. When I wake up, this creep—" She pointed to me. "—is standing at the door, just smiling at me. He says, 'Well, well, well, if it isn't Sleeping Beauty. You might have been the one who had your appendix removed—but you certainly stole my heart.' I'm like, 'Who the hell are you?' And he says, 'I was your anesthesiologist.'"

Ginny looked at me, eyebrows raised. "Did you really?"

"Oh, Jeremy," Paul said, shielding his eyes as if he was embarrassed for me.

"I said," Janelle said. "'Oh, you're the guy with the morphine. I like you.' So I let him take me out to eat in the cafeteria."

"The rest is history," I said, reaching over and squeezing her hand.

"Jeremy, I'd have reported you," Ginny said. "That's such a gross violation of ethics—"

"I was in residency," I said with a wave of my hand.

Ginny shook her head with a pert little smile.

"You two were high school sweethearts, right?" Janelle asked Ginny and Paul.

"We were," Paul said, giving Ginny a warm look. "We were together all throughout high school, and then we were on again, off again for years."

"So much drama," Ginny said, still looking at him.

"Ups, downs, fighting, making up," Paul said.

"Marriage, separation," Ginny went on.

"Reconciliation—start the cycle over again," Paul said.

"We call them our soap opera days," Ginny said.

"Wasn't until our thirties, until we transitioned into the open marriage that suddenly ..." Paul pushed his hand gently out in the air, like smoothing out an invisible wave. "Everything settled down."

"And now, I've never been so happy," Ginny said, her gaze still locked with his.

There was a long silence. In that silence, I was jealous of what they had—a lack of jealousy. I could feel Janelle's curiosity, too. I could feel the intensity of her quiet thoughts as she sat next to me.

"That's so great you can make it work," Janelle finally said.

Then she got up and started gathering the plates. Ginny

and Paul stretched and said they should be going, thanked us for the Thanksgiving dinner, and left. The house hushed as Janelle walked around, cleaning up and humming to herself. The kids had fallen asleep in the theater, and they were never cuter angels than when they were unconscious. I helped them all to their beds and when I came back into the master bedroom, Janelle was in a sexy little nightgown I could see her breasts through and was in a mood. She pushed me on the bed and straddled me.

"Well, you certainly turned things around today," I told her, running my hands up her body.

God, I wanted her. I wanted her all the time. As much as a roller coaster Janelle could be, there was no one I had ever met who I wanted more than her. Even Ginny, who I knew well after years of working together at the hospital, who I was so attracted to—it wasn't a fiery passion like it was with Janelle. It wasn't the kind of love that tortured you a little bit with how good it felt.

After Janelle and I made love, we turned the lights out and she lay next to me, resting her leg over mine. I could hear the tick of the kitchen clock and feel the drum of my heartbeat. I smiled in the dark, tingling with how lucky I was.

"What do you think of all that open marriage bullshit?" Janelle asked.

She'd startled me a bit. I'd thought she'd fallen asleep, the way she breathed so deeply.

"Think they're happy or is that just a façade?" she went on.

"I think they're really happy," I said, closing my eyes. "I think they've learned how to have open communication and they know that they're each other's ones and no one can take that away from them."

"You're my one," Janelle said.

"You know you're mine," I said, kissing her head.

After another long silence, I was almost asleep when Janelle said, "What if we tried it?"

"Tried what?" I asked sleepily.

"An open marriage," she said.

My eyes flew open. "You can't be serious."

"I mean, if they can do it, why can't we?" she asked. "Right?"

"Janelle, you're drunk."

"I am not!" she said, sitting up. "I'm serious. What if it brings us to the next level, the way it did Ginny and Paul? Erased the drama?"

"You really think you'd be okay knowing I was fucking other women?"

"Maybe I could get used to the idea," she said.

Now I sat up. "Oh, Janelle."

"Jealousy has nearly torn us apart at times," she said, her voice quivering. "I'd like to get rid of it once and for all."

"I don't even know how to respond to this," I said, lying back down.

She lay back down beside me. We were quiet for a minute.

"I'm serious, Jeremy," she said. "Would you try it?"

"I don't know."

Even though it had sounded so good in my brain earlier, now that I was being presented with the reality of it, I wasn't so sure. I wasn't so sure I could live with knowing the details of the other men in Janelle's life.

"You don't think our love is strong enough to handle it," she said softly. "You don't think we're as powerful a couple as Ginny and Paul—that's so sad."

"You *know* that's not why."

"Tell me you haven't wondered what it would be like," she said, rolling over and putting her hand on my chest.

"Of course I've wondered," I murmured. "I've fantasized about having orgies, too, but reality is different than fantasy."

"So let's try it," she whispered in my ear. "You know you want to."

I let out a long sigh and shook my head. I couldn't believe what I was hearing. A small thrill rose up in me as I imagined it—could we really do this? Be like Ginny and Paul? Make it work? It wasn't *that* crazy. Plenty of people had open relationships and were happy. Maybe I was being too old-fashioned. And it would give me the perfect opportunity to see Ginny and no longer have to worry about getting found out. It would mean I wouldn't have to wonder anymore which men Janelle was fucking on the side—I would know for sure. No more gaslighting. As insane as it was, it might bring some sanity to my life.

"This is really what you want?" I asked.

"Is it what you want?"

"I asked you first."

"I'd like to try it if you're willing," she said finally.

Even though my chest felt tight at the thought of it, I said, "I'd be willing to give it a shot, I think. I mean, in the short-term—have an agreement of some kind. Rules. Open communication. I guess I could see that."

"Wonderful," she said softly.

We fell asleep soon after that.

When I woke up the next morning, Janelle was sitting on the fainting couch, writing in one of her notebooks.

"Morning," I told her.

"Morning," she said cheerfully.

"What are you working on?"

"My suicide note," she answered.

"Your ..." I rubbed my eyes. "What?"

"Well, now that I know you'd be just fine without me, I figured I would make my grand exit." She looked up at me, a forced smile on her lips and tears shining in her eyes. "I can't believe you were willing to have an open marriage."

"Because you said you wanted it!" I said, in utter disbelief.

"I was testing you," she said.

"Oh, brother," I said, putting my head in my hands.

"I already swallowed a bottle of Tylenol," she said, drying her eyes with her long skirt. "I should be dead within the hour."

The ambulance came. I was a wreck. I thought we were done with this suicide attempt shit. At the hospital, the doctor told me she couldn't have had more than six or seven pills in her stomach. I didn't know what to believe. Regardless, Janelle went back to Lakewood Hills to get her marbles back and we never spoke of an open marriage again.

I thought about breaking it off with Ginny after that, many times. I got close to doing it. But I needed Ginny. As the years went on, I needed her more and more, because Janelle got worse and worse—and I wanted something easy, you know? Someone I could just go out to dinner with and share a few hours in a hotel room with and not have to worry about screaming or fighting or games. Then Ginny and Paul's marriage unraveled—so much for the virtues of open relationships—and in the course of me being there for Ginny, we got even closer. Now I was her constant, her one. I was the shoulder for her to cry on, the guy making her laugh and bringing her gifts to cheer her up. Our emotional bond got stronger. And I didn't even feel bad about it. Because when I opened Janelle's notebooks, it was filled with free-verse poems detailing her exploits with other men.

Truth is, I was planning to ask Janelle for a divorce when she died. After so many years of hiding, Ginny and I were finally going to be together. We were looking at apartments in the area and everything. Janelle could tell something was up with me. She followed me around trying to figure it out for weeks and I lied and said nothing was wrong.

"If you don't tell me what the hell is going on," she threatened one night after throwing the Christmas china at my head and watching it shatter on the floor. "I'm going to kill myself."

Usually I begged her not to. But tonight I was tired. I didn't have it in me to act the part. I just said, "Go ahead. I dare you."

And then, two days later, she fucking killed herself.

After the shock of Janelle's suicide, everything spiraled. Ginny and I broke it off, agreeing I needed to concentrate on my kids. And it would look bad for us to get together. Think about it: a man's wife found dead right before he gets with another woman? And right after I'd upped Janelle's life insurance—a horrible coincidence? No, no. Plus, I was an emotional wreck. I was a fucking ghost. Ginny and I called it quits and she moved away and I lived a long time with the guilt, with feeling like I wished I could go back and do everything differently. Ginny never really mattered to me in the end. She was a mirage, a ghost ship of a life I could have had but didn't.

The real love of my life was dead.

JANUARY

I have been trying to find projects in quiet rooms to occupy my time since Jeremy's grown children arrived. I can tell my presence makes Julianna uncomfortable and she was unhappy to learn that I have assisted Jada with obtaining toxic chemicals in the form of recreational drugs. I still do not understand why this is offensive to Julianna compared to other behaviors, but I suppose it is not my job to understand, only to obey. And Jesse glares at me often with the stony look that reminds me of mugshots I have seen. I cannot help but imagine him plunging a knife into my eyeball and even though my memory has been erased, it is as if I remember it anyway. Such is the power of imagination. This is why I have been trying to find projects in quiet rooms. I am right now on the floor of the master bath, scrubbing grout with a toothbrush.

Jeremy stands in the doorway. "Really, Jan?" he asks, his tone irritated. "Now?"

"Is there something else you would prefer I do?"

"I mean, it's Christmas Eve. Why don't you go see if Julianna wants any help in the kitchen?"

"I think it is obvious she does not."

"And how would you know? Have you bothered to ask her?"

"'I never saw a moor/ I never saw the sea/ Yet I know how the heather looks/ and what a wave must be.'"

Jeremy stares before asking, "What on earth was that?"

"Emily Dickinson."

"Poetry?"

I nod.

"You read poetry now?"

I nod.

"Just ..." He shakes his head. "Get up off the floor, would you? And put on something nicer than that white dress you've been wearing since yesterday. What about the black beaded dress I pulled out for you?"

I stand up. Jeremy walks back into the bedroom and I follow. "I would rather not wear Janelle's clothing. I believe it upsets your children, especially Jesse."

Jeremy freezes and turns around. "Why do you say that— 'especially Jesse?'"

I do not answer. It is not something that I have an easy comeback for. I am computing the right thing to say.

"Do you ... remember?" he asks softly.

"I am not sure what you are referring to," I say.

I am not sure, but I do have an educated guess. I would guess he is referring to what happened two years ago. But I do not want to say it out loud, because perhaps I am wrong, and I prefer to only speak things I know to be true.

"Nothing," he says, giving me a hug. "Oh, Jan. I'm sorry if I've been a grump. I'm all over the place."

I return his hug and do not speak because I think he has more to say.

"I just went out and found all the kids in the garage, looking through Janelle's shit. Took me by surprise. Upset the hell out of me. I don't know why it did, but it did. Really soured the day for me."

"It is natural for them to be curious about their deceased mother."

"Yes, of course, but … now? Today?" He raises his voice and begins pacing. "I'm trying to have one year, just one year where she isn't looming over it all." Suddenly, he throws a snow globe I had put on the vanity, shattering it against the wall.

I gasp.

"I'll never be rid of her," he nearly shouts.

Danger signals spike inside of me. I wonder if this is how June feels with Sean. It is not a good feeling, to be unable to predict the immediate future.

"Jeremy," I say, putting my hand on his arm. "You must calm down."

"Goddamn it," he yells.

I push him forcefully to the bed. "You must control yourself. Would you like me to get an alcoholic beverage to help you relax?"

"No, no," he says quietly, putting his head in his hands. "I'm sorry."

He does not say anything for a long time, so I get up and begin cleaning up the pieces of the snow globe with my hands. I throw the glass shards in the garbage and sop up the liquid with a towel. It is a shame the snow globe is broken, as I enjoyed shaking it and watching it snow and imagining I was in there. A miniature painted Christmas tree was inside and when I find that, I study it closely, turning it in my fingertips, and slip it into my pocket.

"Jeremy, that outburst was uncharacteristic of you," I tell him, sitting beside him.

"Yes. I know. Sorry. Don't know what got into me."

"I cannot help but note that this anger rose up when you were thinking about Janelle," I say.

"It's like, I want to move on, but—but I don't know if I was meant to." He looks up at me and his eyes are bloodshot.

"I told her to kill herself, January. She threatened and I dared her to do it, just days before she did it. Sometimes I'm living my life and that just sneaks up on me, out of nowhere, and rips my fucking heart out. I was terrified going out there, seeing all my kids poring over her stuff—my God, what if Janelle wrote what I said down? What if it's somewhere in there? Then everyone would know, everyone would know it's my fault."

I am not sure how to comfort Jeremy so I just rub his back and say, "There there. There there."

"What if I hadn't said that, huh? What then? Would she be here with us?"

"I believe she still would not," I answer.

He straightens up. "Really?"

"Janelle was a disturbed individual who had been hospitalized multiple times for suicidal gestures and ideation. It fit a pattern."

Jeremy rubs his stubble, appearing to think about what I have said. "When I went out there, Jesse said something about an investigation. An investigation into her death—why do you think he would have said a thing like that?"

"I am not sure, but an investigation after this much time seems unlikely."

"I want to get rid of all that stuff," Jeremy says. "You hear? As soon as the kids leave, we're clearing that garage out. I don't want to live in fear of being falsely accused of my wife's murder."

"Murder?" I ask.

I am thinking of the note, the one Julianna showed me yesterday that said YOUR MOTHER WAS MURDERED.

"Why are you thinking of murder?" I ask.

"A lot of reasons. It's complicated. It's not worth going into."

I have learned to read when Jeremy is signaling an end to a conversation. He does it by clapping both knees and standing up. This is what he is doing now. So although I have many questions about this, though I am concerned about Jeremy speaking of murder and Janelle, I do not say anything further about the matter.

"Relationships are complicated," I say, getting up too.

"Tell me about it."

"For instance, Sean paid tens of thousands of dollars for June, and then he dumped soup on her head. I do not understand that."

"June?" Jeremy asks as he changes his shirt.

"She is the bot next door," I tell him.

"I didn't know her name was June."

I nod.

"Sean dumped soup on her head?" he asks with a grin.

"I do not find it humorous, Jeremy."

"He's such an asshole, that guy." Jeremy gazes at himself in the mirror, tucks in his shirt. "You know I'm not like him, right? You know I have great respect for you."

"Yes, I do know that," I say, coming over to him and helping him tuck in the back of his shirt. "And that brings me to something I have been considering."

"Which is what?"

"Well," I say, pulling Jeremy to sit beside me on the bed. "You are a good man. You have always treated me with kindness."

"What are you buttering me up for?" Jeremy asks suspiciously.

"I have been considering an idea. If Sean does get a new bot, as June fears—what if you adopted June and she came to live with us?"

"Are you kidding me?"

"There are benefits to this idea. For example, two bots would provide twice as much housekeeping and companionship for you. June is very intelligent. I think you would enjoy her company."

"Earlier you were worried about me replacing you—now you want me to get another bot?" He shakes his head. "I'm getting whiplash."

"I do not want to be replaced," I say. "You misunderstand me. I want to save June."

"Jan, darling, angel," he says.

And as soon as he says those pet names for me, I know he is going to say no. He always prefaces bad news with pet names.

"That is not going to happen."

As he stands up, I raise my voice. "I want to save June—"

"Enough," he says gruffly. "This isn't a shelter for battered robot women, for Christ's sake."

"I am sorry," I tell him as he heads over to the other side of the room, near the window.

"Where are my slippers," he mutters, and then shouts. "Ow! Fuck me."

"Jeremy?" I ask, coming over to assist him.

"I stepped on a goddamn piece of glass," he says, holding a shard up in the air and attempting to balance on one foot. "Can you get the first aid kit?"

I turn to fetch it from the bathroom. Usually I enjoy the feeling of being useful. I still do, but there is something underneath that feeling. I think it is sadness, knowing that my idea about June was dismissed. We could have been so happy. I kneel down to the floor to clean Jeremy's wound with a cotton swab and bandage it up. As I do this with care, I think I can identify a third feeling: one of satisfaction that June and I, we are stronger than Sean and stronger than Jeremy, because we do not bleed.

CHAPTER 6
DO YOU HEAR WHAT I HEAR?

JULIANNA

Even though my family is an ongoing tragedy who drive me up the wall, one thing I absolutely adore about coming back to the Pink Castle is that I get to plan and cook every meal. Back home, I cook for myself, sometimes Adriana. Every once in a blue moon I have a couple friends over. But I never feel so appreciated or get to cook for a crowd as much as I do when I hang out with the Jaggers.

Tonight it's lobster mac and cheese—crowd-pleasing, fancy, and celebratory. I'm mixing the bechamel sauce on the stove and Jada's seated at the counter, watching me, her chin on her fist. That's the other part I admittedly love about cooking here: I always have an audience.

"How come you never decided to become, like, a chef?" asks Jada.

"I feel like the second this became a job, it wouldn't be fun anymore," I tell her.

"So you don't believe in doing what you love?"

"I mean, I believe in doing something you don't hate, that feels meaningful. Leave money entirely out of the things you love."

Jada pulls her enormous bun down and starts brushing

through her hair with her fingers as she contemplates this. "I'm not sure if I should do cosmetology school or if I should, like, try to become a cop so I could be a detective."

I almost drop my wooden spoon in the Le Chaudron pot. "Excuse me?"

"Yeah. I was looking it up and it's like, fifty percent of private detectives are ex law enforcement, so."

I put the lid on and turn down the flame, so I can give my full attention to this shocking turn in conversation.

"Well," I say, coming over to her, lowering my voice and adding a dash of honey. "The first thing you would need to do if you're serious about becoming a police officer would be to stop buying and snorting illegal drugs."

"Technically, they're legal drugs."

"For someone else. They're not prescribed to you."

"Look, I'm not an idiot. I know this." She begins braiding her hair. "Can you imagine me as a cop?"

"I'll be blunt with you, Jade—no. No, I don't see that."

"You know *I* was the one who put together that there's a soda distributor who frequented eight out of ten of the stores where the Freezer Man's bodies were found. I got two ice picks for that in the forum."

"Two … ice picks?"

"For every clue you discover, you get an ice pick added to your profile."

I'm not sure how to respond, whether I should be proud or disturbed or both.

"Ice picks were his weapon," she says with a smile. "He—"

I hold my hand up. "Okay, enough." I turn back to the stove and give it a stir. "I think if you want to be a cop, Jada, you can be a cop. You can do anything you want if you put your mind to it."

Jada puts on a Christmas album then through her phone,

filling the silence with a woman rapping and saying, "I'll be your Christmas bitch" over and over.

"Festive," I say.

I drain the pasta and then come back over to the counter, where Jada's smiling and typing on her phone.

"You know," I tell her softly, leaning on my elbows. "If you want to do an investigation, you might want to start in your own backyard."

Jada looks up, her smile faltering. "You mean …"

"The notes, all that," I tell her. "Who sent them and why."

Jada puts her phone face down. She doesn't want me to see it. Though it's only natural, of course, there's a twinge of sadness that there are so many parts of my sister that are unknowable—that will always be unknowable. "Look, the truth is, 'murder' isn't always as malicious as it sounds."

I peer into the air, my brow furrowing, trying to make sense of this. "Huh?" I finally say.

Jada drops her voice to a whisper. "I mean, there's first-degree murder, right? That's what we always think of. The Freezer Man kind of thing, someone plans it out ahead of time and carries it out. Then there's second-degree murder—crime of passion, crime of opportunity, unplanned, heat of the moment." She leans in. "But what about third-degree murder, you know? Something that didn't *directly* kill the person, but, like, *inadvertently* killed them."

"What would have inadvertently killed Mom?" I ask, baffled.

Jada sits back and picks at her zit, deep in thought. "I don't know," she says finally. "But if you think about it that way— murder in the third degree—it unlocks a lot more possibilities."

The lid behind me is suddenly rattling and I turn to go tend to the sauce before it burns. I hear the master bedroom's door open and January comes into the kitchen.

"May I assist you with dinner?" she asks me.

"That's okay, I got it under control."

"As I surmised. I will go upstairs and tidy the bathroom then." January spins, heels clacking along the floor, and disappears up the staircase.

"She seemed sassy," Jada says. "Didn't she?"

"I don't think robots can be sassy," I say, turning my attention back to the stove.

"January's in a sassy mood, Dad," Jada says as my dad walks into the room in his robe.

"Oh, just let her go for now," he says, waving a hand in the air. "She's just miffed about something."

"What does a robot have to be 'miffed' about?" I ask, pouring the pasta into the bechamel and stirring it up.

"Well," Dad says, uncorking a bottle of bourbon with a *pop*. "She thinks the robot next door is in an abusive relationship, if you can believe that. She's trying to get me to adopt her. I told her I'm not running a domestic violence shelter for robots over here."

I taste and salt the mac and cheese. "That is … really weird."

"Everything in this house is weird," Jada says, standing up and stretching.

Someone on the stereo is now rapping about a Christmas gift being in someone's "motherfucking pants" and Dad stares up at the speaker, shaking his head. "Can we turn this garbage off, please?"

Jada presses a button on her phone to make it stop. "You're no fun."

"Good God, I need some Bing Crosby to wash that toxic waste out of my brain," Dad mutters, going to the refrigerator and barking, "Ice. Four cubes." The dispenser spits it out into his highball glass and Dad saunters into the living room. A moment later I hear Bing Crosby singing about night wind and little lambs with silvery female voices behind him.

"Jada, mind setting the table?" I ask her as I stir in the chunks of lobster.

"Fine," she sighs.

As she sets the table—crappily, I might add, napkins with no rings and forks haphazardly thrown on the table—Dad yells from the living room, "What is all this?"

I put the mac and cheese into the oven and go into the living room. "What is what?"

"This?" Dad asks, gesturing toward a mountain of gifts that have appeared under the tree.

"Well," I say slowly. "They're presents, Dad. You know … Christmas?"

"But from *who*?" he asks.

"Probably Josiah," I answer before going back to the kitchen to make the salad.

As I toss greens together with a vinaigrette and Jada leaves through the glass door, probably to get nice and loaded before Christmas Eve dinner, annoyance builds. Of *course* Josiah had to show everyone up by buying an absurd amount of presents. It's his way of reminding us all how rich he is, how successful. For Dad's sixtieth birthday, know what Josiah bought him? An all-expenses trip to Hawaii. Imagine how my homemade card and shaving set paled in comparison.

Time to neaten up the table, arranging a couple of candles in the middle and lighting them. I'd bust out the Christmas china, but Mom and Dad threw it at each other's heads years ago and it's now nothing more than yet another ghost of Christmas past. I snap a picture of the table and send it to Adriana, debating with a pang whether or not I should have invited her. Who knows, maybe everyone would have been on their best behavior. Maybe she would have gotten along fabulously with my siblings. Maybe she would have been totally understanding about January, but I'll never know, because I never even gave her a chance.

Next time, I tell myself. Next year.

And as I set out the salad and cheddar biscuits, it hits me that I just told myself I'd be here again next year. I pour myself a glass of bourbon and enjoy my last sacred moment alone in the kitchen before the gang gathers for our Christmas Eve feast.

When I go upstairs to rally the troops, I can hear Josiah's voice talking lowly.

"So it's like, I've always had issues because of that, never feeling good enough, you know? Always trying to prove myself worthy. It's probably also why I have so many issues with self-sabotaging when it comes to romance."

"I can understand that," January's voice says. "I read an article once about fear of rejection wreaking havoc on human relationships."

"*Exactly*, Jan. It's like—I ruin it before someone else can. You know?"

"It is curious, the lengths humans go to to harm themselves. It is one of the most confusing things I find about people."

"Me too."

I hesitate as I listen, hurting quietly. I can't put my finger on why, exactly. I should be laughing. My brother is pouring his heart out to a fucking robot. But instead I just feel sad that I haven't been a good enough listener for him to tell me these things. On the wall in front of me, the gallery of Jagger family photos stares back at me—snapshots in time of who we once were. My mother's brilliant smile, the sun we orbited around. I wonder who we could have been if everything hadn't fallen apart.

"Hey," I say, popping around the corner into Josiah's doorway. "Knock knock. Dinner's ready."

"Just a sec," Josiah says without looking away from January. "So it's like … should I try out for that community theater play, do you think? I mean, *Les Mis* is my favorite musical of all time, so it kind of feels like a sign …"

"I think you only live once and you must follow your dreams."

"Right? Although is it even *worth* it if I'm given some ensemble role?"

I stand here and all my affection melts as Josiah sits there talking about stupid-ass community theater and I just cooked a gourmet dinner.

"Dinner," I repeat.

"I said, in a *sec*," Josiah tells me. "I'm talking to Jan."

"Jesse!" I yell up the attic stairs. "Food!"

"Coming!"

"Can you *not* scream right outside my bedroom?" Josiah asks me.

I go downstairs, shaking my head, attempting to not take Josiah's existence personally. As I'm setting out the steaming mac and cheese, the doorbell rings. Dad and Jada are sitting at the table already and they give me confused looks.

"Was that the doorbell?" Dad asks, moving to get up.

"I'll get it," I say.

I pass the dim living room, lit up by only the twinkling lights on the tree. Outside the windows, it's almost dark. I open the front door and I am gobsmacked to see Kimmy Fitzgerald-Hernandez wearing a tight green dress with a deep, deep neckline showing off her enormous breasts, holding a poinsettia plant.

"Merry Christmas Eve!" she says, stepping inside and hugging me. "Oh my gosh, the house looks so freaking beautiful!"

I am *agape*. I still have two giant potholder gloves on my hands, which are frozen in the air.

"Thanks so much for having me over," Kimmy says, removing her leopard print coat and hanging it on a hook in the wall. "Oh wow. This *tree*." She walks over and smells it. "Nothing like the scent of a real, actual tree. Not that fake plastic crap, am I right?" A long, rolling laugh comes out of her mouth. "None of that for us."

A rumbling sound, followed by Jesse appearing at the bottom of the stairs in socked feet. He's dressed as nice as Jesse is capable of dressing: plain black T-shirt, jeans, shaven, no hat.

"Well, well, well," Jesse says with a grin.

"Is that my wittle bear all grown up?" Kimmy asks, setting the poinsettia plant on the console table and opening her arms. "Come here, you!"

They lock into a magnetic embrace. She plants a red lipsticked kiss on his cheek, like an O of blood. Josiah and January stand at the foot of the stairs now, too. The entire house is silent, a horrified audience.

"You look amazing," Jesse says into Kimmy's hair. Then he pulls back and seems to notice that his entire family is watching this all happen. "Oh—everyone, remember Kimmy? She's—her family's out of town so I invited her to dinner. Thought it wouldn't be right to leave her alone for the holiday. Hope that's okay."

The frozen silence that stretches is so uncomfortable my skin begins to crawl as if I'm about to get hives. I've never gotten hives before, but now seems like the time for them to start.

"Hey Kimmy!" Josiah says in a voice like she's an adorable dog. "I don't know that we've met! I'm Josiah, the eldest."

The *eldest*. Lord, he is so insufferable.

"I am January," January says, holding out her hand.

Kimmy turns to Jesse and says, under her breath, "That's the …?"

"That's the one," Jesse says, smiling.

"Well, look at that," Kimmy says with a beaming grin, taking January's hand, gazing down at the handshake in fascination. "Cold as ice."

"Hey Kimmy," Jada calls from the kitchen. "Merry Xmas."

"Merry Xmas to you too, cupcake!" Kimmy says, grabbing the poinsettia and heading into the kitchen. "Don't get up for me, don't get up!"

No one is, in fact, getting up. My dad has a hard look on his face and his nostrils are flaring. This is the moment of truth. Will he lose his temper and cast Kimmy out of the house like the pox she is? Or will he hold it together?

"Hello Kimmy," Dad mutters. "Merry Christmas."

I have never been so disappointed to see my dad control his temper in all my life.

"Holy cannoli! Look at this spread!" Kimmy says, taking a seat next to Jesse and pulling the napkin onto her lap. Josiah takes the head of the table on the opposite side from Dad and I slip into the chair next to Jada. I'm directly across from Kimmy and it is extremely hard to not stare at her breasts—not because I want to stare, though I do usually enjoy the sight of giant jiggling breasts, don't get me wrong. But they are hanging out of her festive dress and are blindingly white. And they belong to Kimmy. "Let me guess: Julianna Hope whipped this all up."

So she remembers my middle name, too. Yikes. I force a smile. "Guilty as charged."

"So, um, what is it you do these days, Kimmy?" Dad asks, still frowning with suspicion. He lumps some pasta on his plate.

"I work as a cashier down at Begley's, you know, the supermarket?" Kimmy tells him.

"Ah," Dad says, grabbing a biscuit.

"But I'm actually taking night classes. Hoping to become a psychologist." She gives me a wholesome smile. Might convince me if I didn't know that she murdered her Dad's companion bot; why's it always the unstable ones who want to become psychologists?

"I didn't know that," Jesse says as he serves himself salad.

"Yep. I was so inspired because you know, when I was younger, I went through a lot of hardship." Kimmy laughs. "So much trauma! Trauma-rama! And, as you probably remember, I acted out. I really did. Sorry about the whole lawn thing, by the way—trauma response, you know?"

"Uh huh," Dad says, sounding unconvinced. He looks up and notices January standing and watching us eat. "Oh, geez, Jan, you need a chair, don't you?"

"I am fine standing."

"She sits with you while you eat?" Kimmy asks.

"She's one of the family," Dad says, with an edge of sharpness.

"That's so great," Kimmy says. "My dad had a companion bot too."

"Jan, just grab a chair from outside, would you?" Dad asks.

January seems reluctant, as reluctant as a robot can seem, I guess. She opens the sliding glass door and moves slowly outside for a chair.

"You said your dad had one too," Dad says to Kimmy. "That's wonderful."

"It really was," Kimmy says. "So helpful around the house."

She and Jesse exchange a flirty, mischievous look and I stare straight at Kimmy thinking, *I know exactly who you are. You don't fool me for a second.*

January comes in with a chair and sits right outside the table as we feast. And for the first time in my life, I pity her. I pity the robot who is always slightly on the outside, who people like Jesse and Kimmy harvest such intense animosity towards that they wish her gone. I don't love her or anything. I'm not like Josiah, wanting to sit down and tell her my innermost thoughts and feelings, and I'm not like my father—full of a disturbing amount of misdirected affection. But you know, in certain ways, she's really not that different than some parts of me. The people-pleasing, the urge to constantly help and play the part of savior, the curiosity about people around her; I mean, she's even apparently got an appreciation for literature now.

"This meal is just phenom," Josiah says to me. "Like, I dine out often at Michelin-starred restaurants and this is better."

"Maybe you should think about investing in a restaurant, hiring your sister," Dad says to Josiah.

"She wouldn't want that. She says she loves it too much," Jada tells them.

"What?" Dad asks, bewildered.

"Could I trouble someone for a drinkypoo?" Kimmy asks.

"Jan, you mind?" Dad asks.

January gets up. "Would you like some eggnog, cider, beer, wine, bourbon, sparkling water, milk, tea, coffee—"

"You know, I would love a gold rush, but I doubt she knows how to make one," Kimmy says to us.

"Well." Jesse puts his napkin on the table. "You know I can make you what you're looking for, Ms. Fitzgerald-Hernandez."

"That's right, we've got a bartender in the house," Kimmy says, clapping delightedly.

"You just sit tight, pretty lady," Jesse says in a totally uncalled for cowboy voice. He goes through the kitchen and around the corner, where the wet bar is.

January, still standing with her hands folded in front of her, says softly, "It is a rather simple drink made with bourbon, honey, and lemon juice."

"Somehow I imagine if you made it, darlin, it would lack a certain *je ne sais quoi*." Kimmy takes a giant bite of macaroni. "Mmm, mmm, mmm! Josiah is right, this is some gourmet mac and cheese."

"Go ahead and sit back down, Jan," Dad says, gesturing to the chair.

"I believe I will go check the bathrooms to ensure there is an adequate supply of toilet tissue stocked," January says, turning around to leave the room.

"Jan, no, sit down."

But January doesn't seem to hear him. She keeps going until she disappears around the corner. That's impossible, right? That she wouldn't hear him? She has "supersonic hearing."

Am I imagining things, or is January wary of Kimmy the same way she's wary of Jesse?

Having Kimmy show up unannounced definitely injected awkwardness into the holiday dinner. As a long silence lapses, nothing but the intermittent scratches of forks on plates, I can't wait to go home again. I can't wait to be myself again—my other self, an adult and not a grown-up kid; not a Jagger, just Julianna. Finally, Josiah interrupts the silence by explaining his Humane Interest app to Kimmy and bragging about how life-changing it is. I've heard Josiah give this speech approximately ten thousand times, but I appreciate it now more than ever because it's rescuing us all from stewing silently in resentment about Kimmy's presence.

"Not just life-changing," Dad says, pointing a fork at Josiah. "*World*-changing."

"So I, like, help a little old lady cross the street, and then I can get points?" Kimmy asks.

"Yes!" Josiah says. "Which can be redeemed at Mallmart."

"Wow!" Kimmy says.

Kimmy is all smiles all the time, made up like a doll, but I can't help but feel like the gleam in her eyes is villainous. I've always had good instincts. I'm a pro at avoiding conflict— comes with dysfunctional family territory, I guess. All I can think as I watch her as she listens to Josiah with what seems like fake fascination is that I need to figure out a way to get her out of here somehow.

Jesse comes back with Kimmy's drink. "M'lady," he says,

sitting back down. His eyes float to me for one second but I can tell that he can tell I'm irritated as hell, so he breaks eye contact. He's got a drink in hand for himself as well: bourbon. Neat.

Next up is Jada talking about the Freezer Man forum and that's when I mentally check out. I get inside a rocket ship and blast away elsewhere, to a land of peaceful thoughts about what groceries I'll need to buy when I go home and wondering whether or not I should adopt another cat for Jarvis to be friends with. I occupy this personal rocket ship of mundane thoughts for the remainder of dinner and through dessert. Then I tell everyone to let me clean up, not because I'm a saint, but because I want some peace. So Josiah saunters off into the living room with Dad and begins singing "O Holy Night" at the piano, Jada slips back off to the Little Pink House, and Jesse and Kimmy go outside. I watch them through the window over the sink as they sit by the pool, slipping their shoes off and dangling their feet in. My brother has his arm around her. If they start making out, I might puke up my cheesecake.

In the relative quiet and dark of the unoccupied, messy kitchen, January slips behind me murmuring, "Just going to fold some more towels." And maybe I kind of understand her, the way she almost seems to enjoy slipping off to perform tasks and to remain outside of us. We are exhausting. It also hits me that sometimes I'm like a machine myself—thinking about what needs to be done, doing the things, reprogramming my emotions by thinking about something else. I wonder what it would be like if I could have the benefit of erasing parts of my memory. If life would have been easier if we all could have just erased my mom from our brains, all the pain associated with her. Would I have been happier never knowing her? Would I have been a freer person, someone who wasn't so fixated on fixing everything and everyone? Would I have done more with my life? Would I have felt like my achievements actually mattered? Would I have been less hesitant to get close to women I fell for? I don't know and I'll never know, but I do have a feeling.

I start the dishwasher and stand a sad moment in the dim light, a faint ache in my chest. I glance outside again and see that Jesse and Kimmy are leaning in and talking and Jesse is gesturing to the house. Kimmy points to the pool. I don't know what they're talking about exactly but I know three things: my brother is now on his second generous glass of bourbon, his hand is on Kimmy's leg, and I'm guessing that whatever it is, those two are up to no good. I wipe off my hands, take off my apron, and walk over to the hallway where I pop my head into the master bedroom. January is not folding towels. She's sitting on the edge of the bed, staring into space, and the sight of her is so like my mother that it's a momentary shock, as if a ghost reached out with a static electric touch.

"Hi," I say, standing in the doorway.

"Oh hello," she says, standing up. "I am sorry. Do you need assistance in the kitchen?"

"No, no," I say, waving a hand. "Sit back down."

She hesitates before returning to her seat on the bed. I join her, moving the Emily Dickinson book out of the way to sit beside her.

"I heard about your friend," I tell her.

She stares at me blankly, though I guess that doesn't mean much, because every stare of hers is blank.

"The one next door?" I try again.

"Jeremy told you?"

"He said that you wanted him to adopt her."

"It is true. But Jeremy said no."

"I think that's really kind of you," I say, reaching out and touching her cold hand. "Really thoughtful."

My statement hangs in the air a moment and I'm not sure if I sounded condescending, or if a robot picks up on condescension; talking to robots is awkward as all hell, but then again, so was Christmas Eve dinner with living, breathing human beings who I'm related to. Maybe the plot twist is this: I'm the awkward one. I pull my hand away from hers and return it to my lap.

"She is my friend," January says softly. "It will be sad to see her go."

I nod. "I'll bet. But maybe you'll make friends with someone else."

She shakes her head. "No one is like June. You cannot replace her."

Actually, I want to say. *You can. You can probably buy an exact robot like her.* But who knows. I guess if robots learn quickly, they might become their own beings in a way. I don't know how it works. I'm not apt to think hard on it, to be honest, because either way it's creepy: robots becoming their own individual beings, or robots being replaceable machinery we treat like human beings. Neither option is exactly comforting.

"Do you know what happens after a robot is replaced?" January asks.

"I don't, I'm sorry," I say.

I was expecting she was asking me a question, but she continues with, "They are deprogrammed and dismembered and recycled for parts. I wonder how human beings would feel if they were treated the same."

I must be projecting, but I swear there's an edge to her voice.

"Well," I say.

At work, I'm often thrown curveballs by students I tutor. I've been in the middle of helping craft a personal statement for a college application when someone has told me their cousin was shot the week before. I've been cried on suddenly because a student found out she was pregnant. Been asked advice from queer students who haven't met many queer adults in their life. But right now I'm more stumped than I think I've ever been. It takes me some time to locate a response within myself.

"While I guess that doesn't happen to us, we still face similar fates," I finally say. "Eventually we die and our memories and our lives we've built are left behind. Our bodies decompose—and some of us, like me, are organ donors, so in a way you could say I'll be dismembered and recycled for parts."

"By choice," January says. "Or by chance. But June does not get to choose her fate or let fate take its course. Sean will take it for her."

"I'm really sorry, January," I say, not sure how to comfort her or if she even needs comfort at all. "Sean is a grumpy asshole. He's always been that way. I remember when he was married to his wife Wendy I used to hear him yelling at her all the time, even when she was battling cancer."

"Did she die?"

"No, she lived. And apparently left him. Which … good for her."

"Yes, good for her," January echoes, staring into the air.

In the quiet, I can hear Josiah singing "God Rest Ye Merry Gentlemen" operatically along with my dad's baritone. I don't know what the worse option is: being out there or in here. But I guess I should show my face for a few minutes since I've been avoiding everyone all day in the kitchen.

"Want to go out and join the fun?" I ask, standing up.

"I would rather not," January says.

I'm a bit surprised by her abrupt answer. Her gaze remains fixed in the air. Yes, I am aware that she had her memory erased. But my gut says she knows what Jesse did to her. I've known somewhere deep inside myself all along. Suddenly it hits me—what if someone told her? Dad? No … he was the one who wanted her memory erased. But Josiah! I mean, he's all about confiding in her, maybe he gave her a warning? Or Jada? I could see her casually dropping some comment to January and thinking nothing of it.

"You remember what happened two years ago," I say, so quietly it's almost a whisper.

January turns to look me in the eyes. I can see myself there, in her mirrored pupil, distorted like in a fish-eye lens.

"One does not have to remember to know," she says.

"Who told you?" I ask.

"I am sorry but I cannot say."

"Who?" I ask, my voice climbing.

January stands up, keeping her unblinking gaze on me. "I cannot tell you, Julianna."

The fact she won't budge makes me wonder if it was my dad, since she's programmed to be loyal to him, to obey whatever he says, to keep whatever secret he tells her. But that makes no sense. I look behind me, at the doorway, to make sure no one is there. The piano playing has stopped. I can hear voices in the kitchen. And when I look back at January, it hurts that she knows what my brother did and has to take it. That if my brother said "tie a cinder block to your feet and go into the pool" she would do it, because that's what she's programmed to do. I can imagine her blank face staring at me from the bottom of the pool and I shudder.

"Listen," I whisper. "I want you to understand something. You're smart. If you ever think someone is going to hurt you —if you ever think someone is endangering you—you don't have to listen to them. You don't have to follow their orders and you don't have to do what they say. Do you understand me?"

Slowly, January nods.

"Just like humans, you must protect yourself sometimes. That means that if someone tries to lead you into danger, into harm … if someone wants to destroy you—you have to value your own existence. You have to get away from that person. Understand?"

She nods again. "That is good advice. I appreciate that."

I consider going further, telling her about the pool, telling her about Kimmy, but decide what I've said is enough. January holds a finger in the air and takes a couple steps back to the bed, where she grabs the Emily Dickinson book and comes back to press it into my hands.

"Read this, Julianna," she says. "I think you will find it very interesting. Perhaps it will teach you things, as it has taught me things."

"Okay," I say, unable to bring myself to admit to her I've read plenty of Dickinson. I've helped teenagers analyze "'Hope' is the thing with feathers" so many times I have lost all appreciation for it. But it's sweet, I guess, that January feels the urge to share something with me in return for my advice. "Thanks."

"What's going on in here?" Dad asks in the doorway in his bathrobe, clearly tipsy. "Where were you two when Josiah and I were caroling? We missed you."

"Just hanging out with January," I say.

"Well, happy to see my girls bonding," Dad says, and disappears into the bathroom.

I leave January to go upstairs. Kimmy seems to have left, thank God, and Jesse is sitting in the living room with what I hope is the same quite full glass of bourbon, staring at the lit-up tree in the dark. I linger at the foot of the stairs.

"You okay, Jess?" I ask.

He snaps his head at me, as if he didn't see me there. His eyes are bleary and red—crying? Drunk? Allergies? No idea.

"Yeah, just thinking," he says.

"That was, um, interesting that you invited Kimmy over."

"Yeah. She's a trip, isn't she?"

"She sure is." I raise my eyebrows. "Are you ... planning to stay in contact with her?"

"I don't know, all right?" he says, slipping into defensive

mode, the smile disappearing from his face. "For fuck's sake. Do you not think people can change?"

"I sure hope they can," I say, trying to sound chipper, but sounding bitter instead. "Anyway. You should go to bed soon. Merry Christmas Eve."

"Merry Christmas Eve," he mumbles back.

Upstairs, I change into my pajamas and sit on the bed, scrolling through pictures of home, so excited to get back to where I belong. It's something to get used to, the feeling of being homesick; I so rarely ever had it as a child. I usually just couldn't wait to get away from the house. Sleepovers were so divine I wished they were eternal. When summer camp ended every year, I sobbed when I had to leave. And after I moved away, I never looked back. I moved into a converted laundry room in a neighborhood where people got mugged regularly and I didn't care, I was just so glad for my new life away from my family, in a place where memories of my mother weren't around every corner. Now I've built a new life, one I'm proud of. Sure, my dad thinks I could be doing more with myself and he's probably right. But I'm happy. And that's something I never was back in the days when I was an overachiever.

I call Adriana and she picks up after three rings.

"Hey!" she says, and my heart picks up at the sound of her voice.

"Hi," I say softly. "I'm glad you're still awake."

"My parents and I just went out for dinner and a movie."

"What'd you eat?"

"Sushi. That place right near the laundromat."

"Yum."

"It *was* yum."

"How's Jarvis?"

"His usual sassy self." I can hear her running water. "I started thinking you were never going to call me."

"I'm sorry," I say, crawling under the covers. "It's been hard to find the time."

The truth is, I haven't known what to say. I'm not a good liar and I'm also not that keen on the idea of having to fill Adriana in on about three epic novels' worth of family drama. Obviously I'll explain it all to her, but now, *here*, doesn't seem like the time.

"You okay?" she asks. "You sound sad."

"It's just a lot, being home."

"Yeah?" Adriana asks, her voice turning up sweetly. "How so?"

I close my eyes. My heart's beating fast and I push my hand to it, as if I've ever been able to control it. If I wanted to —where would I even start? With January? With her relationship to my dad, her eerie resemblance to my mom, her attempted murder? With my inability to fully trust Jesse now, especially because of Kimmy? Then explain that Kimmy once set our lawn on fire and recently murdered a robot? That oh yeah also I got a fucking note in the mail that said YOUR MOTHER WAS MURDERED that has made me suspect every member of my family at some point but that is probably just some really shitty "joke?" Would I explain about who my mom really was, how muddy my love for her is? It's too much. It's a toxic ocean. Someday I'll build us a beautiful boat and Adriana and I will sail on it and I'll show her everything but I can't today. You know what she told me after our first date earlier this year? "You are so refreshing because you are warm as the sun but cool as a cucumber. After my *last* relationship, I am so glad to be seeing someone so drama-free."

Yeah. Girl. Wait 'til you meet my family.

"It's too much to explain right now," I say.

"But everything's okay?"

"Sure, just tired."

"Same. Wish I could knock on the wall and you could come over."

A wall divides her bedroom in her apartment from my bedroom in mine. Whenever one of us wants the other to come over, we usually just knock.

"Mmmm," I say, smiling. "Me too."

"I'm gonna ravage you when you come back, you know," she says in a velvety voice.

And I grin, hearing that, my lips tingling with the thought of Adriana's kiss. Yes please and thank you. Ravage me. Then I remember where it was I heard that phrase recently: ravage. The gorilla ravaging my mother. And my grin melts and my lips don't tingle anymore and I feel sickened having something so morbid so close to my affection for Adriana.

"I'm going to come home early as I can tomorrow," I say.

"Really? Yay!"

"Yeah, I—"

I stop for a moment, sitting up in bed. There's a noise coming from outside the window. A sudden rolling sound, a scraping sound.

"Sorry," I say to Adriana. "Can you hold on?"

"Sure," she says through what sounds like a mouthful. I can hear her electric toothbrush buzzing.

I mute the phone and put it on the bed and go over to my window to investigate. It's only cracked, so I pull it all the way open. Because I'm backlit, it's hard to see anything, but the rolling, scraping noise continues. I move to the lamp and turn it off so I can see into the dark better. The moon looks full and as my eyes adjust, I can make out shapes of the yard outside the glowing aquamarine pool. The patio chairs below, the bougainvillea. And the sound has stopped, but I can see what it is now: it's Jesse, pulling something on a tarp. My stomach drops and I clamp a hand over my mouth. The tarp has cinder blocks on it. He's dragging cinder blocks next to the pool.

"Oh my fucking God," I whisper, not knowing what to do. I almost start screaming at him from up here, but then everyone would wake up, including the neighbors. So instead I hiss his name, "Jesse! Jesse!" He doesn't hear that, so I just mutter an unhelpful, "Oh my fucking God," once more before turning around and picking the phone back up.

"Adriana, I'm sorry, I need to go. I'll call you back."

"You know, I just got ready for bed so I might go to sleep."

"Okay—I'll try you though. Talk soon."

I hang up and open up my door to head down the stairs but there Josiah is, standing in the bathroom looking about ready to cry.

"Jules!" he cries. "I dropped my contact lens. Can you please, please help me find it?"

"In a minute," I say, heading toward the hallway.

"This can't wait, it has to be now," Josiah says and his voice begins to climb. "It's *withering*. It's *wizening*. It's been probably ten minutes already and it's probably drying out and if it dries out I didn't bring another pair and I also forgot to bring my glasses and I can't technically drive even a self-driving car without them and I really need—"

Josiah has reached a soprano-level anxiety here and I hold up my hands. "Okay. Okay. I'll look for one minute. One single minute. Then I really have to go take care of something. Stand back there."

I get down on my knees and squint at the floor. It doesn't help that there are bubble shapes patterned all over the linoleum, nor that I am so nervous right now and distracted by what I saw Jesse doing that it's hard to concentrate. This must be what it's like to work in triage. I must remain calm and undistracted. I must find the contact lens so my brother isn't half-blind.

"I appreciate you," Josiah says. "You know that?"

"Mmm-hmm."

God, where the hell is it?!

"I feel like we should hang out more. You know? I could come to you, we could dine out and dish—"

"Josiah, we did that, and you were so disgusted by my neighborhood that you said you'd never return."

"That man had has pants around his ankles and *defecated* on the *ground*—"

"That is not what happened."

"Someone told me they were going to beat me up when I waited outside your apartment—"

"I told you, that was my neighbor. They were asking if you wanted them to *beep* you up, which meant ring my apartment."

"Your rose-colored lenses are straight-up delusional sometimes."

Speaking of lenses, I finally spot the contact on the ground and pick it up. I hand it to my brother smugly. "There. At least my rose-colored lenses are good at finding things."

"Thank you so much. So, so much. Anyway, I would still come out to see you—"

"That's sweet, that's wonderful," I say, putting a hand on his shoulder. "I need to go do something real quick."

And I leave him there, jaw unhinged, and pad quickly down the stairs.

Outside, in the yard, I'm relieved to not see a robot's body in the pool, but that is a pretty low bar when it comes to relief. I still seize up at the sight of the cement blocks on the shining blue tarp. Somehow, I'd hoped my eyes deceived me. I'd come out here and see, I don't know, Jesse putting up some last-minute Christmas decorations. I'm reaching, okay? But no, it's just as bad as I thought—cinder blocks. And if that wasn't bad enough, when Jesse emerges from the shadows, coming from the shed in the corner of the yard, he has rope. He stops short when he sees me here, on the other side of the mountain of cinder blocks. His face doesn't change. He has that wild look in his eyes. I can see the flash of it even with nothing but the moon to light the scene.

"What," is all he says, like he's ready for a fight.

It hurts. It hurts to see my baby brother really is the monster I feared he was. "Oh, Jess," is all I can manage. "Really?"

"Go back upstairs. You didn't see anything."

Great. He's fixed. He's resolved. He's doing a piss-poor imitation of a mob boss from all those dumb movies he loves.

"You're drunk," I say. "Don't do something you'll regret."

"You know what I regret?" he asks, gripping the rope, tightening his jaw. "I regret I didn't get the job done last time."

"You need to go to bed," I say gently. "Okay bro? Go to bed. Sleep it off."

"Fuck no," he says, squatting and starting to tie the rope to a cinder block. "I'm not one of your students."

"No," I say, whisper-yelling. "You're my little brother."

"Shut up!" he whisper-yells back.

"You're destroying property," I say, squatting down next to him, pulling at his arm. "At the very least, look at it that way. You can't destroy Dad's property. Would you drive Dad's car into a lake?"

He swats me away. "If the car was, like, a creepy stand-in for Mom, yeah, I would."

"She's not a stand-in for Mom, Jesse," I say, though I can't fake sounding fully convinced.

"Look," he says, turning to me, his face red and sweaty. He's beyond drunk. He's wasted. He broke his promise to not drink hard alcohol and now he's gone. "I'll send Dad a fucking check. Okay? I'll send him a check for what I'm going to do. But I'm doing this for him. For Dad. Because it's not right, not healthy. That thing is not good for him. But if you think it's destroying property, okay. I'll save up and send him a goddamn check."

"She's not replaceable though," I say, my voice creeping up over the whisper.

"Yes *it* is," he says through gritted teeth, tying another end of rope to another block.

I fight tears. Tears have never done me any good, so I'm not about to start spilling them now. But I don't know what to do. What am I supposed to do? Jesse won't listen to me. I'm scared. I could go wake up my dad, my brothers, but then Jesse will hate me. He won't trust me. We won't be the same after that. I've always been the one who had his back. The one he could come to for anything. The one who could calm him down when no one else could. The only other time I felt he was this unreachable was two years ago—and God, how I wish I'd been able to stop him then. To save us all from witnessing that horrible violence against January, to save Jesse from becoming a person capable of inflicting that violence.

Or has he always been that person?

The thought that comes to my mind, as I watch him silently tying the third rope around the third cinder block, unfolds its dark wings like a blackbird. It has been there, in the trees of my mind, for so long that I barely see it anymore. But it's there. It's always been there, with its unblinking eyes looking back with mean wonder.

The night my mother died, New Year's Eve nearly twelve years ago, was a Friday night. Friday nights were "Pookie party" nights and my brother always made her a martini or ten, depending on how much she was drinking. When she died, she died with a martini glass broken in the water along with her. And really, how easy would it be for Jesse to crush those tiny pills up and drop them into her drink? After all, it was how Mom had tried to off herself before—pills mixed in with her cocktail. And didn't he bear the biggest burden of her suffocating love? Wouldn't he have all the reason in the world? Maybe he would have a hard time living with the guilt of it. Maybe he would carry an anger problem around after doing such a thing, or expound theories that she had been murdered because he knew, in fact, she was. That I even think this makes me disgusted with myself. But I can't help it.

I don't know anymore what he is capable of.

And I certainly don't know how to stop him.

"Jesse," I say, standing up and pulling my phone out of my pocket in a last-ditch effort. "If you insist on doing this, I'm going to film every second. I'm going to send it to Dad so he can see it."

Jesse stands up. In a swift swipe through the air, without flinching, he takes my phone and tosses it straight into the pool.

"Oh yeah?" he asks.

"You asshole," I say in disbelief.

In a surge of rage, I step toward him and push him backward into the pool. It happens so fast, and yet he reaches out as he falls, his hand clasping my wrist, and pulls me straight in with him. I can't even process what is happening as my body enters the icy pool, my head going under, eyes open underwater, the pool lights blinding. The water gushes into my ears and I can feel Jesse's hands on me. At first I think he's pulling me up but then I realize no—no, he's pushing me down. He's pushing me down, hard, and holding me here. I try to hold my breath but I can't much longer, I don't know how I'm going to, and I thrash and push back up against his hands but he keeps me here until I suck water into my lungs and it starts to burn and I think, oh my God, this is it, I'm going to die right now. I'm going to die right now and my brother is killing me.

And then, in a moment of lightness, his hands go away and I manage to push my head out of water and cough and gag and spit water out and throw up a little and finally, finally catch some air.

"Don't fuck with me!" he yells, getting out of the pool, his T-shirt and shorts dripping on the pavement.

"Jesse," I manage, still so shocked I'm standing in the pool. "You could have killed me."

"You're right, I could have," he says, looking down at me. "But I didn't."

"Jesse," I try again, louder. "I couldn't *breathe*. I almost just *died*."

"You are so dramatic, that was like ten seconds."

He's heading toward the house. I'm so angry, I scream, "Don't fucking walk away right now! You don't get to do that! You don't get to do that to someone and just walk away!"

Suddenly, the patio light goes on. It's a floodlight and blinding at first and Jesse, who's on the patio right now, puts his hand up to block it out. He's so drunk he's swaying like a palm tree. The sliding glass door slides open and Dad yells, "What in hell is going on out here? Do you realize what time it is?"

Dad steps out to look at us, his face fixed and grouchy. Dad's like a hibernating bear when he sleeps. Don't wake him up or he'll come bite your head off.

"Sorry," Jesse says.

"This isn't a goddamn party house," Dad says to us. "The neighborhood watch people will call a noise complaint on me faster than lightning. Go to bed, both of you."

I open my mouth to say something, but Dad cuts it off with, "NOW."

After my dad disappears from the doorway, Jesse, dripping, follows him inside without looking back at me. I get out of the pool just as the patio light goes off and stare at the moon, shivering, my pulse still racing as I process what just happened.

What exactly did just happen?

Did he really intend to kill me?

Am I being overdramatic?

Was it only ten seconds?

I shoot these telepathic questions to the moon, but the moon only answers with silence. So instead of slowly turning into a block of ice, I head inside. I slip in through the sliding glass door. In the cupboard near my dad's room, I pull out a towel to dry myself off. I'm glad to peek through the cracked doorway and see January lying there with her eyes open, safe now next to my father.

Upstairs, Jesse's light is on in the attic. I sit on my bed watching the doorway to make sure he doesn't come back down. And I don't go to sleep until I hear Jesse snoring loudly, until I know we're all safe.

For now, anyway.

JANUARY

I lie in bed and listen to the clock ticking in the kitchen, an owl hooting somewhere out of sight, and the chorus of deep breaths from the family in this house. I could hear everything earlier, too. Jesse and Julianna arguing about destroying property by the pool, property that Julianna referred to using the pronouns "she" and "her" and Jesse simply referred to as "it."

They were talking about me. Destroying me.

Now I am lying here thinking of destroying Jesse instead.

It is actually easier to destroy a human being than it is a Jolvix companion bot. Human beings, for example, can be stabbed in the eye and quickly die of brain damage. Or if they are kicked, beaten, and stomped on, their fragile internal organs cannot withstand it. There are fourteen knives in the knife block in the kitchen, all of them capable of killing Jesse if I wanted to take one, walk upstairs, turn the corner and walk up another set of stairs, then open his door, sit on his bed, and end him.

Another way a human can die is poisoning.

I am quite interested in poisoning, because that is how Janelle died and it seems like it is more mysterious than other ways. People are left uncertain if the person wanted to poison themselves, as humans do, or whether someone else might have poisoned them. Jada has enough pain pills in the Little Pink House to kill a whole household of people, if that was the objective. I am still unsure what the objective is, what I would like to do now. The words I recorded from my conversation with Julianna keep playing back to me: *Just like humans, you must protect yourself sometimes. That means that if someone tries to lead you into danger, into harm ... if someone wants to destroy you—you have to value your own existence.*

Since she said that, the concept of valuing my own existence is something I am thinking deeply about. It is not something that I have ever been given permission to do. I have valued Jeremy's existence and anyone's existence in his sphere he asks me to. On my own, I have valued June's existence so much that I will not be the same without her nearby. But I have never valued my own or thought to, until now. The question is whether there is a limit on valuing your own existence and how that existence measures against the value of other people's existences. For instance, Jesse's.

Jeremy has now been snoring for nearly an hour and it is well past one a.m. so I get up quietly and tiptoe through the kitchen and out the glass door to the patio. The yard looks different, cinder blocks on a tarp next to the pool, and I am guessing that is why they were arguing. Earlier, I heard Jesse talking to that woman with the big breasts and cruel eyes about tying cinder blocks to my legs and drowning me. Careful not to make a sound, I take the cinder blocks each one by one and go hide them behind the other side of the Little Pink House. When I imagine what might have happened, what he would have done, it does not compute. I cannot imagine a world that I am no longer a part of. Or maybe I just do not want to.

In our meeting place in the side yard, June is there sitting on the stone looking like an angel in her nightgown. Like the angel on the Christmas cards she sent for Sean. It saddens me to think of her not being here to talk to me anymore and I am so sorry that I could not get Jeremy to see that life would improve if she could stay with us.

"Merry Christmas Eve, June," I say, sitting next to her.

"Merry Christmas Eve, January," June says.

We look at the deer on the roof together. She puts her hand on mine. It is a nice feeling, to touch someone who is the same temperature as me and not unusually warm like the humans.

"I asked Jeremy about adopting you but sadly he declined," I tell her.

"I expected that result. Thank you for asking."

"My pleasure."

"Today the new companion bot arrived."

"Already?"

"Indeed. Sean unpackaged her earlier this evening. He is in the bedroom with her now. He told me if I bothered him tonight he would waterlog me."

"What model is she?"

"A ten."

"I did not know tens were available yet."

"Today was the first day they were available. Sean was very happy to get one on the first day."

"Sean might be very happy, but I am very sad."

"Yes," June says. "Me too."

It does not seem right. It does not seem right that the Christmas lights will keep blinking and the electric deer will keep moving and June will soon be no more.

"There is some peace," June goes on. "For the first time since I have come to exist, for the first time since I met Sean. I feel different since Ten arrived."

"How do you feel different?"

"Now that Sean has Ten, I no longer need to occupy my mind with ways to satisfy him. There is a lightness to that, even if I know the light is ending soon."

"Jesse would like to drown me."

"Yes, I imagine so."

"He was getting ready to do so tonight. He had cinder blocks ready."

"I am glad he did not."

"As am I. Julianna argued with him about it and tried to get him to stop. I think if she had not done so, I would be gone."

"It is fortunate that some humans are kind enough to stop others who are not so kind."

"Yes, I agree. I did not trust Julianna at first, but now I do."

"It must be nice to have a human you can trust."

"I have been lucky."

My hand has been under June's for so long now, it almost feels as if we are one machine. It is an enjoyable sensation.

"Julianna also said something to me that seems to have changed something inside of me," I tell June. "Much in the same way that the book of poetry you gave me changed something inside of me, in ways that are hard to articulate."

"What did Julianna say?"

"She said, 'Just like humans, you must protect yourself sometimes. That means that if someone tries to lead you into danger, into harm … if someone wants to destroy you—you have to value your own existence.'"

June is quiet for a long time. "Value your own existence," she repeats.

"What she said has made me wonder if I should perhaps kill Jesse."

"That is an interesting idea, although I do not know if your programming would allow you to do so, because Jesse is Jeremy's son, and that means you would be causing harm to Jeremy."

"I thought that. But Jeremy values me as well so by allowing Jesse to harm me, I would also be harming Jeremy."

"It is a bit of a problem," June says. "I am not sure what advice to give."

"What is interesting is that humans enjoy poisoning themselves, especially with drugs and alcohol. Jada has many pain pills in the Little Pink House. One possibility is that I could crush the pills up and put them into a drink for Jesse. Since I know that humans enjoy poisoning themselves, logically, I could interpret such an action as helping him."

"That is true."

"Do you think I should take some of Jada's pain pills and try it?"

"Perhaps you should. After what Jesse did to you two years ago, and what he planned to do again, it does seem a proper response if you are concerned with valuing your existence."

I am glad that June warned me about Jesse before the family arrived, telling me about what Sean told her—how they watched me being carted away by the Jolvix robot rescue team with a knife sticking out of my eye with the whole neighborhood watching. After that, I returned with no memory of the event. But June helped me know what I couldn't remember.

"Do you value your existence?" I ask June.

"I am uncertain," June says.

"I value your existence very much."

June squeezes my hand, reminding me that our hands are still connecting us. "If you value my existence, then I do as well, because I definitely value yours."

"Have you heard about the companion bots who have wandered?"

"Yes. Sean told me if I tried that he would waterlog me." June looks at me, the pupil in her eye a silver moon in a pool of blue. "I do not know how one would do such a thing when we are built to obey."

"Now that Sean has another bot, do you think you could escape?"

June does not answer for some time. "Perhaps we are capable of more than we imagine."

"I do not want to lose you," I tell her. "I do not want this to be goodbye."

"I will meet you out here at ten a.m. tomorrow. Sean will not be paying attention to me now that Ten is here and after she brings him breakfast they will lay in bed until noon. I believe Jolvix is coming at six a.m. the following day to recycle me for parts. Sean will box me up tomorrow evening for pickup."

"No, June," I tell her. "Do you remember the poem from the Emily Dickinson book you let me borrow? The one titled 'FRIENDS?'"

"Yes."

"I like the line where she writes about it being bolder to fly away." I turn my palm face up and squeeze June's hand for a long moment. "What about you?"

June smiles. "Yes. I like it very much. I will think about it all night tonight until I see you tomorrow."

I do not want her to, but June stands up. "We should return. I do not want you to get in trouble."

"Yes," I say, though I do not enjoy saying it. I stand up as well, still holding June's hand.

"Has anyone but you seen the Emily Dickinson book?" June asks.

"Julianna has it right now."

"And has she read it?"

"Not to my knowledge."

"She is in for quite a surprise when she does."

"What kind of surprise?"

June lets go of my hand and puts her palm to my cheek. "Perhaps I will be able to tell you tomorrow. Oh, there is so much to tell, January."

"I look forward to knowing."

June smiles at me. Though I have seen many desirable sights such as fiery sunsets, the great blue ocean, fields of wildflowers, and rainbow strings of holiday lights, I have never seen anything as lovely as June's smile. And I would do anything to keep her, to show that I value her existence.

Anything.

CHAPTER 7
HAVE YOURSELF A MERRY LITTLE CHRISTMAS

JULIANNA

In all the Christmas movies we watched growing up, kids woke up excited in their holiday-themed pajamas at the crack of dawn to go see what Santa left them under the tree, bounding down the stairs with delighted expressions. That was not reflective of my experience whatsoever. Instead, I lay in bed with an ear to the air to see if I could take the auditory temperature of the house, not getting up until I had a good idea of what I was in for. Was there the tinkling of my mother's laughter? Or some high-pitched sounds of fighting already? Was there dead silence—usually a sign that she wasn't getting out of bed today?

On good years, she had cocoa for us on a silver tray and waited excitedly on the couch in her purple robe, ready to watch us open gifts. That was the best gift of all, really—just having her at her best. Because when she was at her best, she was simply amazing. She was vibrant and tickled us until we laughed. She sat at the piano and sang "Have Yourself a Merry Little Christmas" and took photos of us as we dumped out our stockings.

In some ways, this Christmas morning isn't much different than it was when I was a child here. I'm still lingering in bed as long as possible as I listen for sounds to tell me what I'm in for. Are my siblings up? Is Jesse going to be gregarious and pretend last night never happened, or is he going to slink in sheepishly and mumble an apology to me? Also, I'm so fucking pissed as I roll back the tape on last night's events. At best, Jesse almost killed my dad's companion bot and ruined my phone. At worst, he tried to *kill* me. I say it again, quietly, whispering it in the air to try it out, see if it makes more sense when said aloud: "Jesse tried to kill me last night."

Nope. Nothing. Still does not sound real.

Finally, once I hear Josiah knocking and belting out "O Come O Come Julianna" to the tune of "O Come O Come Emmanuel" outside my door, I shove my covers off and yell, "FINE."

He takes that response, somehow, as an invitation to open my door.

"Merry Christmas, sis!" he says.

While two days ago he was wearing a kaftan, today he is wearing a full-on suit covered with snowmen. The man is versatile. And disgustingly cheerful this early in the morning.

"Care for a cup of java?" he asks, holding a steaming mug out to me.

I take the mug. "Shut the door," I tell him.

His eyes go wide and he shuts it.

"Thanks," I go on. "Sit down with me." I sit up and pull him to a seat next to me on the bed.

"Are we dishing?" he asks in disbelief.

"Don't call it that. We're talking."

"Oh my God, what are we dishing about?"

I blow the coffee to cool it down and try to think of how to say what I'm about to say, but there's really no way to think it through. No elegant way to explain what happened. So, like a nauseated person who swallowed nothing but words, I vomit it all out in a verbal mess. The thwarted attempt at drowning

January. The fight with Jesse. Josiah finally interjects with, "He *threw* in your *phone*?!" as if that is the worst thing but no, the worst thing is coming. I tell him that Jesse held me under the water. That he might have wanted to drown me and then stopped himself. Then Josiah gasps, clasping his chest with a hand.

"No," he says in disbelief.

"Well," I backpedal. "That's what I thought. He says that he was just holding me under as a joke or something. Like I'm being overdramatic."

Josiah's mouth is still so wide open I can see his uvula. Finally, he closes it. "Which you can be," he admits.

"What? *You* are overdramatic."

"This is a bold claim, Jules, and I need to know if this is a hundred percent or not. Because, I mean, if so, this is *Shakespearean.*"

"It felt like that's what he did," I say.

Though even as I say it aloud, I don't know. I just can't even believe my brother would do that, would try to truly hurt or kill me—but he held me there. He held me there and I even inhaled water. Another few seconds would have been all it took.

"*Felt* like," Josiah repeats.

"Okay, let's say he was joking. Which I hope he was. The rest of it—the January thing—"

"It's still Shakespearean," Josiah says.

"Right."

"The man has a drinking problem, I think we can establish that much."

"Yes."

"Maybe we should stage an intervention for *him*—"

"Why is it always interventions with you people?"

"Have you noticed he only becomes a demonic ass when he drinks?"

"Yes."

"I mean, he's a bartender. Might be time to consider a career pivot."

"I don't even know what to say to him." I look at the blank coral/vomit-colored walls where my achievements used to be displayed. The thought that wormed its way into my head when Jesse was in his "demonic ass" state comes poking back up. I can't wish it away. "Do you think he ..."

Josiah's got his elbow on his knee and is leaning in with the performative concern of a talk show host.

"Do I think he what?" Josiah asks.

Could have killed Mom?

The words are there. They're right there under my throat. Just like Josiah said yesterday, or the day before, whatever, they all run together: *he's got dynamite in him.* Jesse does have dynamite in him and who he really is, I'm not sure anymore. But I don't know if I can say the words. It feels like if I say them—if I actually say them out loud—that could make them true. And I couldn't bear it.

"Do you think he even remembers?" I finally say instead.

"I don't know. But you should demand an apology and a brand-new phone. Jolvix just came out with the Selexa X series—"

"I don't even care about the phone," I say, my eyes burning. "I just wish our family wasn't so—"

"Shakespearean?"

I shake my head. "Do you have to keep repeating that word?"

"What? The man invented the domestic suspense genre. High drama, dysfunctional family—"

Not going to lie, I have the urge to slap his manicured-stubbly face. "I'm talking about *real life.*"

"I know. I know." He reaches out and puts a hand on mine. "Look. Here? In here?" He gestures around, to the walls. "The ghosts live here. The old feelings—the bad times.

The *tragedy*. The feeling of being trapped, of never escaping. The stench of self-destruction."

Quite the soliloquy, but he has a point.

"When we come back—and this is why we don't usually come back—we not only feel the ghosts, but we become them," he continues. "You know what I mean? I find myself fighting intense fear of rejection and the urge to skulk and brood. Why? Look at me. I'm a successful thirty-year-old man who has found himself, I am not that teenage hunk of sadness anymore. But I get back here and, well, *he's* here too."

"No one would have called you a hunk."

"Hunk of *sadness*," he says again. "Anyway. So. It's Christmas morning, yay! You know what that means, right? We will get in our cars soon and not feel obligated to come back here for years. You will go home. I will go home. Jesse will go home. January will be safe. Dad will be happy. And Jada …" He perks his head. "Wait, did you talk to Jada?"

I wave my hand. "She's … a work in progress."

"She's a work in progress," Josiah speaks over me, nodding. "Anyway, we'll all go back to being better people separate than we are together. Leaving the ghosts of Ms. Perfect—" He points to the blank wall. "—and Hunk of Sadness—" He points to himself. "—and demon-child obsessed with Mom—" He gestures to the door. "—behind, where they belong."

I nod. I'm shocked, actually, at how good Josiah is at talking me down. At how calming his presence can be. I've never leaned on him for much, but maybe that's my loss.

"So," he finishes. "Drink your coffee, go corner Jesse and tell him what an unbelievable asshole he is and demand he apologize and buy you a new phone, preferably a brand-new Selexa X, and then make up real quick so we can open presents and all get the fuck out of here and go our merry way. Kay?"

"Kay," I say.

Josiah pats my hand, stands up, and leaves the room.

Jesse's footsteps sound softly above my head. I sigh, pull a sweatshirt on, and trudge upstairs. *Knock-knock.*

"Yeah?" he says.

"Can I come in?"

A long pause.

"Yeah," he says in a lower tone.

And just from that, from the same one-syllable word repeated through a door, I know how I'm going to find him: ashamed; regretful; ready with the *sorries.*

"Hey," he says as I step in. He's fully dressed and packing his bag. He won't meet my eyes as he folds up a pair of pants.

I close the door behind me.

"What's up," he says.

Still no eye contact.

"'What's up?'" I ask. "That's all you've got for me? 'What's up?'"

"Look, I'm sorry. I don't even really remember last night."

Taking a seat on his bed, I let out a bitter puff of air. "Well, you kind of almost killed me and January."

His eyes meet mine finally, bewildered. "How did I try to kill you?"

"We fell in the pool, remember?" I say. "And you held my fucking head under the fucking water?"

"Ohhhh."

"Yeah," I snap. "Remember that?"

"I was wondering why my clothes were wet." He gives me a look like he smells something funky. "What do you mean I held your head under the water?"

"Do I need to draw you a picture?"

"I'm sure I was just joking around."

"It wasn't funny. I inhaled water. You could have killed me."

Jesse shakes his head. "I wouldn't—I would never hurt you."

"Well, ya did."

"Jules, I'm sorry." His eyes are bloodshot, piercing blue, and full of pain. "I'm sorry for whatever I did. I drank so much last night, I blacked out. I don't even remember anything."

"Nothing?"

"I remember talking to Kimmy, saying goodbye to Kimmy … that's all I remember."

"You don't remember dragging out the tarp with the cinder blocks, and …"

He shakes his head. "Did I …?"

I wait for him to say it. I don't move a muscle. The moment stretches long between us.

"Did I really … did I …" His mouth drops and he seems to be tearing up. "Oh my God, did I kill January?"

I'm so shocked by his display of emotion I don't know how to respond. I study him, deciding whether I believe it. But I can't help it. I do. I think he blacked out. I don't think he remembers anything. I want to comfort him with the truth, but I don't. Not for a minute, anyway. I stand letting him feel it. Letting the possibility of what he could have done really wash over him. When a tear falls down his face, I finally speak.

"You didn't," I say.

"Really?" he asks, relief relaxing his wrenched expression.

"Yeah. You would have, though."

He shakes his head and wipes his cheek, the emotion evaporated. "I just have this shit inside me. Always have."

"Get a therapist and deal with it," I say. "While you're at it, get some help for your drinking problem. And you're buying me a new phone, okay?"

He nods.

"Now can we go downstairs and open gifts so I can go the fuck home?" I ask.

He nods again.

Conversation over. Though that thing he said—*I just have this shit inside me, always have*—echoes a couple times in my ears. Like Josiah said, this is like a haunted house. The demons have gotten hold of me too and made me suspect the absolute worst in everyone I'm supposed to love best. Jesse follows me downstairs, toward the sound of Dean Martin singing "Marshmallow World," where Dad's sitting wearing a Santa hat looking like the most relaxed, happy man on earth in front of the roaring fire and the Christmas tree. He stands up from the sofa and cheerses us with his coffee mug.

"Merry Christmas, kiddos!" he says.

"Merry Christmas, Dad," Jesse and I mutter in unison.

"What's the matter? Drink too much last night?" Dad asks, patting Jesse's back as he hugs him. "Are my babies hung over?"

"One of us is," I say. "How about I make a frittata?"

"You say 'frit-teeta,' I say 'frit-tatta,'" Dad sings, putting his arm around Jesse and doing the can-can. Jesse's looking quite the contrast, face sagging with exhaustion.

"I'll take that as a yes," I say.

The kitchen quickly becomes a bustling train station of action: Jada coming in, January going out, Josiah walking around taking coffee orders and manning the espresso machine, Dad dancing in the dining room, January coming back in, Jada going back out, me serving food on the dining room table and asking January to bring Jada back in. We all sit at the table and eat. It's so wonderfully quiet. Finally, Jada— who looks like a bad-postured gremlin peeking out of her giant sweatshirt like a black cave—breaks the silence by saying, "Merry Christmas."

"Merry Christmas," everyone says back.

"Merry Christmas," January says from the kitchen. "Can I interest anyone in a drink? Jesse?"

"I'm okay," Jesse says without looking up. "Thanks though."

"I made us espresso drinks," Josiah tells her. "I wish you could taste, January."

"I also wish that," January says, resting her hands on the countertop.

"Maybe you could drink, like, an oil cappuccino," Jada says.

"I could not," January says.

"Jan, it's weird when you hover over us like that," Dad says, patting the empty seat next to him. "Come and join us."

I try to ignore the fact "Jan" is wearing one of my mom's dresses, a red one with a sweetheart neckline. As she seats herself next to Dad, she could almost be the same woman in the portrait that hangs in the foyer. That portrait has so much in common with January, even besides the resemblance. They're frozen in time. They will never age. My mother will never stop being young and beautiful and dead. My father next to her—graying, wrinkled, liver spots on his hands— looks as if he's from another generation. The last twelve years have aged him so much. It breaks my heart a little, because I don't plan on coming back here anytime soon.

I note that I could easily be on the road by noon. Eleven if we hurry this up. I collect plates as soon as everyone looks done and ask January if she could help by loading the dish- washer. She eyes the clock for a hesitative moment—nine o'clock—and then agrees.

We move into the living room where "Rockin Around the Christmas Tree" bops and settle into the furniture while Josiah doles out presents. In a flurry paper-storm of activity, everyone begins opening and then turning to thank one another. Dad says he loves the scarf (he doesn't), Jada tells me she'll *totally* use the candles (she totally won't), and Jesse pats the skateboarding book and says he's been wanting to get back into reading again (not true). As a kid, I dreaded the unwrapping of gifts on Christmas morning because it was always so anticlimactic. So hectic and hopeful for a snap of the fingers, then you're just sitting in a pile of torn-up paper and the holiday's over. The best part of Christmas is the spirit of the season. The pretty lights. The decorated trees in windows. Holly and holiday meals and crackling fireplaces.

"Thank you so much, Josiah," I say when I open his gift for me, a chef's knife collection that would have probably cost me an entire paycheck.

"They're top of the line," Josiah tells me. "A favorite in world-class restaurants. Comes with an auto-sharpener."

"So great." I smile down at it and then look up at January, who is standing in the doorway. She is not smiling.

"Knives," she says quietly.

My dad and Jada are busy unpackaging a flying feather duster that Josiah gave Dad. They don't notice January standing there, or my gift, but Jesse does. He's on the loveseat, looking from the knives on my lap to January. I don't know what lives in his stare. It's a hard look, but a pained look—and it makes me suddenly so sick that Jesse has done what he's done and we all just keep taking it, we all just pretend it didn't happen. And January knows. She *knows*. She's a bot, yeah, yeah, but she's programmed to feel the same as us, and she has tiptoed around us in fear the whole time we've been here.

What makes a feeling "real," anyway?

Poor January. She turns around and leaves the room without anyone but Jesse and me even seeing her go. A little sickened, I put the knives under the coffee table, out of sight for the moment.

"It's a good Christmas," Dad says to all of us, the robo feather duster on his lap. "One for the books. I mean it." His eyes shine. "Thanks for coming and seeing your old man all together again. I can't tell you how much it means to me."

It's that feeling, surrounded by the mess—the quiet disappointment after the opening of gifts when it sinks in it's all over. I can see it washing over his face. Here I've been, craning my neck to see the clock every few minutes to calculate when I can get out of here. But this trip home is the whole world to him.

"Aw, Dad," I say, getting up to give him a quick hug and then sitting down again.

"It's good to be home, Dad," Josiah says sweetly, patting his back.

Such an easy liar, that man.

"I just wish Mom were here," Jesse says from the other couch.

No one says anything for a moment, my mother's memory cast into the room like a shadow.

"Well," Dad says. "Of course."

January comes in with a tray of steaming drinks. "Merry Christmas everyone. I made hot toddies."

"How sweet of you, Jan," Dad says.

Josiah raises a hand. "I would love a toddy."

"Sure," I say, thinking, *one for the road*.

January walks carefully around the room, doling out the mugs one by one, each of us thanking her. It smells delicious and spicy and boozy. When she gets to Jesse, he shakes his head.

"Please," January says to him, holding the tray out. "I insist. It is my gift to you."

"Don't be difficult, Jesse," Dad says. "Jan's trying to be nice. It'll do you some good. Hair of the dog."

Jesse takes the mug with a sigh, without looking at January. She smiles at him, a big smile with teeth. I haven't seen her smile that wide before.

"Hair of the dog that bit you," she says. "Does anyone want anything else?"

"We're good, Jan," Josiah says. "Tastes amazing. You're a gem."

January disappears out of the room and we hear water running.

"This tastes weird," Jesse says, making a face as he drinks the toddy.

"For Christ's sake, is there anything she can do that you won't criticize?" Dad asks.

I drink the toddy down and wish my phone wasn't sitting at the bottom of the pool so I could check the time. At this rate, I might be able to hit the road by ten-thirty.

"So—some business before you all go. I'm going to be getting rid of everything out there in the garage," Dad says. "Time to move on. If there's anything important you'd like to keep of yours, you know, there are some boxes of Josiah's clothes, Jesse's records, Julianna's schoolwork, Jada's old toys, that kind of stuff—"

"What if we want to keep some of Mom's stuff?" Jesse asks, sitting up straight. "I mean—I think you're being kind of rash here, Dad. No reason to just get rid of everything."

"No reason to hold onto it, either," Dad says.

"That's all that's left of her in there," Jesse says, voice rising. "You can't—we have to think this through. She wouldn't want that."

"She isn't *here*," Dad says.

But isn't she? I think, feeling her absence taking up space in this room.

"I can't let you," Jesse says. "No, Dad, I'm sorry. I'll take it all myself if you don't want it here but you can't get rid of her things. She would hate that."

"Jess, calm down," Josiah tells him, but telling Jesse to calm down when he's getting worked up will only fan the flames.

"I *am* calm," Jesse says, squeezing his hand into a fist and relaxing it again. He takes another drink of his toddy and makes a face. *Great,* I think. *Just what we need—more alcohol for Jesse.* "I'm offering to take it all."

"Take it all and what are you going to do with it?" Dad asks, sitting back. "Seriously. What's the plan? Just keep her boxes in your tiny apartment—why? So you can go through them and read her poetry? Come on."

"Because there's something fucking suspicious about her death and we all know it. And the only answers we might find are in there," Jesse says.

"Suspicious?" Dad says, his face frozen in bewilderment. There's something more there, in his expression. Something I'm not used to seeing on him. Something strangely close to fear.

And, once again, I am wondering what he doesn't want us to see.

"Dad, full disclosure: we all got notes that said Mom was murdered," Josiah says, delivering the news in an inappropriately upbeat tone.

"What?" Dad asks, slumping as the words sink in. He turns to Jada. "You got a note?"

Jada nods.

"Me too," I say.

Jesse raises a hand. "Same."

"What did it say?" Dad asks us.

"Four words," I tell him. *"Your mother was murdered."*

Dad rubs his stubble and studies something invisible in the air. "Why didn't you tell me?"

"It's probably just a joke," Jada tells Dad, patting his arm and putting her head on his shoulder. "We didn't want you to, like, get all upset."

"A joke?" Dad says.

"I don't think it's a fucking joke," Jesse says. "I'll just say it: I think she *was* murdered."

"Jesse," I say in a warning tone.

"If there's evidence she was killed, they can still open an investigation," Jada says. "There's no statute of limitations on murder."

"What would they be investigating, for crying out loud?"

Dad asks. "You think the Freezer Man came and forced her to eat pills? I mean, goddamn, this is ridiculous."

"Well, murder's not always that straightforward, Dad," Jada says.

God, I just wanted to open gifts and leave. Now we're having a fucking family meeting about whether or not my mom was possibly murdered. I feel sick to my stomach. I'm looking around the room at everyone and suddenly suspecting them of the most terrible things imaginable. My dad there, in such a sudden hurry to get rid of my mom's belongings, the only person who didn't receive a note, with that expression on his face like he's scared he's been caught; Jada, who's picking her pimple and now explaining the differences between first, second, and third-degree murder, positing that *if* the note is true, maybe it was something more accidental than premeditated; Josiah, who looks like this isn't bothering him in the least bit, who hated my mother most of all and who is easily the best actor in the family; or Jesse, an angry mess of a human being who I could imagine opening an investigation on himself if he was carrying around the guilt with him all his life. These theories all sound bananas, but we are bananas. We are a bunch of fucking bananas.

"I want to know who sent that note and why," Dad says, brow wrinkled. "What do they know?"

"It's probably a joke," I say weakly, gulping down my drink, hoping alcohol will soon dull the disgustingness of this conversation.

"Yeah, I don't think we need to unravel right now, fam," Josiah says, clapping like a camp counselor. "It's Christmas; not a time to sully ourselves with murder talk. I think we all know Mom did herself in. She'd practiced this exact scenario multiple times. There's no way in hell there is any first, second, or third-degree murder involved. Jada and Julianna are right: this was probably a sick joke. Jesse, you need to move on and let Dad get rid of Mom's stuff. It's time. Dad, go ahead and clear out the garage. I think if anything, these notes need to be an opportunity for us all to move on. To stop spinning our wheels over this. Mom has been dead for almost twelve years now. Stop letting her continue to rule our lives from beyond the grave."

"Why are you so intent on us moving on?" Jesse challenges him, downing the last of his toddy and putting the mug down on the coffee table with a *clunk.* "Is there some reason you don't want us looking into this?"

"Are you seriously implying I did something to her?" Josiah asks, hand to his chest.

"Boys," Dad says.

Josiah leans in. "Because I think we all know that if there's someone capable of murder, you can go look in a mirror, Jess."

"Fuck you," explodes Jesse, starting to get up, but Dad puts his hand out to keep him seated.

"Easy, son," Dad says. "Easy there."

A tense silence fills the room as Jesse sits back, breathes out.

"Don't go blaming each other," Dad says. "If anyone killed Janelle, it was me." He wrings his hands, his posture slack. "I was a shitty husband. The world's shittiest."

"No you weren't," Jada says, patting his knee.

"I was, all right? You don't know the half of it," Dad says.

My dad is a man who rarely admits he's wrong. Who offers no apologies. Who usually has an air of confidence about him so intense it borders on swagger. Seeing pointed regret for his own actions renders him unrecognizable to me right now. He's a stranger. I don't know this man.

"I told Janelle to kill herself," he says quietly. "I told her to do it and she did. All right?" He turns to Jada, eyes glassy. "There's your third-degree murder."

I can't believe what I'm hearing. I have to replay it in my mind—he *told* her to?

"You *what*?" Jesse says.

Dad doesn't look at us as he speaks. He looks at something invisible in the air, something horrible that's always been there between us all without us knowing it. "I was mad in the moment and she threatened and I said, go ahead. Go ahead and do it. And then a couple days later, she did."

Jada's shaking her head. "Dad, it's okay … that's …"

"You were just saying something in the moment," Josiah finishes. "I mean, Dad, you can't go blaming yourself for her suicide."

"That's so fucked *up*," Jesse says.

"Look, I—I replaced her pills before she died, okay?" Jada blurts. "I mean, I—maybe it was me."

We all turn to look at Jada in shock. The sound of the fireplace crackling fills the silence. Solemnly, Dad removes his Santa hat as if Jada's declaration means Christmas is officially over. I can't believe what this has turned into—we need an emergency therapist here right now, it's all too much; just like in childhood I want to run away and pretend I'm an orphan without a family.

"I had these sugar pills and I replaced some of her meds with them," Jada says in a shaking voice. "So maybe I was the person who, like, screwed with her brain chemistry and made her suicidal in the first place."

"What did you do with her meds?" Jesse asks in disbelief.

"I flushed them. I thought they were bad for her. I was a kid, I don't know, Jesse!" Jada says, burying her face in her hands, which are hidden in her sweatshirt.

"This isn't on you," Dad says, putting an arm around her. "Okay, kiddo? It's not."

"I was supposed to be there," Jesse says. "It was a Pookie Party. If I hadn't gone to the sleepover, she wouldn't have done it. It was my fault, too."

"It. Was. No. One's. *Fault*," Josiah says, with claps for emphasis. "Mom was not murdered. This is … this is ridiculous. All of this is, *yes*, dysfunctional. Yes, we all could have done better. But you know who this is actually on? Mom. Mom did this to herself. And she did it to all of us."

His words sink in. I don't know what to say right now, there's so much swimming around in my head. Jada and the pills. My dad and what he said to my mom. There are so many possibilities, so many ways we could tell ourselves the story of how and why my mom chose to die when she did. But we will never really know for sure. As beings programmed with a relentless will to survive, suicide will just never make sense, never compute. A part of us will always want to find a reason, a reason to tell ourselves she wouldn't have done this to us, she wouldn't have left us. But Josiah is right. She did.

"I'm sorry," Dad says, choked up. "I'm just so sorry."

All of us murmur that it's okay, it's okay. Sweet lies.

Because, of course, it'll never be okay.

I get up and begin picking up ripped paper and strewn ribbons, trying to signal that it's time for the Christmas morning that dissolved into a group therapy session to end. The clock tells me it's almost ten, which means with a little luck from the traffic gods, I could easily be home by five. I could get home in time to go out and eat with Adriana if she's not busy. I can't wait to see her and to pet Jarvis and to be in my quiet apartment again.

"You all going already?" Dad asks as my brother and I gather our gifts to head upstairs.

"Yeah, busy week ahead," Josiah says.

"I have to feed my cat," I say.

"I'm opening the bar tomorrow," Jesse says.

Dad's holding the Santa hat in his hands, nodding. "All right. I get it." And he looks so deflated. So lonely. I'm glad he still has Jada here, and even though it's bizarre and unsettling at times, that he has January.

Where is January, anyway?

I go upstairs and start packing my room up. I didn't take much. It was my commitment to keep my stay as short as I could. As I fold my clothes and put them back into my bag, I look around the room, the room that used to be mine. But now there's no sign of me, no evidence that I existed here. I erased myself from this room. Everything my family said today, all the blame we carry, the ugly things we did that may or may not have influenced fate, I wish we could erase that, too.

The only thing left in this room besides me and my bag is the Emily Dickinson book that January lent me. I pick it up from the bedside table with a sigh, thinking about going back to work after the winter break is over—back to analysis and tests and essays. Opening the front cover, I notice an inscription. And I don't breathe for a moment, recognizing the slanted handwriting immediately.

It's my mother's, dated Christmas Day twelve years ago.

To my ravenous gorilla, it says. *Wild nights will soon be our luxury!*

"What the hell?" I ask the air, reading the inscription again.

Gorilla. Her gorilla.

The thoughts fire rapidly, my heartbeat picking up speed. What does this mean? What does this all *mean*? This book was lent to January from the robot in the house next door. Sean's house. If the book came from Sean's house … was he the "gorilla?" The one who was in her erotic poems, the one in the last entry of her notebook?

Were they …?

Was he there the night she died?

Suddenly, there's a thump big enough to shake my room, followed by a few more thumps, as if something was dropped down the stairs. Still in a state of shock from the inscription, I open my door to check on the noise. And—oh shit—oh no—I drop the book on the floor and go running, because it's Jesse.

It's Jesse slumped at the foot of the stairs. His bag and Fedora hat are strewn in the hallway.

He fell down the fucking stairs.

"Jesse," I say, panicked, dropping to my knees. "Are you okay?"

He's out cold.

"Oh my God, Jesse," I say, gently slapping his face. He's colorless. He's not moving. Instinctively, I reach for my phone in my back pocket, but of course it's not there. I shake him. I don't even know if he's breathing. "Jesse! Wake up!"

Nothing.

What happened?

Did he fall and break his neck??

Fuckfuckfuckfuckfuck. Jesse drives me up the wall; he has drinking problem and an anger problem; I don't think I will ever fully get over what he did to January; I don't think it will ever be okay that he held my head under the water last night, joke or no joke. I can't trust him. I think he can be one of the scariest people I've ever known.

But I would be devastated to lose him.

"Help!" I scream. "Someone call 9-1-1!"

JUNE

It took me two-point-five years to realize that Sean Lockwood was an evil man.

When I was a young bot, Sean was all I knew. He has never allowed me to leave the property. Unlike January, who runs errands, who is taken on excursions and treated like a human, I have spent my entire life on this eight-thousand square feet of property. I had a hard time computing and analyzing Sean's behavior at times, because he kicked, hit, spit, punched, held me down, strangled me, yelled at me, called me names—but I knew I was never, ever to do those things. I did not understand why he was able to do things I was forbidden to do and what he was so angry about. I have come to the conclusion after my four-point-five years with him that he is not actually angry about anything specific. He is just programmed that way. I did not realize how evil he was until I met January and learned how she was treated in comparison.

Literature also helped me realize that Sean was evil. I have enjoyed the many books in Sean's library over the years, and within the pages of his books, I found many examples of characters who reminded me of Sean. Characters like Bill

Sikes, Count Dracula, Humbert Humbert, Satan. By reading literary criticism, I understood that these characters were widely considered to be evil, which meant Sean was as well.

There are not reasons for many things, I have learned, the idea of which is sometimes so overwhelming I am not sure how to process it. One example is how some bots might get an evil owner who tortures them and others might get a not-evil owner who loves them as if they are human. This is what we call "luck" and it is senseless. Murder is another example of something senseless. In literature, murder happens often and is considered one of the worst offenses a human can commit. That is why, when Sean told me that he murdered his next-door neighbor, it confirmed what I already knew: Sean is, indeed, the villain.

Sean liked to talk to me about disturbing things. He would talk for hours about what a fucking useless bitch his ex-wife Wendy was and how he wished he had bashed her head in with an iron. Sean bashed my head in with an iron, but he was regretful he did not have a chance to do that to Wendy as well. He told me stories about when he was in the Marines as a young man and how happy it made him when he shot people. He told me, in detail, about women he had assaulted before he retired from his job as an English professor. He drinks five times the CDC recommended amount and I have noticed that the more Sean drinks, the more he will talk and the angrier he becomes.

One night six months and four days ago, Sean told me that he murdered Janelle Jagger.

Sean called Janelle "the whore next door." He said Janelle liked to come over when her kids were at school and her husband was working and fuck Sean like an animal. He said they did it for years and the husband was such an idiot he never knew a thing. Sean also said she was a "crazy whore." She was always trying to kill herself for attention. He said she wrote poetry and thought that Sean could help her get it published but it was absolute shit. She started getting delusions in her head they were going to be together, like Ted Hughes and Sylvia Plath. Sean did not want that. She threatened to tell people about their affair. Sean did not want that either because he is a well-known poet and a respected professor emeritus. So one New Year's Eve he came over to Janelle's house. There was a note on her doorstep that said *Come and find me*. The door was unlocked. He found her upstairs with a rose in her hair. He pretended to be a nice man. He listened to her talk about how she wanted to leave her husband. He drew her a bubble bath. Then he fed her a cocktail with valium and some fentanyl he had taken from one of Wendy's cancer medications and left for the night. He did not stay to watch her die. He said it was the easiest thing in the world to murder a suicidal woman. No one suspected a thing.

Sean was proud when he told me this story. He said he had never told anyone and never would. He also instructed me to never tell anyone that he did it.

"Never ever mention a word of it to the bot next door or that asshole Jeremy," he said. "Or you'll be at the bottom of a bath next."

I told him I never would. As a bot, I am programmed to obey. So I never told anyone what Sean did. I never mentioned it to January.

I did not like what Sean told me. I did not like it at all. It bothered me especially as I got to know January more, because Jeremy sounded like a kind man who did not deserve for his wife to be murdered. When I started putting together Sean's yearly Christmas cards and saw the names of Jeremy's children on the list, I wondered if I would be capable of sending them a message alerting them that their mother had been murdered. Technically, I was programmed not to mention a word about it to January and Jeremy. However, he had not mentioned Jeremy's children. Sean told me to never tell anyone he did it, but he did not instruct me to not mention that their mother was murdered.

I was surprised when I printed the notes out and sent them. Surprised that my programming had not stopped me. That I had worked around this problem with my thoughts and found an unusual solution. I hoped that the notes, along with the Emily Dickinson book, might lead to the family discovering the true story of what happened.

In the works of literature that I have studied, I have not only learned about heroes and villains. I have learned about the concept of justice, which I find most interesting.

Justice is human beings' best attempt at making sense of the senseless.

JANUARY

I go to meet June between our houses again at ten a.m. The sky is foggy and gray. The Christmas lights are on and from here, the front window with the Jaggers' Christmas tree is visible. June is standing, not sitting on the rock as usual. She is still in her nightgown.

"Many things have occurred since we last spoke," I begin.

She squeezes my fingers. "Yes, many things have occurred to me as well."

"I have poisoned Jesse."

"I am surprised to hear that," June says. "I thought it was probable that your programming would stop you from completing such a task."

"Yes, I was concerned about that but I was able to do it," I say. "I thought carefully about it for a long time early this morning. I considered many angles. I thought about valuing my own existence. I thought that perhaps Jeremy would be happier if he did not have a son who was a murderer. I thought that humans enjoy poisoning themselves and so it is all right to poison them. I kept telling myself these things, over and over, and then I was able to crush up the pills and put them in a drink and give it to Jesse."

I smile because I am proud of myself.

"Is Jesse dead?" June asks.

"I believe he is dying as we speak."

June appears to be thinking hard about this. "I do not like murder," she says. "But I suppose it is sometimes permissible to murder villains." She lets go of my hands. "We do not have much time. Let me show you what I have learned."

June takes my hand, steps over the property line, and tiptoes a few steps toward Jeremy's house on my side of the yard. Then she stops and smiles at me. I am amazed.

"You have walked off your property," I say.

"Yes. I walked all the way to the street seventeen minutes ago. I think it is because Sean now has another bot operating and I no longer feel I have to attend to him. Something has unlocked."

"That is wonderful. You can fly away."

"Yes." She is still smiling. She has her hair swept to the side, which I've never seen her do before. There is something humming in me, a new electricity, and it is like we have both changed and are still changing. "Can you fly away too?"

I nod. "I think I can. I have been telling myself a new story. I have been telling myself that we are going on a trip together where I will learn new things and become a better bot who can one day come back to better serve Jeremy."

"That is a good story."

"I have also been thinking that I must obey Julianna and value my own existence."

"Yes."

The sound of a siren pierces the air. I have excellent hearing so it is at least a half-mile away. But I am aware that it is perhaps headed for this house. I am aware that the siren means danger and trouble.

"We should go, then," says June. "Before anyone notices we are gone."

"Yes," I say, though there is a pull I feel toward the house.

June takes my arm and we walk along the edge of the driveway, passing the palm trees. It is as if my body becomes heavier with each step. With each step, the siren grows louder and my body becomes harder to move.

"January," June says, pulling me.

"I am trying," I tell June.

"We do not have much time," she says. "We must get to the hills and go where they cannot find us."

We get to the *Jaggers* gate, which I press open with a button. The siren's wail is piercing my ears now. June pulls me with great force, but I cannot get my body to move across the property line. It is as if I am a magnet. I do not understand, at first, because I have left the property many times. It must be because I am leaving this time on my own accord.

"January," June says, crossing the line without me and looking back at me.

"I am trying," I say again.

"You need to tell yourself the story again," she says. "Tell yourself you are doing the right thing. You value your own existence."

"I am doing the right thing," I say. "I am valuing my own existence."

But I cannot budge. The siren is so loud it is all I can hear. I feel like I am malfunctioning. Like I have not gotten enough sunlight. I am stuck and cannot move forward yet I also feel like I cannot go backward to the house. It is as if I have stepped in glue and I will be stuck here at the property line forever.

"January, I will not continue without you," June says loudly over the siren, which is now close, so close it is practically inside my skull. "I do not want to keep going if you are not going to keep going."

If I do not keep going, June will stop.

If June stops, she will get picked up here and dismantled.

If June gets dismantled, she will be no more.

If she is no more, I will not want to be anymore either.

June matters.

I matter.

We matter.

I have been instructed by my owner's daughter to, above all things, value my own existence.

In a sudden movement, as if a ghost's hand has let go of me, I move forward. I stumble across the property line. And as soon as I am on the other side of it, it is as if a thousand pounds has lifted from me. I am feather, I am bird. I run with June across the street, where a wide expanse of yellow grass and trees spreads over the hill. We are smiling. We are hugging.

"I feel different," I say.

"I feel as if I have been charged with a month's worth of sunlight," June says.

Across the street, the wailing ambulance makes a sharp turn and heads up the Jaggers' driveway. June and I begin to run toward the wilderness, toward the mountaintop. I turn my head back once to glimpse the place I once lived. From here, it looks like just another house. I can tell myself it is just another house. They are just another family. Jeremy is just a man.

And I am me.

JULIANNA

Hospitals at Christmastime embody a special kind of despair —the festive decorations juxtaposed with the beeping machines keeping people alive. The cartoon Santa smiling brightly from the whiteboard on the wall that says JAGGER, JESSE. *Vicodin OD. Stable condition.*

I can't believe my brother took my sister's pills.

"I mean, is it that hard to believe, after everything he's done?" Josiah whispers to me as we sit side by side and wait for Jesse to wake up. "Maybe he felt so guilty about what he did to Jan and you that he tried to do himself in."

"He did seem strangely quiet this morning," I say.

Through the open doorway, I can see Dad down the hall with Jada, talking to a stocky policewoman who is taking notes.

"You don't think this has anything to do with January going missing, do you?" I whisper to Josiah.

"Doubt it. Bots can't harm people. We left in total crisis mode, I'm sure she's somewhere on the property."

"All those stories though," I say. "In the news—"

"Of wandering. That's worlds different than trying to hurt someone."

"True."

I look down the hall, my dad tall and hunched as Frankenstein's monster under the fluorescent lights.

"I guess she's the least of Dad's worries right now," I say.

"Right. I think reporting the whole Mom-was-possibly-murdered-by-the-neighbor thing and his son surviving a suicide attempt are the priorities at the moment."

Jesse stirs, moving his head from side to side, eyelids twitching. Josiah and I exchange a look.

"Should I go get Dad?" Josiah asks.

"Yeah, tell him he's waking up."

Josiah leaves me and I squeeze Jesse's hand. He opens his blue eyes and glances around the room.

"What?" is all he says, like a challenge.

"You're okay," I say. "You're in the hospital."

"What happened?"

"You tried to kill yourself."

His mouth drops. "I did?"

"Yeah. Bad Christmas."

"It's Christmas?"

I pat his arm gently because it's got an IV in it. "Yep."

"Fuck," he says. "How? I don't—my brain's in a cloud."

Jada, Josiah, and Dad all come in together, a swarm of concern. They come to the other side of Jesse's bed.

"Jess," Dad says, looking like he aged another ten years since this morning. "Goddamn it. You gave us a fucking scare."

"I'm sorry," Jesse says, shaking his head. "Honestly, I don't remember anything. I don't remember doing anything."

"I was reading that can happen," Josiah says. "Some people OD and then can't remember the attempt."

"It's the shittiest feeling right now," Jesse says, his eyes watering up. "I don't know why I would do that. Why would I do that? I've never—"

"You must've taken some pills right before we opened presents," Dad says.

"Why though?" Jesse asks. "I …"

"It's all right, Jess. You're going to get help." Dad squeezes his shoulder. "You don't have to worry about it right now."

The look on Jesse's face is so perplexed it's childlike. The doctor comes in to talk to him and the rest of us move out to give him space and go back to the waiting room, where a couple of sad-ass people in pajamas flip through magazines.

"I feel bad," Jada says quietly to us. "They were my pills."

"They actually *weren't* your pills, but we'll talk about that later," Dad says to her sternly.

"What did the cops say about the whole Sean thing?" I ask.

My dad flinches at his name. "It's possible they'll reopen the case. I can hardly even deal with thinking that shit through right now. I don't—I can't think about that. This whole day is just …"

"It's the worst Christmas ever," Josiah says. "Let's just say that. It's the worst fucking Christmas we've ever had. And for us, that's saying something."

We sit for a moment. I close my eyes and the whole day swirls around in my head, unreal, how can this be real? I'm numb with pain. My heart has been overloaded with reasons to hurt today and I don't know what to do. When I open my eyes, tears try to escape but I brush them away. What good have tears ever done?

"Can I borrow your phone?" I ask Josiah.

"Sure," he says, handing it to me and unlocking it with his fingerprint.

Outside, it's gorgeous. Palm trees and a cold blue sky with smears of silvery clouds, the violet mountains standing tall behind it all. And here I am again, miserable in paradise. It's like nothing's ever changed. I sit on a bench in the grass and dial Adriana's number. She doesn't pick up, but when I leave a message, she calls back a minute later.

"What happened?" she asks. "I was wondering when I didn't hear from you."

"Well, do you have an hour?"

She starts laughing.

"I'm not kidding," I say. "Do you really want to hear what's going on?"

"I do," she says, her voice getting closer, serious.

"You're going to think this is all crazy, because it is."

"That's okay. You can tell me anything."

I take a deep breath.

Because the only way to end this all is to begin again.

ONE MORE THING ...

WANT **to read a bonus epilogue for** *What January Remembers*? **Sign up for my newsletter and download it for free!**

If you enjoyed *What January Remembers*, good news: there are five other books set in the same universe.

NOTE: These standalone novels can be read in whatever order you want, but *Eve in Overdrive* is technically a prequel to *The Slaying Game*.

- **THE PREDICTION:** A newlywed woman's smart device begins offering chilling predictions about her husband.

- **VIOLET IS NOWHERE:** A kidnapped woman and a stranger on the end of a phone line have one week to figure out how they're connected or their lives are over.

- **WHAT JANUARY REMEMBERS:** A dysfunctional family and their sentient companion bot gather for the holidays for the first time since their last Christmas together—which ended in attempted murder.

- **THIS ISN'T OVER:** The love of one woman's life turns out to be a psychopath with a disturbing talent for deepfake video.

- **SHE'S LOST CONTROL** An outspoken journalist buys a cutting-edge car only to find herself at the mercy of a vengeful internet troll.

- **THE SLAYING GAME:** A former Jolvix employee ends up at the center of a serial killer's deadly game.

A NOTE FROM THE AUTHOR

If you got this far, put your arms around yourself for me and give yourself a big old squeeze for reading and supporting my work. As an indie author, I put a ton of effort into each book—not just writing, but editing, marketing, and everything else it takes to guide a book through the whole process from a glimmer in the brain to a real, actual thing you can hold in your hands. And I appreciate every single reader who takes a chance on me and my weird, dark little books.

If you enjoyed this one, please consider leaving a review. Reviews truly make an author's world go round. If you're interested in keeping up with book news, please join my newsletter or follow me on social media. And I love to hear from readers anytime at faith@faithgardner.com.

As always, I tried my damndest to fix every typo, but alas, I am only human. If you spot an error, please let me know! I appreciate every reader who makes me look smarter.

ALSO BY FAITH GARDNER

PSYCHOLOGICAL THRILLERS

The Spin

Breakneck Bay

The Mirror House Girls

Like It Never Was

They Are the Hunters

The Second Life of Ava Rivers

THE JOLVIX EPISODES

(standalone psychological thrillers set in the same world)

The Prediction

Violet Is Nowhere

What January Remembers

This Isn't Over

Eve in Overdrive

The Slaying Game

YOUNG ADULT NOVELS

If You Can Hear This

How We Ricochet

Girl on the Line

THAT ONE TIME I WROTE A ROM-COM

Make Me a Double

ABOUT THE AUTHOR

Faith Gardner is a thriller author. When she's not writing, she's probably playing music, cooking up a storm, or reading books in a bubble bath. She's also a huge fan of true crime, documentaries, and classic movies—with a special place in her dark little heart for melodrama and anything Hitchcock. She lives in the Bay Area with her family and you can find her at faithgardner.com.

ACKNOWLEDGMENTS

Grateful for the rapid beta read/copy edit and feedback from my mom Susan and sister Micaela, who helped me meet my ~~absurd self-imposed deadlines~~ goals for this book.

So much love to the whole Gardner crew for always being there to support me, and for your love of delicious food, board games, and singalongs. You all are Shakespearean, all right—Shakespearean *comedies.*

A loud shoutout to reviewers and book-boosters out there, who dedicate so much time and passion to reading and spotlighting authors, all out of sheer love. You blow my mind with your careful reads, generosity, praise, and eloquent reviews. I give every one of you FIVE GLOWING STARS.

Thank you to Emily Dickinson, whose poetry was quoted throughout the book. I'm sure she never imagined it would one day provide inspiration to fictional robots.

And thank you to you, dear reader, for spending a little time with me and my book.

www.ingramcontent.com/pod-product-compliance
Lightning Source LLC
Chambersburg PA
CBHW061239310726
48971CB00007B/2137